Praise for *The Shadow of the Shadow*

"What a wild and wonderful story! A great rip-roaring novel, and thought-provoking social history as well."

— *St Louis Post-Dispatch*

"In this action-packed thriller Taibo successfully mixes fictional characters with historical personalities and events . . . reflecting a spellbinding image of a lawless period in Mexican history."

— *San Francisco Chronicle*

"An engrossing fable that recalls B. Traven's classic *The Treasure of the Sierra Madre*."

— *The Philadelphia Inquirer*

"A beautifully written story . . . With his superb storytelling and endearing characters he has written a different kind of crime novel. . . . Highly recommended."

— *Mystery News*

"A gem of a whodunit . . . A wildly witty, philosophical and radical yarn that keeps its readers not only stumped by red herrings and false leads, but intellectually stimulated and politically disquieted. A wonderful murder mystery as well as a searing and absorbing look at the effects of revolutions and political upheavals."

— *Village View*

"A lively, offbeat crime novel . . . A fun, refreshing read with a historical backdrop that adds a rich flavor not found in most crime novels."

— *Albuquerque Journal*

"Mexico's foremost crime novelist masterfully evokes a bygone era. His quirky characters are as endearing as they are well-drawn."

— *Library Journal*

PENGUIN BOOKS

THE SHADOW OF THE SHADOW

Born in Spain in 1949, Paco Ignacio Taibo II has lived in Mexico since 1958, and has been a nationalized Mexican citizen since 1980. For many years a professor of history at the UAM-Azcapotzalco (Metropolitan University of Mexico City), he is currently president of the International Association of. Crime Writers. The author of numerous novels, works of history, and short-story collections, many of which have been published throughout the world, Taibo lives with his wife and daughter in Mexico City. His crime novel *An Easy Thing*, published by Viking in 1990, marked his English-language debut.

Paco Ignacio Taibo II
THE SHADOW OF THE SHADOW

Translated by William I. Neuman

PENGUIN BOOKS

PENGUIN BOOKS
Published by the Penguin Group
Viking Penguin, a division of Penguin Books USA Inc.,
375 Hudson Street, New York, New York, 10014, U.S.A.
Penguin Books Ltd, 27 Wrights Lane,
London W8 5TZ, England
Penguin Books Australia Ltd, Ringwood,
Victoria, Australia
Penguin Books Canada Ltd, 10 Alcorn Avenue, Suite 300,
Toronto, Ontario, Canada M4V 3B2
Penguin Books (N.Z.) Ltd, 182–190 Wairau Road,
Auckland 10, New Zealand

Penguin Books Ltd, Registered Offices:
Harmondsworth, Middlesex, England

First published in the United States of America by
Viking Penguin, a division of Penguin Books USA Inc., 1991
Published in Penguin Books 1992

10 9 8 7 6 5 4 3 2 1

Translation copyright © Paco Ignacio Taibo II and
William I. Neuman, 1991
All rights reserved

PUBLISHER'S NOTE
This is a work of fiction. Names, characters, places, and incidents either are the
product of the author's imagination or are used fictitiously, and any resemblance to
actual persons, living or dead, events, or locales is entirely coincidental.

Originally published in Mexico as *Sombra de la Sombra*, Planeta, 1986.
© Paco Ignacio Taibo II, 1986

THE LIBRARY OF CONGRESS HAS CATALOGUED THE HARDCOVER AS FOLLOWS:
Taibo, Paco Ignacio, 1949–
The shadow of the shadow / Paco Ignacio Taibo II ; translated by
William I. Neuman.
p. cm.
ISBN 0-670-83177-8 (hc.)
ISBN 0 14 01.3083 7 (pbk.)
I. Title.
PQ6670.A42S5   1991
863—dc20   90-50577

Printed in the United States of America
Set in Times Roman
Designed by Virginia Norey

For my compadres Rolo and Myriam,
and for Rogelio Vizcaíno
who, as my lawyer,
attended the rebirth of this novel.

For the Tobi Club

"How strange, the shadow of a man!"
—*Maxwell Grant (Walter B. Gibson)*

"There's a certain grandeur in all this mixed-up madness."
—*Jesús Ibáñez*

THE SHADOW OF THE SHADOW

SHADOW
SHADOW

1

IN WHICH THE CHARACTERS
PLAY DOMINOES

"Go ahead and play your double-twos, my friend," said Pio-quinto Manterola, with a smile. "I dare say even a poet of your esteemed character can't find a way out of this one."

The poet sank down in his chair, took off his hat, and drummed his fingers on top of his head, keeping time to a song no one else could hear. With the other hand he flipped over the double-twos and slid it across the marble tabletop.

"They'll screw you coming and going, partner," said the law-yer Verdugo from across the table. As if to make it clear the game had gone beyond the point of no return, he downed his glass of tequila with a single swallow, paused for breath, and with a scarcely audible "excuse me" reached over and emptied the Chinaman's glass as well.

The Chinaman played the two/three, leaving Manterola with the last of the threes.

With only two rounds left to go, Manterola pulled a soiled handkerchief from his jacket pocket and blew his nose loudly, breaking the others' concentration.

Almost, though not quite, forty years old, the journalist Pio-quinto Manterola looked much older. Prematurely bald on top with tufts of curling hair sticking out from under his British tweed cap; a faint scar, red at the edges, running from behind his left ear and down his neck; round-lensed glasses perched on a protruding hooked nose: he had the kind of appearance that routinely drew a second glance from passersby, an ap-pearance that gave him a vivid and erroneous air of respect-ability.

"Pass," said Verdugo the lawyer.

"Permanently, sir," said Pioquinto, playing the two/five.

One by one the lights went out in the bar of the Majestic Hotel, number 16 Madero Street, downtown Mexico City. The last click of the pool balls cut softly through the air. Soon the only light left would be the one bulb hanging from the ceiling under its black metal shade, casting an increasingly stark circle of light around the four men at the table.

The poet played the five/one; Tomás Wong the Chinaman passed; Verdugo the lawyer tossed out the double-ones with a sigh; and Manterola went out with the three/four.

"Count 'em up, gentlemen," said Pioquinto Manterola with satisfaction.

Tomás the Chinaman got up and walked over to the bar. He focused on a bottle of Havana brandy smiling at him from its place on the shelf. Following his stare, the bartender found the bottle, took it by the neck, and poured the Chinaman a generous glassful. It's an old trick that worked for Tomás nine times out of every ten, so long as there was a professional behind the bar.

"I count twenty-six, inkslinger. Mark it down," said the poet.

Again, the bones danced across the marble tabletop while the bartender—somewhat more prosaically—wiped down the counter with a dirty yellow rag. Then he went out to cover the abandoned pool tables at the back of the bar. A cuckoo clock, ridiculously out of place with its little Swiss chalet and its broken beakless bird, struck two.

Two o'clock on an April morning in 1922, for example.

Tomás the Chinaman sang softly to himself as he strolled back to his chair:

> *Oh, Beautiful Tampico*
> *tlopical paladise,*
> *the gloly of the lepublic,*
> *whelevel I go, I'll lemebel you.*

I'll lemebel you . . . It had been a long time since he sang that song, not since the last time he sang it softly (so softly only she could hear it) to a German prostitute he lived with for a few months in Tuxpan back in 1919 (her pink chiffon skirt blowing gently in the breeze, the ocean like a rolling curtain in the distance).

The poet finished mixing the bones and raised his hands over the table like a proud chef about to serve his favorite meal. Fermín Valencia was just over thirty years old and just under five feet tall. He was born in the port of Gijón, Spain, but the land of his birth was only a shadowy memory for him now. He left at the age of six with his widowed father who came to Mexico to set himself up as a printer in Chihuahua. The poet needed glasses to see anything at a distance but he almost never used them. Instead he sported a tremendous mustache which, along with his tall leather boots and the red handkerchief around his neck, served as memories of the years he'd spent fighting alongside Pancho Villa in the Northern Division from 1913 to 1916. It was hard to know what to think about that face, sometimes peaceful as a child's, sometimes convulsed with an inner fury. It was hard to tell the difference between wit and bile, hard to distinguish the amiable youth from the tortured razor-sharp man. There was something broken somewhere inside the poet. The only constant was his smile, a smile that expressed very different things at different times, depending on life's ups and downs and the humors of the body.

Pioquinto Manterola stretched his legs out under the table, arched his back over the back of his chair, and put his hands behind his head. "A bit rusty tonight, aren't you?" he asked the lawyer.

"Nothing lasts forever, sir," said Verdugo dryly.

The Chinaman took his place at the table and started to draw his bones, lining them up in a single neat row then shuffling them around two or three times until he was satisfied.

Two women stepped through the door. They were dressed comfortably but with style. And yet there was a hint of something wrong about the way they looked, a kind of falseness highlighting the desired imitation, the sense of professional elegance.

"These women want to talk to you, *licenciado,*" said the bartender.

Verdugo slid himself into an upright position and placed his wide-brimmed hat over an unruly mop of hair. He smiled at his friends.

"Duty calls, gentlemen. If you don't mind, I'll just open up the office for a few minutes."

His three companions watched as he greeted the two women, steering them toward a nearby table with a gentlemanly wave of his hand. As if by magic the light over the table switched on. Professional bartenders like Eustaquio were well versed in the vices and habits of their regular customers. Now, three tables over from where the others sat and inside a second circle of light that matched their own, Verdugo the lawyer tipped back his hat with a flick of his index finger and settled down to listen to his clients. Taking advantage of the break in the action, the bartender approached the domino table with a pair of glasses and the bottle of Havana brandy.

"Excellent, barkeep," said the poet, "only next time try to keep your fingers out of the glasses. It's simply a matter of hygiene."

Eustaquio ignored him and with Olympic indifference poured the liquor into the dirty glasses.

"What's our friend up to now?" Manterola asked the others.

"I heard him say yesterday he'd agreed to draft a petition to the regent on behalf of the ladies of the evening. There was something about it in your paper today, didn't you read it?"

"To tell you the truth, lately I don't even read my own stuff."

"Seems like everybody's gotten into a big huff because the city wants to move the red-light district to La Bolsa. The ladies and their madames over on Daniel Ruiz, Pajaritos, Cuauhtemotzin and Netzahualcóyotl are asking for a little more time. They say La Bolsa's too dangerous. There's no police there, and no sewers either. I think he said they want to move over to your neighborhood instead."

"To Santa María?"

"That's what he said."

"I suppose it could be worse. Better than a lot of the riffraff you see out on the street nowadays."

The Chinaman watched his two friends with a dreamlike air. Taking advantage of the pause, he'd gone off inside himself to a place he didn't share with his friends, a place all his own. The place of his frequent silences. A private place inside the mind of this thirty-five-year-old Chinaman who, regardless of the fact that he was born in the Mexican state of Sinaloa, spoke with a marked accent, swallowing his *r*'s and putting the characteristic *l* in their place, maybe as a way of affirming his differentness, as a way of getting back at this country where the Chinese were persecuted with an absurd cruelty. Tomás Wong—ex–oil rigger, ex-sailor, ex–telegraph operator, currently employed as a carpenter in a San Angel textile mill—inhabited many worlds, including the world of his private silences and the world of the most bitter workers' struggle the Valley of Mexico had seen in many years.

Verdugo got up and said good night to his clients, who kissed him and fussed over him, chattering amiably. The light went out over their table.

"Another game, gentlemen?"

WORKING-MAN BLUES

The surrounding hubbub of the newsroom was just what he needed to forge that tiny island of silence his thoughts shared with the rhythmic (he would say musical) tap-tap of the typewriter and the ring of the bell signaling the approach of the right-hand margin. He needed that nurturing chaos, the newsroom filled with lines of singing chorus girls, his coworkers arguing the finer points of local politics at the top of their lungs or disputing the latest and always doubtful results from the old Condesa Track (recently converted to the new sport of auto racing), slamming the doors on their way in and out, while Rufino the messenger boy howled disconsolately from a toothache, and some unrequited lover shamed by one of Manterola's colleagues fired a gun into the air, threatening to kill himself.

This was the music of the spheres for Pioquinto Manterola. Only in the midst of that journalistic free-for-all could he truly retreat into his own thoughts, only there could he really enjoy his work. A few years ago he'd gone out to Tlaxcala to write a novel but he'd never gotten past the first page, undone by the silence of the countryside.

So it was nothing out of the ordinary on that afternoon to find Manterola chain-smoking Argentino ovals out of a wrinkled pack while he ran page after page through his typewriter like links of sausage in a chorizo factory.

He was writing the sad story of the capture of Mario Lombardi and his multinational gang (with an Italian capo and a Cuban and a Colombian in its ranks) who had busied themselves during the last two months drilling through the walls of the Coliseo and Ambos Mundos Hotels and the Paris Jewelry Shop.

Lombardi, a mechanical genius, confessed that he would leave the dirty work to his companions while he saved his own talents for the fine art of safecracking and picking the locks on suitcases and chests.

It had only been half an hour since Manterola's interview with Lombardi (hot out of the oven, as they say) and the thing that impressed him most were the criminal's parting words:

"I worked for years in New York City before the cops tumbled to my game. But this town is something else, you can't get any work done around here. When they finally kick me out of the country I'm going to tell all my friends: 'Stay the hell away from Mexico.' "

Manterola was fascinated by the ambiguity of the whole thing: Lombardi telling his friends not to go to Mexico. What for? Because the police were too tough? Because there was never enough loot in the safes he cracked? Because the weather was no good? Because there was too much traffic?

Once he'd filled four double-spaced pages he ran quickly back over them, checking for errors, stuck the last page back into the typewriter to add a few lines praising the work of the secret police under the leadership of Special Agent Chief Valente Quintana, and finally went back to the beginning to scrawl a headline:

STAY AWAY FROM MEXICO, LOMBARDI WARNS FRIENDS

He threw his cigarette onto the floor, ground it out energetically under his shoe, and ran downstairs to the print shop.

"I need three columns, first page, second section."

The editor left off setting type, leafed through Manterola's manuscript, and nodded.

DEATH OF A TROMBONIST

The poet Fermín Valencia stood combing his mustache in front of a broken piece of mirror stuck with a few big-headed nails against the bluish wall. First he combed it down so the hair completely covered both his lips, then with two quick strokes he launched it skyward, first on the left, then on the right.

He stood for a minute admiring his handiwork, but even the jaunty mustache couldn't lift him out of the blackness of his depression. In disgust, he threw the comb onto the bed, covered already with books, dirty clothes, boots, his Colt .45 and cartridge belt, and a heap of empty whiskey bottles (Old Taylor, Old Continental, Clear Brook—all the product, despite their names, of the Piedras Negras National Distillery in Coahuila). He stared unhappily at the mess. He'd slept through what was left of the night, which wasn't much, in an armchair by the window to avoid having to clear off the bed at five o'clock in the morning when he'd gotten in after dominoes and a long late-night walk.

Closing his eyes in the face of so much desolation, he stuck his arms out in front of him and, playing blindman's buff like he used to as a child, walked unsteadily toward the door. His hands touched wood, he turned the knob, and went out.

Passing apartment B on the ground floor, he suddenly realized it had been days since the landlord had been by to pester him. It wasn't for lack of money the poet's rent was always exactly a month and a half overdue. That was just his way of creating some kind of order in the midst of so much chaos. And besides, he loved to get old *don* Florencio's goat.

"*Don* Florencio?" he called out softly, rapping his knuckles on the door.

There was no answer and the poet went out into the street.

The First Artillery Regiment Brass Band was playing in the park ("in dedication to the honorable citizens of Tacubaya," according to the program: "Sonoran Echoes," followed by A. Castañeda's "Alvaro Obregón March," and finishing up with selections from the opera *Aïda*). The poet was never one to turn down something for free, especially concerts in the park. He liked the Secret Policemen's Marching Band the best and after that the Mexico City Police Corps Orchestra which, in the time of Police Chief Ramírez Garrido, had learned to play the "Internationale" with such enthusiasm that it became a regular practice number for them and they would play it when tuning up before their concerts.

The poet strolled past groups of workers from the nearby munitions factory, bank tellers, and lonely señoritas shouldering bright parasols, until he came to the place where *don* Alberto the butcher sat along with his family on the chairs they'd brought with them into the park.

"Take a load off, *don* Fermín. Pull up a chair," smiled the butcher.

"Thanks, *don* Alberto, but I think I'll walk awhile. I'm just trying to get the blood going and shake off some of this melancholy." He smiled out of the corner of his eye at the butcher's daughter Odilia, who had recently had the honor of being elected "Miss Congeniality" by her coworkers at Munitions Factory Number Three.

The poet strolled on to the beat of the band in his high-heeled boots, hands clasped behind his back, weaving his way through the crowd. He glanced around at the musicians sweating in their heavy uniforms, Odilia with a pair of enormous yellow bows tied around her braids, and a gang of boys trying to fly a small toy airplane but succeeding only in knocking men's hats off or crash-landing into the round bellies of good-humored petit bourgeois picnickers.

"The sun up/ every day it comes/ a gift/ Gladly we would

repay it/ but our hats are empty," the poet wrote in his head, trying to memorize a little piece, a few words, a single line so that he could retrieve it again later on. Maybe it was true for other people that writing was the act of giving life to the blank page. But the poet lived a life filled with invisible pages all covered with his invisible thoughts which he tried in vain to recapture, late into the night or mornings round about dawn, with a real piece of paper on the desk in front of him, disconsolately empty.

He dropped anchor at a little juice cart near the bandstand.

"What'll it be today, boss?" the vendor asked him.

"I'll have a glass of lemonade, Simón."

The vendor, wagging his little goatlike beard back and forth, poured out a glass of lemonade and made another mark on a wrinkled piece of paper. He had agreed to pay the poet twenty-five glasses in exchange for the lines that graced the front of his cart in a multicolored gargoylish script:

> *Simón's drinks are sweet and frosty,*
> *fruity, fresh, top-notch, first-rate.*
> *If anyone thinks they're not tasty,*
> *with one punch I'll set him straight.*

The poet took a sip of lemonade and glanced at the band as it hurried through the final strains of the Alvaro Obregón March. A sudden movement caught his eye. A man whose face the poet couldn't quite make out was climbing the stairs at the back of the bandstand. He approached the trombonist from behind, pulled a small gun from his vest pocket, and without the slightest hesitation held it to the musician's temple and pulled the trigger.

The killer looked out into the crowd and for a moment his eyes met with the poet's myopic gaze. Fermín Valencia rubbed his hands vigorously over his face while the band played on unaware of what had just happened in the back row. The murderer jumped over the bandstand railing and ran off through the groups of Sunday strollers. The poet brought his hand to his waist, confirmed that he was unarmed, and watched as the man crossed the avenue and disappeared into a side street. The music stopped and the startled cries of the crowd rose to replace it. As the shocked musicians hovered around their murdered comrade, the poet tried to get a grip on what he'd seen. A man had climbed onto the bandstand, approached the trombonist from behind, and shot him through the head. He was wearing a vest, the poet remembered that much. And his face? There wasn't any face, just the vague image of a peaked cap, the kind a rich man's chauffeur might wear. And he'd held the gun in his left hand. A southpaw. Wouldn't this be a hell of a story for Pioquinto Manterola, the poet thought. If only his eyes were better . . .

He approached the bandstand and climbed up through the crowd, swinging his elbows to clear the way. In spite of his diminutive size the poet commanded respect, maybe because of his magnificent mustache or the look of uninhibited desperation burning in his eyes.

He saw how the blood oozed from the small black hole in the dead man's temple, pooling up on the bandstand floor. He stared for a long moment into the dead man's wide-open eyes: "the stare of death," how many times had he seen it before? He'd never been able to decide whether that look reflected the final brutal pain of death, the slipping off of the mortal coil as it were, or whether it was the first glimmer of what lay beyond. In the face of this uncertainty the poet had become an atheist: something told him the blank stare of death corresponded to the first glimpse of God, and if that was the case, he'd decided long ago he didn't want to have anything to do with Him.

"Stand back!" he shouted at a pair of grief-stricken trumpet players. "What's the dead man's name?"

"Sergeant José Zevada," answered the captain and conductor, savagely twisting his baton between his hands.

The poet leaned over the dead man and pulled his eyelids shut. Then he stuck his hands into the dead man's pockets and emptied out the contents, naming each item out loud as he sorted through them:

"One snotty handkerchief, one photograph of a beautiful young woman, one darning egg, one peso, fifty-five cents in change . . ."

IN WHICH THE CHARACTERS PLAY
DOMINOES AND ACCEPT THEIR LOT AS
THIRD-CLASS CITIZENS

". . . one silver fork, one bundle of newspaper clippings held together with a rubber band, one sapphire ring, two diamond rings with silver bands, and two large turquoise rings . . ."

"This trombonist of yours sounds like a walking jewelry store," observed Verdugo, setting the two/three onto the marble tabletop. His plan was to force the Chinaman to play the antepenultimate six, so the journalist could crucify the poet on the double-sixes.

The Chinaman avoided the trap, playing a one.

"And the newspaper clippings, what were they all about, my esteemed collaborator?" asked Manterola, leaving off taking notes for a minute to wipe his sweaty face with a handkerchief. The poet made an elegant wave of his hand, like a magician performing a trick, inserted two fingers into his vest pocket, pulled out the bundle of clippings, and dropped them onto the table.

"Ask and ye shall receive."

"Now that's no ordinary helper," said the lawyer, impressed.

The journalist played the three/five, to the lawyer's great consternation. If anyone was going to be crucified at this point, it was going to be him.

"Pay attention, man," he admonished Manterola. "The moment of truth is at hand and you've got your mind on your work."

"Sorry," apologized the journalist, while the poet played the double-fives, a big grin on his face.

Manterola picked up the bundle of clippings. With Verdugo forced to pass, the Chinaman played the two/four. The journalist went on the offensive with another three.

"Have you read them yet?" he asked.

"Of course. In all the world there was never born another man as impatient as I."

"Do you realize it's getting to the point again where you have to carry a gun in this town?" the journalist asked the others. "Seems like we let ourselves get out of the habit for a while."

"Not me," said the lawyer, drawing his .38 automatic. "It cost me thirty-two pesos at La Universal. I clean it and oil it every month, and take it back once a year for a complete going-over."

"How about you, Tomás?" Manterola asked, losing interest in the game now that he'd practically got it in the bag. Without showing any other sign of having heard, the Chinaman drew a large Spanish switchblade from his boot. He pressed the button and a polished steel blade, nearly a foot long, sprang out with a clean snap.

"General Villa used to clean his fingernails with one of those," said the poet.

"They must have been vely dilty," said the Chinaman without changing his expression and without taking his attention off the game.

"Game's over, gentlemen," declared the journalist, slapping his last domino onto the table with a sharp crack.

The echo ran the length of the nearly empty cantina and mixed with the forced laughter of three officers drinking at the bar.

"I never understood where you got your accent from, Tomás," said the poet, getting up from the table. "After all, you were born in Sinaloa."

The lawyer counted the remaining dominoes and jotted the score in a small notebook he kept just for that purpose.

Manterola suspiciously eyed the three young officers, two captains and a lieutenant. From the very last batch to come out of the Revolution, no doubt. Probably from one of the last campaigns against the Zapatistas and the final Agua Prieta Revolt, where they would have won their stripes. They'd reached a thoroughly advanced state of inebriation and waved their hands about dramatically as they talked. Manterola didn't like them. He didn't like soldiers in general, men in uniform. It was an aversion he shared with his three friends, though perhaps for different reasons.

"How'd you get onto the bandstand in the first place?" he asked the poet.

The poet climbed onto the back of his chair. "Let's just say that in spite of my size, people manage to perceive something of my inner strength. And besides, the place was a complete madhouse."

Verdugo started to mix the bones. The Chinaman stood up, crossed the room, and leaned his elbows on the bar.

The bartender got the message, followed his eyes just to make sure, and took down the bottle of Havana brandy.

"You serve Orientals in this place, mister?" slurred one of the officers.

"They say they're absolutely the filthiest creatures that ever walked the earth," added the lieutenant, smoothing his trim little mustache. "I hear they all live in those nasty little shops of theirs and fight the rats over the crumbs for dinner. Then they go to sleep on the countertops." The officers had spent the earlier part of the evening drinking second-class aguardiente at first-class prices in the ballroom upstairs. Obviously, they weren't familiar with the house rules. Two different worlds made up the Majestic, one upstairs and one downstairs. There was no love lost between them and they didn't mix. María Conesa might be singing upstairs for some high government minister while downstairs, when the pool tables were really jumping, you might run across half a dozen of the toughest, ugliest Spaniards that ever cursed the face of the earth, and with more blood on their hands than the whole rest of the city put together. And this was a city with a blood debt you couldn't clear up in a very long lifetime.

The Chinaman looked the officers over one by one. His disdain could easily be misinterpreted as fear by the drunken men. It would be a big mistake.

"Don't you officels have any medals?" he asked.

"The Mexican Army doesn't need to put its honor on parade for some slanteyes like you," scoffed one of the captains. Back at the table, the poet and the journalist exchanged looks. Verdugo got up and walked toward the bathroom, near the front door. He unfastened two of the buttons on his vest and with the same motion released the safety on his gun.

"What about in youl house? Don't you have any medals in youl house even?" asked the Chinaman, fixing the men with a withering stare.

"My friends here each have two citations for valor and a medal for being wounded in the line of duty, you lousy Chink," sputtered the lieutenant, feeling incomprehensibly trapped by the absurdity of the Chinaman's question.

"Tomás!" the journalist shouted from his seat at the table. "Let's not have any bloodshed, please." He turned his back to the bar and took over where the lawyer left off, shuffling the dominoes. The poet kept his eyes on the officers.

"You gentlemen ready to pay for your drinks?" the bartender asked the three soldiers, well aware of what was about to happen.

"I was only going to suggest you take youl medals and hang them flom youl fucking mothel's asses," said the Chinaman.

Tomás found himself obliged to deflect the lieutenant's fist with a quick chopping blow to the forearm. At his post near the door the lawyer drew his gun and shouted in a booming baritone:

"Keep it clean, gentlemen. The first one who goes for his gun is a dead man."

The two captains turned to look at Verdugo while Tomás smashed his fist into the lieutenant's face. Two bloody teeth dropped from the officer's mouth and he staggered backward. One of the captains hung back with his eyes on Verdugo while the other went to the aid of his fallen comrade, who fell underneath the bar spitting blood. The Chinaman stopped the captain in his tracks, butting him in the stomach with his head. The poet got to his feet. Walking calmly to where the first officer lay on the floor, he placed a foot over the hand slowly inching its way toward the gun at the man's belt.

Gripping his stomach, the captain dropped to his knees and started to vomit. Then the Chinaman moved toward the third man, who grabbed the bottle of Havana brandy off the bar and, brandishing it in front of him, backed toward the door. But the lawyer came from behind and brought the barrel of his gun down hard on the man's temple. He fell in a heap on the floor.

"Sorry to spoil your fun, Tomás, but I was afraid you were going to hurt the poor guy," he said.

The bartender came out and saved the rest of the bottle of brandy from spilling onto the ground.

Tomás walked back to the bar, rubbing his right hand.

"You missed the party," said the poet to Manterola, who continued to scramble the dominoes.

"Not on your life. I turned around when the action started. I was just keeping quiet a little for show. I've known Tomás for three years now and I've seen him do this two or three times. It's always the same. I tell you, the man's made of iron inside. And I love to watch the way he fights with his hands. It's like nothing I've ever seen."

"That may be true enough, but when there's gunplay involved, the guys in the white hats don't always win," said Verdugo the lawyer, returning to his place at the table.

"That was a good move on your part, no doubt about it," acknowledged the poet.

The Chinaman continued to rub his hand while the bartender poured him a drink from the salvaged bottle.

"Have you got a pan you could put some cold watel in fol me?" he asked.

"The thing that gets my goat," said the poet, "are these boys who get their heads all swelled up when they get inside a uniform. They act like every civilian's a second-class citizen."

"But that's exactly what we are, second-class citizens. Haven't you ever figured that out? You can't expect to get any more out of this country than you're ready to give," pronounced the lawyer, lighting up one of his short cigars.

Two of the officers lay passed out on the floor, while the third threw up under the bar. The Chinaman took the washbasin from the bartender and stuck his swollen hand into the water. The bartender went back out and stripped the three soldiers of their weapons.

"Anothel game?" asked Tomás, taking his seat.

Using the bandana from around his neck, the poet wiped the sweat from his hands. It had always been that way for him, this same cold sweat breaking out in the face of violence.

"Second-class citizens? I think not, gentlemen," said the reporter. "Third-class is more like it. The second-class citizens are the ones running all over each other to spit-polish the boots of the first-class citizens. After all, who were the real losers in this little Revolution of ours? The old Porfirian aristocracy? Hardly. They're all busy marrying off their daughters to Obregón's colonels. The outcasts, the pariahs, they're the real losers, same as always. The campesinos who made the Revolution in the first place. And us, too, we lost the Revolution without even firing a shot."

"Speak for yourself," said the poet. "You're forgetting all the years I rode with Pancho Villa."

The newspaperman slowly unbuttoned his vest and then his shirt. A whitish scar ran across his chest. He touched it gingerly, as if it belonged to someone else.

"What about the ones who got it from the sidelines? Do we count, too?"

"Naturally," said the poet.

The Chinaman placed his hand back into the water and slowly spread his fingers.

"Is it broken?" asked the lawyer.

Tomás shrugged his shoulders.

"Third-class citizens," insisted the journalist.

"Don't get all worked up about it, okay?" the lawyer said as he drew his seven shiny dominoes from the pile. "After all, what about the fourth-class citizens? Didn't you read how the other day fifteen thousand Roman Catholics came together to pay homage to good old Agustín de Iturbide on the hundredth anniversary of his crummy little empire? For Chrissakes."

"I'm not getting all worked up about it. That's just the way it is, and believe me, I know. If all the third-class Mexicans left town, there'd be no one left to turn out the lights, let alone grow the food for the rich man's table."

"Remember you're talking to a poet," the poet reminded him. "I have a hard enough time putting food on my own table."

"I suppose I just feel like talking, that's all. And unlike our friend Tomás, here, I can't get it out of my system by beating up on a few helpless soldiers."

As the friends talked, the three officers staggered to their feet and with the bartender's encouragement made their way to the door. One of them turned to fire off a last threatening glance, but the bartender mercifully sent him on his way with a friendly shove. The double door swung back and forth, squeaking softly.

The Chinaman extended his long fingers one at a time, his hand continuing to swell in spite of the cold water.

"See what you get for fooling around with the Mexican Army?" the poet scolded him. "And what for? Just because the guy said you sleep on a countertop? If what our friend Manterola here says is true, about us being nothing but a bunch of third-class citizens, what the hell's it matter if we sleep on countertops anyway? I sleep in an armchair, and Verdugo, here"—he gestured toward the lawyer—"never sleeps at all. He's a vampire."

"You want to go first, or you want me to?" Verdugo asked Manterola.

The cuckoo clock chirped out three in the morning.

5

THE WAY THINGS USED TO BE:
ALBERTO VERDUGO

My full name was originally Alberto Verdugo y Sáez de
Miera, and I suppose it's only natural that after thirty-five years
I should have discarded a fair amount, if not all, of so much
nomenclatural baggage. That's why it's all the same to me if
they simply call me "the lawyer Verdugo," or "*licenciado* Verdugo," which means the same thing. It's always amused me
that what I ended up with after all these years is my father's
ancient surname, which has likewise become my nickname: El
Verdugo, which literally means "the executioner," the hang-
man, the one who kills within the law. And it doesn't matter
too much either that I've fallen short of certain expectations,
certain illusions. If that's what you want to call that conglom-
eration of vague aspirations we inevitably turn into pretexts for
living instead of rules to live by. The only thing that makes any
consistent sense is a certain stubbornness on my part, the overwhelming desire to move on. The executioner of dreams, you
might say. But above all, the executioner of the plans they had
for me, that's more like it, the future they so carefully prepared.
The killer of my parents' dreams, that would have had me as
the administrator of giant haciendas, overseer of masses of campesinos, a factory owner with the obligatory annual holiday
pilgrimage to Europe on a Ward Line steamship. On the other
side of the balance was my own rebellion and the bet I'd made
with myself. Like a runaway vehicle on the Paseo de la Reforma
I ran in the opposite direction from where they wanted me to
go, and here I am, still running today, in spite of the fact there's
nowhere I'm running to and the absence of any real victory is

painfully obvious. Gone now are the father and mother who made the straightjacket in the first place, gone is the last trace, the last scrap of cloth the straightjacket used to be. As for me, I've simply gone and turned my lawyer's degree into the modus vivendi for a streetwalker's attorney. There's nothing either better or worse I could have done with that sacred scrap of paper originally destined to hang on some wall in the graveyard of the Porfirian establishment where the rest of my family lived and died. Of course, there's still the three years I spent studying in Italy. Or better yet, there's still my translation into Spanish of the great anarchist writer Enrico Malatesta. The proof is in the pudding, as they say. I can still see my Uncle Ernesto foaming at the mouth like a rabid dog when I put a signed and dedicated copy in front of him on his desk. I remember reading out loud to him in a honeyed voice where it says: "The enemy is not he who is born beyond our borders, nor he who speaks a language different from our own, but he who, without any right, seeks to strip away the liberty and independence of others." And now that the old family home lies in ruins, struck by a stray cannonball in the fighting back in '13, the rubble crumbling underfoot, I can go home dressed as myself and wearing my own wide-brimmed hat, telltale symbol of a man of the night. The same pearl gray hat that's known and recognized in cabarets, cantinas, and bordellos all over Mexico City, stolen off a hat rack from the son of one of old *don* Porfirio's own government ministers (he only wore it on Sundays). Now I can take my hat off, wave it through the air, call out in greeting to the ruins, and say: "Here where you see me now I have triumphed. I have become nothing of what they wanted me to become, I have none of what they wanted me to have. I've left nothing behind. Nothing remains. Nothing remains."

A BODY FALLS

Pioquinto Manterola had just finished writing up the bloody murder of officers Filiberto Sánchez and Jesús González, shot to death in the backseat of their black Ford, license number 4087, the same two officers who only a month before had been showered with praise following the capture of the infamous "Black Hat." Today the men were nothing but a pair of bloody corpses in the back of a squad car. They had been quietly lying in wait for Tufiabla the Arab, who had turned the tables on the two policemen and not so quietly emptied the chambers of his revolver into the back of their car before they could take him in.

With this routine piece of work out of the way, the journalist turned his attention back to the bundle of newspaper clippings his friend the poet had given him the night before. A stiff breeze was blowing down from the mountains, and Manterola got up from his desk on the third floor of the El Demócrata building at 15 Humboldt Street to go close the window. A cigarette hung out of one corner of his mouth. He was feeling particularly beaten down, washed out, old, and maybe just a little bored.

He walked over to the window and looked down in time to see a shiny new Exeter pull up in front of the building. The breeze that had so annoyed him a minute ago refreshed him now. He went back to his desk and looked around at the desolation all around him. At the other end of the office Gómez was relating the latest escapades of the Soviet Nine, the sports reporters' baseball team. Two desks farther on, Gonzaga dozed at his drawing table. Manterola tried to concentrate on the clippings in front of him. They all seemed to be more or less the same, brief single-column pieces that over a period of ten years followed the somewhat dubious career of a certain Colonel Froilán Zevada (the brother of the murdered trombonist?): his contribution to the struggle against the Maderistas, his timely about-face following the Juárez treaty, his bloody triumph against the forces of Emiliano Zapata, his less than exemplary participation in the events of the Decena Trágica, his belated crossover to the side of the Carrancistas, his union-busting police work on behalf of the oil companies at Mata Redonda, his ties to Pablo González. His promotion to the rank of colonel during the fight against Pancho Villa, his once again belated switch over to the opposing side, along with an entire garrison under his command at Tampico during the Revolt of Agua Prieta. And mixed in with everything else, the occasional mention of his presence at some military academy ball, his success in a marksmanship competition, rumors about a midnight duel in the Alameda, an article about a ballistics course he attended in Germany . . .

Nothing out of the ordinary, thought the journalist as he lit up another cigarette. A horse-drawn coal cart passed underneath the window, the animal's hoofs ringing out against the cobbled street, and he got up to watch it pass by. Something you see less and less of all the time, he thought.

It was the kind of afternoon made for daydreaming, for blowing smoke out the window—the kind of afternoon to lie back and let your mind run free, not to let yourself be bothered with the pointless career of some power-hungry colonel, not to let yourself be distracted thinking about how the horse-drawn carts were giving up ground day by day to streets full of Packards and Fords, perverse imported machines (only the tires were made in Mexico) running wild in a city that was built for anything but them. It was a perfect day for daydreams, for long reminiscences, to ring the bells and set the doves of memory free. But which memories? That was the question. The saddest ones? The ones that pricked the spirit like that red sun going down out toward Tacuba? Or cotton-filled memories, like those clouds over there, nibbling away at the edge of a stubbornly blue sky? He flung his cigarette out the window, partly because he was tired of listening to his own thoughts, partly because he liked to watch the little white cylinder tumble down the three stories to the street. The butt paused in midair and then continued its descent, landing on the roof of one of the aforementioned automobiles, from which, at that very moment, a woman emerged. Tiny sparks scattered off the roof of the car into the woman's hat. She turned to stare up; he smiled with embarrassment and quickly pulled the window shut.

Manterola took a step back, like a little boy caught doing something bad, and then it occurred to him the face he'd just glimpsed had been a very, very pretty one.

He walked back to his desk and pulled a piece of paper from his typewriter. Whistling a waltz, he sauntered over to where Gonzaga nodded off at his drawing table, and shook him gently.

"Hey *artiste,* wake up. It's time to go to work."

"What's that, cheggidout . . ." muttered Gonzaga, not quite sure who he was talking to.

They said he smoked opium in the dens off Dolores Street, that he regularly drank mezcal until he passed out with his old Zapatista buddies in some dive out toward Tacubaya, and that he would chain-smoke Veracruz cigars until he was on the brink of nicotine intoxication. But be that as it may, he could draw faster than anyone, and with both hands at once, like Leonardo da Vinci.

"Cheggidout. What you got?"

"Tufiabla the Arab sneaks up on a squad car from behind, a black Ford, license number 4087, and empties his revolver at the two officers sitting in the back seat."

"Is he dressed like an Arab?"

"I suppose so, more or less. Like the Arabs in the market."

"Cheggidout, cheggidout, one Arab coming right up," mumbled Gonzaga, starting to draw what would soon be the central illustration on page one, section two of *El Demócrata.*

Pioquinto lit another cigarette and felt himself drawn back toward the window. What had happened to that pretty face?

Gonzaga sang "Flor de Te" as he drew, a fine pencil in his

right hand and a piece of charcoal in his left for sketching in the shadows. Manterola let out a deep sigh and went back to contemplating the blue of the sky out the open window. Suddenly something caught his eye, and he looked over toward the third-story window of the building across the street. He watched as the glass pane shattered and a man fell through the air waving his arms wildly, his screams reaching Manterola's ears seconds before he crashed to the pavement. Manterola stared across into the broken window and for a pair of seconds stood contemplating the terrified eyes of the same woman he'd inadvertently thrown his cigarette at only a few minutes before. He wouldn't exactly have said that time stood still, but he might have said that time stretched out while he looked from one to the other, from the woman's eyes in the building across the street, to the broken body splayed out on the pavement forty-five feet below. As he watched, the woman retreated slowly and disappeared.

Unable to believe his own eyes, the journalist leaned out the window as if to confirm the fact there was actually a body lying amidst the shards of glass on the street below. It was true, the body was there, starting to attract the attention of passersby. Slow to react for the first time in years, Manterola finally started to move in the direction of the stairs.

"Cheggidout, cheggidout, what's going on?" asked Gonzaga, but Manterola was already out of sight, running down the stairs to go stand in front of a dead man in the middle of Humboldt Street.

WORKING-MAN BLUES

All day long his swollen hand gave him trouble. The foreman had already come around a couple of times to egg him on and step up the pressure. Indalecio and Martín, the Chinaman's coworkers, had tried to cover for him by carrying more than their share of the work and leaving the easiest jobs for him, but it was no easy thing to avoid Maganda's "all-seeing" eyes. The foreman made his way between the looms, repeating obsessively:

"I'm all-seeing. Nothing escapes me. Maybe you think you can fool the boss man, and maybe sometimes you can, but you can't fool me, you lazy sons of bitches. I'm all-seeing."

Tomás Wong liked the noise inside the factory, the thick humidity of the air, the smell of the dyes. As a carpenter he wasn't tied down to a machine but could move freely around the big building, setting a wedge, building a bench—or, like right now, making shipping crates that would travel around the world in the hold of some ship.

"Come on, Chinaboy, take it easy, will you? Look at your hand. Let me cover for you," said Martín, taking the heavy hammer from Tomás and driving in the big double-headed nails.

A ship, a ship roaming the high seas, never stopping . . . except every now and then to fish for a few words, always in a different tongue, always with a different meaning.

"Nostalgia," he thought to himself. "Too damn much nostalgia. Too many memories. You can't live on nostalgia and secondhand news," and instead he tried to think of a way to get back at Maganda the foreman.

He'd had it on his mind since a week ago when, at the end

of the day, the management had tried to strip-search him, Martín and Indalecio, the three carpenters at the Magnolia Textile Mill in Contreras—supposedly because tools had been disappearing from the factory shop. And, of course, they'd refused to go along and there'd been a ruckus at the factory gate. They got their way in the end, and ever since the "all-seeing" Maganda had been trying to get even.

The Chinaman's swollen hand was as good a pretext as any, and Maganda spent the whole day egging the Chinaman on—tightening the screws. The "All-seeing" got a special pleasure out of picking a fight with the workers, humiliating them one by one. He was the kind of man who needed constant affirmation of his own existence, his power. In those turbulent years in the textile industry, he found his place as the perfect battering ram on behalf of an owner class locked in a fierce and violent confrontation with the unions.

The Chinaman left his two companions hammering away at the crates and walked over toward the warehouse to see if the wood had come in for the repair of two old broken-down looms.

At the warehouse door he ran into Cipriano, mill mechanic and the union's general secretary.

"What's up, Tomás? How've the bourgeois dogs been treating you lately? I noticed Maganda's been giving it to you all morning long."

"I sclewed up my hand," said the Chinaman, as if that explained everything.

"Been rearranging faces again, eh?"

The Chinaman shrugged his shoulders. He wasn't much of a talker. He let other people tell his stories for him. It seemed as though his friends were always hearing about his adventures secondhand, if at all, from people who'd known him in other places. At other times.

"Leave it to Tomás to be like one of those inscrutable Orientals," thought Cipriano, quoting the reporters from *El Universal,* which at that time was leading a massive campaign against the tongs, Chinese gangs that controlled the clandestine gambling houses and opium dens on Dolores Street.

"Don't forget about the meeting tonight," he said. "We're going to talk about the dance and solidarity action with the strike at the Magdalena mill."

The Chinaman nodded and walked on without any hurry.

The factory was divided into three giant bays and a pair of warehouses, all arranged around a large flagstoned patio in front of the offices. The shop space, poorly illuminated through small windows high up on the walls, enclosed 350 workers and 10 foremen. According to custom, the factory's French administrators never set foot inside while the mill was in operation. They only went in after the workers had left. Theirs was the world of the offices. The opposite of the Chinaman and Cipriano, who roamed the entire factory, looking for projects here and there, picking up odd jobs. Whenever they could they stopped to chat with the other workers who, tied down to their machines, received the two labor organizers with enthusiasm, like homing pigeons carrying good news. Cipriano had been named union general secretary in the last elections and the Chinaman was elected labor secretary.

Tomás Wong crossed to the end of the warehouse looking for the clerk. When he finally found him, lost among the giant rolls of cloth, the man gave him a dozen vague excuses about why the wood he needed hadn't come in yet. "Somebody's scamming here," thought the Chinaman. That was the kind of game the nonunion workers played. If it had been a union man it would have been different. The union had its code of honor. The workers fought head-on with the bosses. If someone needed extra money he could earn it organizing for the union. The code had been born with the union and passed down from veterans to newcomers. No one had ever bothered to write it down but everyone knew what it said: Never talk to the foremen unless your work requires it; always work out production problems among the workers; cover for sick or tired comrades; support and nourish the apprentice.

Now as Tomás headed back toward the yard loaded down with wood for the shipping crates the "All-seeing" suddenly stepped in front of him.

"You lousy Chinese bum," he growled.

The Chinaman dropped the wood onto the floor. He spoke slowly:

"Look, in the last thlee months two folemen have got themselves killed in the mills hele alound San Angel and Contlelas. You know why that is, Maganda? Because they couldn't lealn to stay out of the way, to not get mixed up with the stlike between the wolkels and the factoly. I don't talk much. You do youl job, I'll do mine, and that's as fal as it needs to go."

"You think you're pretty hot stuff don't you, Chiney? You think you can scare me?"

Tomás only hit him once, with his already swollen hand. Maganda fell backward, a cut over his right eye. He looked up uneasily from the floor, but the Chinaman's cold stare cut him short.

The Chinaman picked up the wood and walked away.

When he reached his comrades, who had watched the whole thing from a distance, he put down the lumber and massaged his hand. The swelling was getting worse.

8

IN WHICH THE CHARACTERS PLAY
DOMINOES AND DISCOVER THAT
THE TROMBONIST AND THE LADY
ARE CONNECTED

". . . a sort of blue-gray gabardine, and a blue velvet ribbon around her neck. White lace cuffs, and a bonnet," explained the journalist.

"Who ever would've thought you had such an eye for feminine attire?" The poet laughed as he mixed the bones.

"It's amazing when you consider the fact I only saw her for a second. When I got down to the street I ran right past the body and went into the building to look for her, but she wasn't there. I swear I looked everywhere."

"Do you think she killed him?" asked Verdugo the lawyer, pouring himself a generous glassful of Havana brandy and stretching his legs out under the table. He wore an elegant pair of new boots purchased with the proceeds from his latest successful case.

"Who can say?" Manterola scratched his rising hairline and pictured the woman's fear-filled face seconds after the man broke through the window and fell three floors to the street.

"You'd think this was some rinkydink little town, the way things are going around here, first the trombonist and now this. And they say this town's getting so big you never run into anybody you know anymore . . ."

"You want to go filst ol you want me to?" the Chinaman asked Manterola.

"That hand of yours is never going to get any better if you

keep on busting heads," answered Manterola, giving his partner the go-ahead with a wave of his hand.

The Chinaman played the double-threes, and the poet and the lawyer pulled their chairs up to the table. The ritual had begun. Now the conversation mixed with the dry click of the bones, forming a tangle of words and dominoes, double-fives and five/fours. The cantina was far from quiet. Two melancholy drunks sat drowning their sorrows at one end of the bar; a kid played an out-of-tune guitar at a table by the door; and a Lebanese fabric merchant, talking at the top of his lungs, was trying to convince his two drinking buddies of the potential profits to be gotten by establishing a new mule route over the mountains to Acapulco, traditional bastion of the Spanish where his countrymen have never managed to get a foothold. And if that weren't enough, Reckless Ross sat at the other end of the bar telling a bored bartender how three years ago in Chicago, before he found himself obliged to "travel around countries the size of a postage stamp giving shows in fleabag theaters," he broke the U.S. motorcycle speed record. His narrative came liberally embellished with the roar of a motor emerging from a throat heavily lubricated with shots of mezcal.

"So what'd you think when you checked out the guy's wallet?" asked the poet.

"Took a little balls on your part, didn't it?" added the lawyer Verdugo.

"Never fear, play away," said Manterola noticing the Chinaman's hesitation.

"You just pay attention, okay? I've got this one lapped up," said Tomás, setting the two/one onto the table.

"Watch it, poet, I smell a trap," said Verdugo, more than anything else to gauge his opponents' reaction.

"I didn't search him," explained Manterola. "A traffic cop had already gotten there by the time I gave up looking for the lady. When I told him I was a reporter he showed me the guy's wallet and that's when I got the big surprise . . ."

The poet pulled his own surprise, playing a two and forcing

everyone else to pass. Enjoying his move in silence, he played the two/three.

"Playing it pretty close to the chest there, eh partner?" nodded the lawyer Verdugo admiringly.

"Just luck is all," said the poet.

"Looks like we're screwed, Tomás," said Manterola.

"It isn't ovel yet," said the Chinaman flatly.

"Anyway, that's when I find out the guy's name is Colonel Froilán Zevada, and I say to myself, 'Now isn't that a hell of a coincidence.' Enough to make a man nervous. Two Zevadas in one week. First yours and now mine . . ."

"I hear you," said the poet. "If you'd only seen the way they blew that trombonist's brains out, you'd know what nervous really was."

"You surely don't expect me to believe that was the first time you ever saw anyone's brains blown out? After all the time you spent in the Northern Division where they'd blow a fellow's brains out at the drop of a hat," said Verdugo.

"And then eat them," put in the Chinaman.

"Go ahead and have your fun, but the fact is it was a little too much to have to watch a fellow's head blown open while he was playing the Alvaro Obregón March."

"I hadn't thought about that," said the lawyer.

The Chinaman turned the game to fours, forcing everyone to pass, and turning the hand over to his partner.

"See what I mean, inkslingel?"

"Trust in the eternal wisdom of the Orient, that's what I always say. *Dios nunca muere.* God never dies."

"Wasn't that Confucius who said that?" asked the poet.

"Don't ask me, I'm an atheist," said Tomás Wong. He smiled.

"Do you remember the photograph of that young woman you found in the trombonist's pocket?" asked Verdugo.

"What? Do you think . . . ?" said the poet.

Manterola looked up from the dominoes and stared at the lawyer. "*Licenciado,*" he said, "you have what they call a powerful recall."

9

THE POET ENCOUNTERS A
DEMONSTRATION

Fermín Valencia heard the blare of car horns as he walked along Reforma toward the offices of a mining engineer who'd contracted him to write "a few love poems at a modest price." The fellow had been struck bitterly by his love for a chorus girl from the Arbeu Vaudeville Theater but, as he himself admitted, was incapable of putting six words together in a row with any kind of feeling.

The poet turned his head and was greeted by an unexpected sight: a long line of cars moved slowly in his direction. At the head of the line were six Fords with about a hundred men marching on foot behind them, followed in turn by some three hundred cars and trucks. Picket signs waved in the air: "Ban the time card," "No more police assaults."

As the protesters drew level with him, the poet made up his mind and jumped onto the running board of one of the passing trucks.

"Got room for a fellow traveler?"

"Make yourself at home," said the driver, sealing their pact of solidarity with a nod.

The poet tried to decide whether to go along with the march or finish one of the verses he was working on for the engineer. But the rhymes in his head took over for him and he floated in that cottony paradise all the way until the caravan of cars and trucks turned into the Zócalo, horns blaring raucously.

Most of the demonstrators left their vehicles parked in the wide avenue and the poet got down from the truck and started off toward his appointment with the engineer. Then from the balconies of City Hall someone started firing on the demonstration. Panic seized the crowd of drivers spread across the plaza, and the demonstrators ran for cover, some toward the National Palace, others toward the shops that fronted the square.

The next day, after conferring with the poet, Pioquinto Manterola would write in *El Demócrata:* "Nobody could have guessed what was about to happen. The tragedy spread its bloody wings over demonstrators and spectators alike."

The drivers counterattacked, hurling stones at the windows of City Hall. Firemen tried to disperse the crowd with water hoses. Then came the charges of the mounted police, which the drivers met head-on in their vehicles. A pair of gendarmes rolled on the ground beside their dying horses. The sirens of the Red Cross and the White Cross added to the confusion. A certain Captain Villaseñor, whom the poet recognized from earlier days in Ciudad Juárez, was swept away by a crowd of taxi drivers charging through the arched doorways of City Hall.

A cab driver lay bleeding from a bullet wound. The poet, hidden under a delivery truck, watched the parade of feet, wheels and hoofs passing before his bulging eyes. Stones flew through the air. The streetcars stopped their circuit around the plaza. Finally the city employees who had started the riot by firing on the demonstrators abandoned the balconies under the hail of stones.

The poet took advantage of a brief pause in the battle to scramble out from under the truck where he was hiding. He made his way out of the Zócalo hanging onto the back of a White Cross ambulance.

The next day he read in Manterola's account how the battle between the drivers, city workers, firemen, and police had ended with five dead and more than twenty wounded.

"And you were there?" the mining engineer asked incredulously a couple of hours later.

The poet only raised his eyebrows, not knowing what to say. It was as if he'd been there and he hadn't. "This goddam town," he thought, not knowing who to blame for the echo of the bullets that still buzzed in his ears.

10

COINCIDENCE, FATE, OR JUST
PLAIN BAD LUCK

The man held out the photo without letting go. The reporter and the policeman tugged on either end of the small picture for several seconds.

"Much obliged, Captain," said Pioquinto Manterola, finally pulling it from the policeman's grasp with a sudden jerk.

"Wait a minute."

"Sir?"

"You know something I don't?" asked the municipal police captain, a thin glassy-eyed fellow groping with his thumbs for the pockets of a nonexistent vest.

"No. I just wanted to get a look at this picture for inspiration in another story I'm working on."

The reporter walked out the door, stepping nimbly over a drunk whose questionable judgment had led him to take his siesta on the station house steps. There was no doubt about it, the woman was the same. And from that point everything was easy enough. A small "F.L." stamped across the lower edge of the picture led the journalist through the dusty streets of Tacuba to the offices of Fotos Larios, a photographic studio used frequently by *El Demócrata*. Half an hour later he emerged from the shop with a photo in his hand more or less identical to the one he'd seen in the station house, but with an added advantage: It had the subject's name and address printed on the back.

He hesitated for a moment before heading down Avenida Juárez. Then marched stoically on under a blazing sun, drops of sweat breaking out over his bald dome and running down the sides of his face. "When it comes to journalists," he told himself as he loped along, "you've got your cavalry and you've got your infantry." Manterola crossed the street, neatly dodging a cart driven by a fellow who'd gotten an early start on his jug of mezcal. The man seemed to have infected his horses with his own distorted sense of direction.

The poet waited in the street composing a bit of deprecatory verse in honor of General Manrique, the new military governor for the State of Mexico, requested by Manrique's second in command, General Viñuelas. He'd been asked to supply an effectively stinging bit of doggerel that would also guarantee the anonymity of his employer. He'd experimented with variations on: "A rose by any other name would smell as sweet; a man by any other name would reek as . . ." but it didn't seem to him either original or to the point. He stood in the middle of the street sipping on a bottle of La Camelia brand soda pop when he saw his friend the journalist bustling around the corner with that peculiar walk of his, like a rheumatic locomotive with a full head of steam, his head jutting out leading the way.

Their friendship dated back to before the domino club. The journalist had rescued the poet from abject poverty, finding him odd jobs here and there in the newspaper world. And the poet had once arrived in time to cut the rope the reporter was trying to hang himself with, victim of an unrequited love. Neither of them was inclined to talk much about the past. The poet liked to think of himself and his three friends as something like the tide scum left on the beach at the high-water mark: the indefinable children of a turbulent decade marked by a social upheaval much bigger than themselves, a series of changes they'd experienced peripherally as spectators, protagonists, and victims.

"Got it," announced Manterola, wiping the sweat off his bald head with a white handkerchief from his vest pocket.

"Is she the same one? Let's have a look at her."

"One and the same. And not only that, I've got her name and address, too."

"Let me see," said the poet, taking a careful look at the

photograph. "That's the one all right. So now what? I never really thought of you as the detective type."

"I was just saying the same thing to myself." He pointed to the bottle of soda in the poet's hand. "Where'd you get that?"

"In a store. Where'd you think? Come on, I'll treat you one."

While the two men stood drinking their sodas in a shop front on San Juan de Letrán, the lawyer Verdugo stood in front of his mirror combing a healthy dab of Tres Coronas brilliantine into his hair. He'd woken up from a nightmare and, after counting the few pesos he had on hand, decided it would be a good idea to combine breakfast and lunch into a single meal. Without having to think too much about it he decided to head over to the Tampico Club near the Ciudadela for a double portion of pork chops in chile pasilla.

With his hair freshly combed and the prospects of a decent meal ahead of him, the aftereffects of the nightmare began to fade. Just then somebody slipped an envelope under his door. It was an invitation to a private moving picture show in the home of the Widow Roldán, courtesy of Arenas, Vera & Co. Ltd. The invitation was signed at the bottom: "Your friend Conchita—social secretary to the Widow Roldán."

He puzzled over the invitation for a while, concluding finally that Arenas and Vera were both strangers to him, not to mention Co. Ltd., whoever that might be. As far as he could tell, his only connection to this Widow Roldán and her luxurious home (or so he assumed from the address in the Colonia San Rafael) was through his old friend Conchita, who he'd rescued several years ago from dire circumstances. From the looks of things, she'd risen considerably in society circles from the days when she used to dance the cancan in second-class cabarets, and was now established as the personal secretary to a wealthy widow. Thinking it would be good to see Conchita again in happier circumstances and sensing the possibility of a free (not to mention substantial) dinner, and also because he'd recently become a fan of the silver screen, Verdugo stuck the invitation in his vest pocket.

He lived in a flat almost entirely devoid of furniture (there was a bed in one room and a single armchair in what would have been the living room) in a neighborhood full of houses under construction half a mile from the Condesa Track, a part of town that was being rapidly subdivided into lots for sale and which the ads in the newspapers had started to call Insurgentes-Condesa. The apartment had previously belonged to one of Verdugo's clients. The man had taken his own life and left the place to the lawyer in his will, with the provision that after ten years it be converted into either a bordello or a gambling house. Verdugo moved in, figuring that after the ten years allotted by his client he would simply walk away and leave the keys in the door. For the time being, and probably forever, the bed and the armchair, a coatrack and a single dish (in which he fed milk to a stray cat that wintered over in the apartment) were the only household items he bothered to keep. Whenever he went out it was with the certainty that he'd left nothing behind and he never felt the need to hurry back.

Now he fitted his pearl gray Stetson onto his head and went out to fight the blazing sun.

As he was stepping off a bus on Balderas he ran into the reporter and the poet arguing about the chances for a Giants-Yankees repeat up North.

"What's new, gentlemen?"

"Discussing strategy," explained the journalist. "Only with this guy you can't talk for more than fifteen minutes about the same thing without him changing the subject."

"The fact of the matter is," said the poet, breaking into a brisk walk down Balderas without waiting for the others to follow him, "that this fellow here is an excellent journalist, but when it comes to detective work he leaves a lot to be desired."

"Maybe it's just that this picture here reminds me of a woman I once held in high esteem," countered the journalist.

Pastel clouds danced around inside his head as he tried both to evoke and suppress his memories at the same time. Painful memories he'd never been able to let go.

Verdugo recognized something in the journalist's voice that

brought his own experiences to mind and he wisely cut into the conversation, interrupting Manterola's reverie.

"What's that? Did you find the woman from the trombonist's picture? Is she the same one you saw when the guy fell out the window?"

The journalist nodded and held out the small photograph.

She was a young woman, no older than thirty, with the fine features and languid eyes currently in fashion. She was thinner than he would have liked, and dressed rigorously in black. Pretty but with a certain hardness about her. She sat in a brocaded chair looking out a window. A halo of sunlight enveloped her face, overexposing the picture and producing a strangely exotic effect. On the back of the photograph were the words: "Margarita, the Widow Roldán," and an address.

"Now there's a coincidence for you," muttered the lawyer.

"What, do you know her?" asked the poet.

"I've never seen her before in my life. But . . . today I got an invitation to go to her house for a private picture show."

"Dammit all to hell, that's just one coincidence too many," said the journalist.

"As for me, I'm starting to believe less and less in coincidence all the time," said the poet. "First someone kills the damn trombonist, then Manterola here watches the trombonist's brother fall out of a window, and now you get this invitation to the widow's house."

"Maybe it's not coincidence, but fate."

"I don't believe in fate any more either, not since Obregón won the Battle of Celaya," answered the poet. "All I believe in is just plain old bad luck."

"Bad luck it is, then," said the lawyer Verdugo.

11

DOUBLE FEATURE

At precisely 8:00, the lawyer Verdugo arrived at the small mansion in the Colonia San Rafael and climbed up the wide porch steps along with three members of the Torreblanca Jazz Band and a pair of artillery officers.

No one was waiting to meet them at the door, and they went on in without having to show their invitations. The customary pre-party chaos reigned in the main hall. A pair of bonneted maids dressed in black rushed about with trays of pastries and two technicians from Arenas, Vera & Co. Ltd. were busy stringing cables to the darkened salon where the pictures would be shown. Verdugo leaned against the mantel of the white fireplace and lighted up an Aguila. The two officers followed his example. Finally Conchita appeared through the swinging door from the kitchen, along with the rich smells of carne asada.

"Gentlemen, please. You should be ashamed of yourselves. When an invitation says eight o'clock it means you're not supposed to show up before eight-thirty . . . Why, *licenciado* Verdugo! Bless my soul!" and with a hurried "excuse me" to the two artillery men she took Verdugo by the arm and led him off into a corner.

"I never thought I was going to see you again, Alberto, and then the other day, by chance, a friend of mine gave me your address. I'm in charge of the invitations, and . . . well here you are. I can't tell you how good it is to see you."

Conchita had been at the height of her career when one of the other actors had inadvertently stuck a foil into her thigh during a performance of *Don Juan,* and she fell screaming off the stage into the orchestra pit. That was the beginning of the end of her artistic career. The real end came a couple of weeks later when, back on stage, she took a bronze jug and attacked the fellow who had stabbed her, breaking his collar bone. She was a small, vivacious young woman with a pair of bright green eyes that in her time had turned many a leading actress green with envy. Everything she said was accompanied by a dramatic gesture, a habit she'd picked up in the theater, a unique kind of body language that gave her words the sense of a double affirmation.

Verdugo took her hand and kissed it.

"Now let's not overdo it, Conchita. I'm flattered enough as it is," said the lawyer.

"What do you mean don't overdo it? When I've got this town's only truly civilized lawyer right here in my own hands . . ."

"I've come as a spy, Conchita," he whispered.

The young woman interrupted her chatter to stare at the lawyer.

"To see how life's been treating you," Verdugo added quickly, retreating in front of those green eyes.

"Oh, well that's different. I certainly can't complain . . . Excuse me a minute while I attend to these simpletons, and then I'll be right back."

She left Verdugo in the hall, hat in one hand, cigarette in the other.

Society affairs in those days tended to bring together a fairly standard blend of young officers on the rise, cultured señoritas, young students in the Vasconcelos mold practicing their Greek, politically ambitious lawyers who spoke and dressed like their hero Jorge Prieto Laurens, well-to-do industrialists, character actresses from the more acceptable variety theaters, and young renegades from the Porfirian aristocracy whose fathers had the good sense to break with the hacienda and make new fortunes speculating in real estate, removing some of the old stigmata from their sons and families and making them more palatable in the renovated world of postrevolutionary politics. For dessert, there was the whole spectrum of hustlers, crooks, high

lifers and confidence men the war in Europe had loosed upon
Mexican shores: Russian counts, French engineers, Catalonian
shysters, high-class housebreakers and specialists in the old family jewels game. There were also a few highbrow reporters and
Sunday poets from *El Heraldo* and *El Universal,* and a smat-
tering of the sons of Spanish immigrant shopkeepers. It was a
society whose insecurities sprang out of its own immaturity,
virginity, and lack of faith. It wasn't Verdugo's kind of crowd,
and he felt out of place as he watched the other guests enter
through the front door, liberating themselves of their hats and
gloves (a vain and pointless accessory in the warm Mexican
spring). For Verdugo's taste the party, if it could be called that,
lacked the necessary contingent of *soldaderas,* anarchists, lottery ticket vendors, horses, dogs and other assorted livestock,
northern cattle ranchers about to make their first million, and
a healthy troupe of the prostitutes who were his good friends.

The press of the late arrivals forced the lawyer and the others
toward the back of the great hall and the rooms bordering on
it. Verdugo somehow got himself dragged into a conversation
about the virtues of the climate in the state of Veracruz, with
the French industrialist owner of a textile mill, and an army
captain, adjunct to the general staff of "Tiger" Guadalupe
Sánchez.

The officer knew General Santa Ana's biography by heart
and made a great effort to insinuate his knowledge into the
conversation wherever possible. Verdugo made an offhand
comment about the practice of witchcraft in the Tuxtlas region
and its common use against the "paleface" foreigners, but his
two companions only stared at him as if they'd just discovered
some rare species of beetle. That was the problem with this
new society: it spent so much time trying to be modern that it
forgot where it had come from. The only ones they were fooling,
however, were themselves.

Verdugo lit another cigarette and turned his back on his two
companions. It was a fortuitous move, because at precisely that
moment their hostess the Widow Roldán made her appearance.
She descended the main staircase dressed in a loose black gown

that hung gracefully from her shoulders on two garlands of white velvet flowers. She wore long white Swedish gloves that reached to her elbows, and a pair of high Russian boots. The blackness of her dress stood out starkly against the whiteness of her shoulders and arms. She smiled languidly, the kind of prefabricated grin that had come into fashion lately in the wake of a much-heralded run of Dumas's *Camille*.

Endowed with a marvelously utilitarian instinct, the lawyer took his eyes off the widow and concentrated instead on the faces of his fellow guests. There was a little bit of everything: envy, fascination, contempt, lust. He paid particular attention to a certain officer stationed at the bottom of the stairs. The man looked at the approaching woman with an expression of— what? Pride? Possessiveness? "There's my man," thought Verdugo, and he glanced up at his friend Conchita, walking at her mistress's side. As she passed the officer in question (a colonel, thought Verdugo, counting the stripes on his sleeve), Conchita stared at the man with barely concealed contempt.

Slowly the guests filtered into the screening room. Verdugo took a seat in the back row where he was better placed to sneak a quick nap if the double feature dragged on too long (*Los ópalos del crimen,* ten rolls, starring Beatriz Domínguez, and *Los Filibusteros,* six rolls, based on the novel by Emilio Salgari).

And lulled by the sound of the pianola, that's exactly what he did.

12

IN WHICH THE CHARACTERS PLAY DOMINOES AND TALK ABOUT A WIDOW, CHANCE, AND A COLONEL OF THE GENDARMERY

"How'd it go?" asked the poet.

"I had myself a nice little nap . . ." said Verdugo.

"No, the dinner, idiot."

"Oh, it was all right, as those things go . . ." said Verdugo, trying somehow to distract the journalist and keep him from playing his last two, leaving Verdugo with the double in his hand.

"And the widow?" asked Manterola, slapping the two/one onto the table.

"She's one of a kind, all right. She manages to be everywhere at once without really trying. Margarita, the Widow Roldán, a hell of a name, if you ask me . . . She's sharp, too. I'd call her a sweetened-up version of Lucrezia Borgia."

It was well past 2 A.M., and the bartender, in keeping with established ritual, went around turning off the lights one by one like someone plucking the feathers from a chicken or blowing out the candles on a cake, until the domino players remained together inside a single circle of yellowish light. There was something Last Supperish about the scene, only with four glasses of Havana brandy in place of the supper. The cantina was nearly deserted. Reckless Ross was sleeping it off under the bar. His days as a hero on the motorcycle circuit long past, he'd taken to drowning his sorrows in mezcal, a drink he acquired a taste for following that famous race in Toluca when he was carried off the course in a stretcher after dropping his bike at sixty-five miles per hour.

"I'm out, señoles," said the Chinaman dryly, playing his last bone. He failed to see the humor in his friends' jokes, their needling of the new aristocracy—as though, despite their self-imposed marginality, they'd never quite managed to break the ties that bound them to the world from which they came.

"You pulled that one out of thin air, Tomás. I had no idea," said the journalist, counting up Verdugo's and Valencia's remaining dominoes.

"So what's the gist of it, man, I want to know what really happened," insisted the poet again, trying to take his mind off the game he'd just lost.

"Well, to make a long story short: What it all boils down to is one gorgeous and shrewd widow, one gendarmery colonel—who I'm sure you'll recognize when the time comes, one personal secretary who, going by appearances, doesn't hold said colonel in very high esteem, one female hypnotist-scientific-mumbo-jumbo-type to cure the widow's migraines and toothaches, one French industrialist's son living off daddy's bank account, one rough-looking Spic, the kind you can dress up in silks but still can't hide the scars, and one police lieutenant who seems to serve as the colonel's errand boy. That's what we could call the inner circle. The rest of the guests seemed as out of place as I was. Or rather, at least as lost and a lot less charming than yours truly."

"I think I can add a new detail," announced the reporter, licking a few drops of brandy off his mustache. "I found out how the Widow Roldán became a widow. Her husband was poisoned."

His three friends turned to stare at the journalist who paused for a moment to relish the effect of his surprise announcement.

"The late Señor Roldán owned a print shop. He died of lead poisoning, or saturnism, as it's known in the printer's trade."

"I remember my father used to talk about that," said the

poet. "He always drank lots of milk to protect himself from the lead."

"Sounds like the widow's late husband didn't drink enough," observed Verdugo.

"So who poisoned him?" asked the Chinaman, his curiosity piqued at last.

"He owned the Industrial Printworks, the largest print shop in the city."

"The CLOM's got a union there," observed Tomás, adding his own bit of expertise.

"What about the woman? I want to hear more about her. What does she look like. I only saw her in the picture, after all," said the poet, losing interest in the defunct spouse.

"Young, beautiful, domineering . . ."

"And, lest we forget, her picture was found in the pocket of a murdered trombonist, and she was there in person when the trombonist's brother *fell* to his death out of a third-story window," added Manterola.

"This much we know," said the poet.

As the dominoes shuffled and clicked across the tabletop, the bartender brought over another bottle of Havana brandy. The sound of the bones was sacred and he set it down gently.

"This colonel you'le talking about is Gómez, isn't it?"

"You guessed it, my friend. Jesús Gómez Reyna, one and the same."

The Chinaman pictured the face of Gómez, chief of the Mexico City gendarmery, the mounted police, the same man who almost a year ago ordered the police attack on the strikers at the Palacio de Hierro Department Store. The same Gómez who ordered his troops to fire on the militant railroad workers. The black beast, the arch-enemy of the anarcho-syndicalists in the Valley of Mexico.

"This woman reminds me of another woman I used to know," said Manterola, choosing his seven bones one by one and standing them up in front of him.

"It's been known to happen," said the poet. "One woman

reminds you of another one, who reminds you of another one, who . . ."

"Gentlemen, please," said the lawyer.

"And the winner by threeeee huuuundred yaaaaards," roared Reckless Ross from the floor underneath the bar.

The cuckoo clock called out the half hour.

13

WORKING-MAN BLUES

The poet opened the center section of the newspaper and admired his work. Anonymous by nature, not really the kind of thing he'd be doing if he had a choice, but there it was in black and white all the same.

Here's a cure that's guaranteed for that gentleman in need . . . Suffering from gonorrhea? Three days, ten pesos.

The competition, *Gorreina,* had an ad alongside his that was unmistakably inferior.

In the left-hand column there was another one of his master works:

Tanlac has successfully cured thousands of Mexicans living in the USA. Countless Mexicans have seen how their relatives and friends in the USA have regained health and happiness with Tanlac, the world-famous cure for all stomach ailments.

He was particularly proud of the ad's semi-religious tone, its sanctimonious air, emphasized by the kindly face of the old man in the accompanying picture, drinking Tanlac and feeling like all the world.

Another one of his best efforts appeared in the bottom left-hand corner, like a variation on a theme:

> *Chronic case of gonorrhea? Here's a cure that's guaran-*
> *teed. You can trust our humble creed: sure as a man's word*
> *of honor. Only three days, ten pesos.*

He liked this one for its military tone, designed to appeal to
the young officers so susceptible to social diseases.

There were a few more of the offspring of his underemployed
pen scattered here and there across the page:

> *Mental fatigue? Brain drain? Reach for marvelous Cere-*
> *brina cordials.*

Both the jingle and the name of the product in that one were
his own invention.

The poet saw his work, which some fools were starting to
refer to as "marketing," as the ultimate joke, something to
while away the sleepy mornings, to pay for his scrambled eggs,
salsa borracha, and tortillas. A way to mark his passage through
the turbulent streets of Mexico City, a way to survive. Maybe
what he liked the most about it was that in the two years he'd
been writing ads for patent medicines (*back pain getting to be*
too much, threatening your stability?—he liked this one for its
magical, enigmatic strangeness) no one had been able to get
him to pop a single pill into his mouth (*Dr. Lovett's Little Pink*
Pills—guaranteed to return you to health, whatever your
ailment).

In his daily perusal of the medical adverts page in the newspaper there was something of the contented air of a rural
patriarch, spiced with an ironic but professional sense of satisfaction.

On this particular morning, he worked at his desk with the
window open and the breeze carrying a rainy dampness into
the room. He glanced over the competition and then settled
back to think up a name for the latest product from the labo-
ratories of F. M. Espinosa and Company, designed to cure

feminine maladies, headaches, weakness, sterility, tumors, liver spots, and other disorders, etc.

He dipped the point of his pen in the inkwell and without hesitation started to write:

Saravia Espinosa. Cures all . . .

14

"MAY I ASK WHY YOU'RE
FOLLOWING ME?"

The woman turned around and stared. "May I ask why you're following me?" she said.

"My name is Pioquinto Manterola, ma'am, journalist by trade. And your face . . ."

They stood in the middle of Alameda Park, in the center of town. The woman held a yellow parasol against the penetrating rays of the sun, while the journalist was forced by a sense of chivalry to doff his English-style cloth cap, exposing his bald dome to the merciless heat. Nearby a small boy sold fruit-flavored shaved ices from a cart.

"I certainly hope you realize that the mere fact of being a reporter doesn't give a man the right to go following a woman all over town. Why, if that were the case . . ."

She smiled. Manterola had spotted the Widow Roldán and a companion walking down the street as he left the newspaper and he'd followed them to the park. Her friend had left her only a few minutes earlier, and the journalist had chosen that moment to close the distance between them.

"Do you want me to stop following you or would you like to hear my story?" asked Manterola.

The woman smiled again and walked toward one of the benches near the bandstand.

"Well?" asked the widow once they sat down.

"Excuse me, but I only know your late husband's name. What may I call you?"

"My name is Margarita. Margarita Herrera."

"Well the story is that I happened to be on the third floor of the building where I work on the day Colonel Zevada fell out of the window across the street. And it was my good fortune to happen to see you there at that very moment."

The woman paled momentarily. "Would you be so kind as to buy me an ice cream? This heat is unbearable."

The journalist nodded and waved to an ice cream man who stood with his cart about twenty yards away. The widow sat in silence, staring at the fountain. Manterola observed her calmly. She'd gained control of herself once again.

A group of *charros* rode past on horseback. Nearby a rowdy pack of truant cadets tossed a sack full of papers into the air.

"You were saying, sir, that you'd had the good fortune to . . ."

"I'm sorry the circumstances were what they were, but I must say . . . that the look of distress on your face made a great impression on me," said the journalist.

"Do you think that I pushed him?"

"I'm a journalist, not a judge, ma'am. I'm not accusing you of anything. It's just my natural curiosity."

"What else do you know about me?"

"I saw your photograph in the pocket of a trombonist who died a few days before the incident with Colonel Zevada."

The woman paled again. She tugged nervously at a silk handkerchief embroidered to match her parasol.

She hadn't tasted the ice cream. Now she let it drop to the ground.

"Señora, if I can be of any help to you in any way . . . You can count on my discretion."

The widow stared at him, searching for some sign in the journalist's face. But her violet eyes probed deeper, until she found the wound left there by another woman, the wound with its vulnerable scar tissue.

"What did you say your name was?"

"Pioquinto Manterola."

The sack of papers fell with a loud thud next to their bench, and for a moment they were surrounded by the riotous cadets.

The widow stood up. When the reporter was about to do the same she stopped him with a wave of her hand.

"You'll be hearing from me very soon," she said, and she walked away twirling her parasol.

Manterola followed her with his eyes. He knew that she'd found his weak spot, but at least he was aware of it. "I may be stupid but I'm not blind," he told himself.

THE WAY THINGS USED TO BE:
PIOQUINTO MANTEROLA

The poet ought to remember it well enough, since he was my only witness. I brought my hand up to my throat and undid the rope around my neck. Then I started to cry. Only, without making a sound. Like a man who can't talk would cry. Not a sound, just these big fat tears rolling down my cheeks, and me, that is the other me, the new me, the survivor, not even trying to stop them.

That's the first thing I remember about myself, about my new life. That, and the feeling that this new life came complete with memories of the old one. Those memories were my reward—the feeling that even though I'd been so close to death I still hadn't managed to leave behind the baggage I'd meant to take along with me when I went. That's when I told myself: "If you want to go on living, then you're just going to have to put up with yourself."

Ever since then I've been easier on myself, more forgiving of my faults, the master of my own misery, you could say, more tolerant of this nearly forty-year-old man who keeps on with his stubborn fight with the minutes and the hours . . . With this time that's been graciously loaned to me, or perhaps I should say: returned.

THE ANARCHISTS' BALL

They closed off Rosario Street, parking a car at one end and camouflaging it with a few clay flower pots for appearances' sake. Then they fenced off the other end of the block and set up the security team, revolvers showing in the men's back pockets. Banners hung on the walls with the emblems of the CGT (General Workers Confederation) and the Textile Federation. Security wore red arm bands, the reception committee wore green ones. Fry stands bloomed all along the block. There were literature tables and, in the middle of the street, a small stage for the orchestra, the singers, and the speakers. At eight o'clock the people started to arrive.

They came from San Angel, Contreras, Chalco, Tlalpan, Doctores, San Antonio Abad, and Tacubaya, dressed in their Sunday best but without the slightest air of pretension, worn-out vests over clean white shirts, buttons polished to a shine, their distinctive wide-brimmed hats freshly brushed. Under their vests they carried their iron, .22 revolvers, Browning automatics, Belgian pistols bought off the docks in Veracruz, short-barreled Colts, knives. Theirs was a festive force in a state of war. Red ribbons hung from their buttonholes with slogans inscribed in golden letters: "Neither God nor master," "Son of the Earth," "Free of chains," "Pariah."

The Barrio Rosales Orchestra arrived shortly after eight and stormed the bandstand.

Jacinto Huitrón was scheduled to speak following the overture (Wagner, oh well). The skinny anarchist scrambled onto the stage as the last notes faded away, and opened fire with the following words:

"Let us invoke the emancipating spirit of Spring! Now is the time for Jupiter to obliterate the steps of the tyrant's throne, for Mars to shatter his weapons of war and devour himself, for Janus to cast down the naves of the temple and crush the worshipers within, and for Croesus to consummate his union with Temis the concubine and cut off his own head with his double-edged sword. Long live Anarchy!"

Fermín Valencia, professional poet, stood in the crowd, cozying up to Odilia the munitions factory worker. But he couldn't keep his eyes off the lay-poet improvising on stage. What drove these crazy anarchists to embellish their political message with third-rate poetry? The band struck up a tango, wild and melancholy, and the workers danced.

By the time Pioquinto Manterola arrived arm in arm with the lawyer Verdugo, the orchestra had switched gears and was sounding off on a lively polka.

Manterola was radiant. It was just his kind of thing. The noise, the gaiety, were like the gloved hands of a thousand fairies caressing his senses. He loved to watch the solemn faces of the textile workers, the men and women with their open, tired smiles, the girls from the Palacio de Hierro sweatshops, the seamstresses from the Nueva Francia bonnet factory, the hatmakers, the young men from Ericsson Telephone halfway between workers and skilled technicians. The two friends cordially ignored the poet caught up in his conquest of the beautiful Odilia, and went on to look for the Chinaman, lost somewhere in the dancing, chattering multitude that filled the street. They found Tomás at a literature table arguing with Ciro Mendoza, a young anarchist leader from the textile mills.

"But we've got to be patient, Tomás," Ciro was saying.

"Patience is fol the bosses," answered Tomás, and noticing his two friends he waved them over.

"Cilo, I want you to meet a couple of fliends of mine. This is Pioquinto Mantelola, and this is the illustlious *licenciado* Veldugo. Veldugo tlanslated Malatesta. Why don't you ask him what Malatesta had to say about patience?"

"Sorry, Tomás, I don't quote Malatesta at parties."

"This isn't a party. Or well, sure, it's a kind of party, but you can quote Malatesta here and nobody's going to mind," said the union leader.

The music was picking up steam and the journalist separated himself from the conversation and drifted off to mingle with the dancing couples. At one of the stalls partygoers threw base-balls at a caricature of Napoleon Morones, eternal leader of the pro-capitalist unions. The prize for hitting the effigy three times was an anarchist songbook. A little farther on they were raffling off the complete works of Bakunin, and beyond that the Estrella strikers were raffling off a goat.

A thin young man with a bow tie was in the middle of a fiery speech. He had the sort of intensity about him that came from endless days and nights dedicated to the struggle.

"The movement doesn't try and tell you how to think, the organization isn't looking for sheep. What the movement needs is militant activists. Criticism isn't something we want to silence, it's something that has to run free like a rushing river . . ."

17

NIGHT MOVES

Verdugo the lawyer stuck one foot in through the window, grabbed his hat, and slipped into the darkened house.

After leaving the anarchists' ball, and over the journalist's objections, he'd decided to make a pass by the widow's mansion. He carried a map of the layout in his head and figured that if he were caught, at the very worst, he could bow out more or less gracefully with a story about a midnight rendezvous with his friend Conchita.

He closed his eyes and waited for them to get used to the dark. He counted to ten, took a step, and tripped over a chair that shouldn't have been there. Groping tentatively, he headed for the banister which would lead him down the stairs to the main floor. Finally, after a few more collisions and a decidedly unpleasant encounter with something that could either have been a cat or a giant rat, he found the stair rail and started to descend. His prodigious memory told him there should have been twenty-one steps, so when he got to the twenty-fifth he started to think that either he'd broken into the wrong house or that, despite his calculations, he was somehow heading down into the basement. Finally, well past the thirtieth step, he was forced to conclude the staircase wasn't the same one he'd seen on the evening of the picture show. Most likely it was another staircase that led from the front of the house into the kitchen, or something like that. He was thinking so hard he hardly noticed when the stairs suddenly ended, the floor leveled out under his feet, and he found himself standing in front of the main fireplace, with its marble mantelpiece, just where he would have expected to find it. He cursed himself, swearing never to trust his treasonous memory again. Then he reoriented himself in the room and with his arms outstretched groped for the door next to the swinging door to the kitchen, which Conchita had told him led to her room. Finally his fingers touched wood and, imitating the cat he'd run across upstairs, he scratched on the door with his fingernails. If Conchita was out he could go on and search another part of the house. He scratched again just to be sure and then heard a noise coming from the front hall. Someone turned on a light. The lawyer opened the door and stepped quickly into Conchita's bedroom. The light from the street shed a vague glimmer over the empty bed. "Dammit," murmured Verdugo.

"No, Ramón, that's not the way it is." He heard Conchita's voice.

A man's hoarse voice answered her, but the lawyer couldn't make out what he said. The sound of their steps approached the room and, as the voices became clearer, the lawyer slipped inside a large wardrobe next to the dressing table.

"She thinks she can run the whole show. But the truth is, we have as much right as any of the others do. As much as her or the colonel."

"You don't understand. They've been doing all right up until now, so let them go ahead with it, I say. Our time will come."

"The fact of the matter, Ramón, is that you let yourself be led around too easily. You're a very servile person when it comes right down to it. It's in your blood," said Conchita, opening the door. The lawyer made himself as small as he could inside the wardrobe, surrounded by Conchita's lacy silk dresses, his head wedged into the tiny space between the clothes rack and a shelf crammed with shoe boxes. The door to the wardrobe didn't shut properly and he could see out into the room through a slight crack.

Now he watched as Conchita stepped inside, trailed by the hard-faced Spaniard he'd picked out on the night of the party as a member of the widow's inner circle. The Spaniard hesitated in the doorway as if waiting for permission to go any farther.

"Can I come in?"

"I don't know, little boy. *Can* you? What are you afraid of?" said Conchita.

The lawyer watched from his hiding place as the Spaniard's face puckered into a grimace, a look of hatred flashing across his eyes.

Conchita sat down in front of the dressing table, out of the lawyer's line of sight. All he could see was her feet.

"Come on in, little boy. And close the door," said Conchita. "Lucky for you I'm not the widow, she would have kicked you out of her bedroom in half a second."

Ramón the Spic stepped into the room and flopped down on the bed. Verdugo could hardly contain himself. He hated to think he was going to have to stand there and witness the amorous relations between Conchita and Ramón the Spic.

"Take your shoes off, you dirty pig. I don't know why I even let you in here."

"Maybe it's because you like to fuck with me," said Ramón prosaically. Verdugo struggled to keep from laughing out loud.

"You're the most vulgar little boy I know, Ramón," said Conchita, moving back into Verdugo's field of vision, but this time without nearly as many clothes on. She wore a transparent white silk nightgown. The hair on Verdugo's neck stood on end at the sight of his friend's shapely, swaying buttocks, clearly visible through the gauzy fabric.

"Ramón, if you don't take your shoes off, I'm going to throw you out of here right now."

"Excuse me, but I happen to like to do it with my shoes on, you know that," said the pouty-faced Spic, standing up and allowing the woman to take his place on the bed. Conchita slid across the covers, letting off little sparks of static electricity.

"Shit," thought Verdugo, staring longingly at the thick curly mat of reddish pubic hair between his friend's legs, until the Spaniard stepped between Conchita and his hiding place, ruining his view.

"What is it with you, anyway? You think it's more sophisticated to do it with your shoes on, is that it? Makes you feel like the goddam prince of Barcelona, or something? And I suppose you're not going to take your clothes off, either. What, are you scared someone's going to come in and find us here?"

"Who else comes here?" asked Ramón as he unbuttoned his trousers.

"Nobody. Who do you think? Hey, stand back a little farther."

Ramón stepped back from the bed and Verdugo could see part of the woman's body, the nightgown rolled up around her hips, an exposed breast, her thigh with the scar of an old wound.

"I don't like to do it this way. Let me get on the bed with you," whined Ramón.

"Shit and double shit," thought the lawyer. "Complete with ideological discussion and everything. By now they could have done it like any normal person and had it over with."

The woman stood up. Even barefoot she was still several inches taller than the Spic.

"There, you're fine right there," she said, keeping a couple of feet between herself and her lover.

"The things a guy has to put up with in this life . . . ," the lawyer thought, trying to adopt the contemplative attitude of a monk and letting his curiosity deflect the guilt he felt as the hidden witness to a scene that didn't belong to him.

18

A TRICK DOOR, A CHINAMAN
AND A CHINAWOMAN

Manterola looked at the body, reread the suicide note, and decided to invest a few pesos and take the forensic specialist out to lunch. This was no more a suicide than Rudolph Valentino was Manterola's uncle.

"First of all, you've got the downward trajectory of the bullet," said the doctor.

"Either that or he was sucking on the gun like a lollipop."

"That's what I was thinking. He had scratches on his lips and a cut on the palate made by some sharp object . . ."

"The barrel of the revolver."

"Naturally."

"That's what I've been saying all along," said Manterola, carving away at his steak. The forensic specialist had already finished his some time ago, and now busied himself gobbling up all the scraps of bread left on the table. Pioquinto looked at him with annoyance.

"Come on, Doc, leave me a piece a bread for the salsa, will you?"

"Sorry, I didn't think you wanted any more."

Well-dressed waiters bustled past their table balancing large trays above their heads, "just like in Paris," dodging customers, lottery ticket vendors, cigar hawkers, a pair of *charros* with their oversized *guitarrón*, a variety singer, and the children running underfoot.

"Let me guess, Doc. There was a fight, someone stuck a pistol in the guy's mouth and pulled the trigger."

"Obviously," said the doctor, who had started out his career as an army veterinarian under General Francisco Coss. His years in the service had left him with a preference for dead bodies.

Pioquinto Manterola wiped the sweat off his forehead with a white handkerchief. The city suffocated in the afternoon heat. The rains were late this year, maybe they'd never come at all.

As they were leaving the Sanborns, Pioquinto glanced at his watch. He had two hours before his deadline. Hoping he could find a few more details to fill out his story he headed off with quick steps back toward the Hotel Regis.

As he walked Manterola thought deep and hard. He needed to know more about the dead Englishman. He needed the ideas to turn into questions, the questions into words, the article to start pulling itself together along a single thread, complete with headline, paragraphs, and punctuation marks.

If he hadn't been hurrying along with his head down and his eyes pegged to the ground like someone looking for spare change, he would have seen his friend Tomás Wong crossing the street between a pair of shiny Lincolns and an old hackney pulled by a rust-colored horse. Tomás was humming an old Irish ballad his friend Michael Gold had taught him several years ago in Tampico. Gold, a New York Jew, had come to Mexico in 1917 to escape the war. Now Tomás was on his way to Chinatown to buy a couple of reams of paper for *Fraternidad,* the union's weekly newspaper.

Tomás was a stranger to Chinatown. Orphaned when he was five years old and living with a mestizo family in Sinaloa until he was ten, he'd never learned to speak Chinese. Growing up among Mexicans and gringos in the oil fields of Mata Redonda and Arbol Seco, he'd never known the great Chinatowns along the Pacific Coast, and he'd moved through the Chinese ghetto in Tampico like an outsider. If he talked with an accent, dropping his *r*'s, it was more than anything else out of a sense of contrariness, a certain pleasure in emphasizing his difference. He had no way of knowing that in recent months the six or seven square blocks of Mexico City's Chinatown, spread out on either side of Dolores Street, had been the scene of a fierce war between competing tongs, merchant societies, revolutionary lodges, the monarchists of the Chi-Kon-ton, and the Triads.

His friend the journalist, just then walking across the lobby of the Hotel Regis, knew far more about these strange events than he did. And Pioquinto Manterola might well have put aside the mystery of the Englishman's "suicide" had he been able to see that just as Tomás turned the corner off Juárez onto Dolores Street, Chief Mazcorro of the secret police, Commander Lara Robelo, and six of their men were advancing from the far end of the block on their way to raid an illegal gambling house.

But neither Manterola nor Tomás realized what was about to happen. It wasn't until Tomás stepped back out of the stationers onto the street, lugging two boxes of paper tied up with string, that he saw everything wasn't as it should be. A fifty-year-old man jumped out of a second-story window, almost landing on top of Tomás. A crowd in the street applauded the old man's escape, and their cheers mixed with the intermittent pop of gunfire from inside the house.

While Tomás might have been a stranger to Chinatown he was no stranger to violence, and as soon as he heard the first shots he pressed up against the wall and covered himself as best he could behind the boxes of paper. He watched as Mazcorro emerged from the house pushing a Chinaman in front of him. The man waved a fifty-peso note in the air, shouting: "I pay, boss, I pay. No wolly." As far as Tomás was concerned, the only fights worth getting mixed up in were the ones he chose of his own free will. Or when it was a matter of defending his ideas, or just plain orneriness. He took ahold of his boxes and was walking rapidly toward the near end of the street when he felt a hand grab his arm.

"Get me out of here," she said. "Please, save me. Get me away from here."

Tomás stared at her for a moment and then resumed his previous pace, only this time with the young woman at his side.

The overwhelming smell of violet-scented perfume filled his nose and made him wrinkle up his face.

At that moment the reporter Pioquinto Manterola wrinkled up his own nose, metaphorically speaking.

"So you're sure the door was locked from inside, are you?"

"I was with the colonel when they broke into the room. Later on he saw it and pointed it out to the rest of us, that the key was still in the lock on the inside of the door," said the hotel employee.

"Have you got a pair of keys to one of the rooms?"

"Of course. What do you have in mind?"

"A little scientific experiment." The reporter grinned, taking the hotel man by the arm, leading him along.

"This one here'll do, I suppose. The guest ought to have his key, and I've got the master."

Manterola knocked softly on the pale green door adorned with golden frets.

A fat-cheeked pink face ringed below by a half circle of neatly trimmed beard peeked through the door.

"*L'acqua non è calda. Mi parti degli ascingomani, sapone.*"

Manterola showed the man his best smile and pushed him gently back into the room.

"Let's have a look at your key, sir," he said, gesturing to show the man what he wanted.

"*Desidera la mia chiave?*"

"That's right. And now you put your key in the lock on this side," he directed the hotel man. "All right, now turn the key. See, the other one stays in the lock. You can lock the door from the outside while leaving the other key in place on the inside of the door. It's because the shaft is so long."

"How did you know?" asked the hotel man.

"Before I was a reporter I used to work as a locksmith . . . What did you say this captain's name was?"

"It's colonel, Colonel Gómez. He was in the bar with a couple of gringos, and when the police arrived he came over to see what was going on . . ."

"*La mia chiave, per favore.*"

"Much obliged," said the journalist, bowing slightly to the fat-cheeked gentleman and stepping away from the door. But his thoughts were already miles away.

When he walked back out onto the street, he was dizzy from so much thinking. He could almost feel the smoke drifting off the top of his bald head. For appearances' sake, and to conceal the nonexistent smoke from any nonexistent observers, he lit up a cigar and crossed Avenida Juárez. On the other side of the street he bumped into his friend Tomás, struggling under the weight of two enormous boxes of paper and with a very beautiful young woman hanging on to his arm, dressed in a sky blue cheongsam embroidered with the image of a dragon.

19

IN WHICH THE CHARACTERS PLAY
DOMINOES AND DECIDE THAT THE
ARCHANGEL GABRIEL IS CALLING ON
THEM TO INTERVENE

It was getting harder and harder to keep their minds on the game, each time the strange plot closing in around them surrounded the marble tabletop with words, impeding their concentration. Dominoes is a game that's meant to be played with its own special kind of banter, full of barbed but imprecise allusions to the game at hand. You shoot the breeze, you joke around, you bluff, but you never say anything to guide your partner, to reveal your hand, to send a hidden message. You talk but you never really say anything, so as not to break the cardinal rule of silence. So there was no way to play a decent game of dominoes with the shadows of three murders, a rescued Chinawoman, an unnatural liaison, and the sound of the rain in Madero Street dancing over the bones.

The characters were doing the best they could, trying not to lose the thread of that schizophrenic night. The bartender noticed their uneasiness, the tension in the game, and put it down to the rain, the rent strike that was shaking the city, the rising unemployment, the day's results at the racetrack, the flu epidemic . . .

"Without wanting to know anything, we know too much already. So why don't we try and see what else we can find out?" said the poet.

"It's your turn, my friend."

Manterola, who'd been playing it close to the chest through the first two rounds to see which way the wind was blowing, now attacked with the double-fours. Tonight he was partners with Verdugo. They all knew how the game would turn out: it was the aggressive play of the Chinaman and the poet against the lawyer's and the reporter's no-holds-barred brand of wily malice. In a normal night the lawyer and the reporter would win six out of ten. Tonight however was anything but normal, and they'd been losing ever since they sat down.

"It's not that I want to defend normalness, Bakunin help me, as Tomás would say, but that was one of the strangest liaisons I've ever seen in my life. And I wasn't born yesterday . . . Now, I'll admit, I haven't exactly had the opportunity to observe the sexual habits of too many of my fellow citizens at such close quarters. My own seem normal enough to me, and maybe that's my problem . . . But picture this: There they are, the two of them, screwing with a good three feet between them, and me stuck in the closet like a peeping Tom."

"Maybe she doesn't love him, or maybe the Spic doesn't wash his hands," suggested the poet, meeting Manterola's fours with the double-twos.

"No. Nobody said anything about hands. It was just that the Spic had a thing about not taking his shoes off."

"It's cleal as a bell," said Tomás with a smile. "If you don't take off youl shoes, at least one yald."

"I hope they didn't splash you," said the poet, trying to knock Verdugo off balance. Despite his sardonic tone, the lawyer still hadn't quite recovered from his strange vigil.

"Only in a moral sense, my dear bard, only in a moral sense."

Manterola hesitated, then played another four, hoping Tomás wouldn't close the hand, and leave him with the six/five and the double fives.

"Oul fliend the joulnalist is playing at suicide," said Tomás, closing the game.

"Shit, I knew it," said Manterola. He poured his partner a glass of brandy as a sort of apology. "Sorry about that, my dear lawyer-voyeur. They don't all come out the same."

"The thing that worries me is that, at least in this case, they don't all go in the same."

"Did you find out anything else?" asked the poet, standing up and stretching. "Apart from your stimulating discovery of coitus telegraphicus."

"Nothing. And I spent five hours inside that damn wardrobe. Even now, when I close my eyes, I feel like there's a hanger watching me."

"We waited for you for a few hours, and then we had to call the game. The bartender couldn't believe it. I think it's only the third time in two years we haven't played. Once when Tomás was in jail for a week, and the other time when I got run over, and now this," said Manterola, proud of their little club's consistency.

Verdugo mixed the dominoes, the monotonous, sleepy click of the bones.

"So who was this dead man that inspired our friend Colonel Gómez to play that clever trick with the doorknob?" asked the poet.

"He was a Brit. An engineer working for one of the British oil companies, El Aguila, I think it was. He was here on a business trip."

Tomás looked up from the bones. El Aguila was part of his personal territory in the land of memories. In the same way that Pancho Villa and his Northern Division belonged to the poet, the haciendas of the old aristocracy to the lawyer, and bloody murders to the reporter, El Aguila belonged to him.

"Blinkman was his name. I didn't have time to dig any deeper. There was just enough time before deadline to get in the story of the suicide that wasn't a suicide."

"Did you say anything about Colonel Gómez being involved in the trick with the key?" asked Verdugo.

The four friends drew their dominoes from the pile in the middle of the table, each in his own way. The poet lined his up in a row, pressed with his fingers on either end and stood them up all at once. The lawyer stood his up one by one and left them in the order he found them. Manterola set his on their sides, and Tomás took a minute to arrange his bones to his satisfaction.

"No, I kept quiet on that score. I figured it was enough for now to unmask the fake suicide. It didn't seem prudent to go any further. Somehow I got the feeling it was something that didn't really belong to me. Like it belonged more to the night and to this table, gentlemen."

"Mantelola, in this town gentlemen lide holses, and I happen to have left my holse at home . . ."

"Tomás is right, we're more the infantry type," said Verdugo.

"But the inkslinger's got a point," said the poet, scratching his mustache with his index finger. "No matter how you look at it, this thing belongs to us. Whether we like it or not. The dead trombonist is mine . . ."

"And I've got the suicide that wasn't a suicide, the English oilman, the widow, and the colonel that fell out of the window . . ."

"And I've got the picture show at the Widow Roldán's, and the tryst between Ramón the Spic and Conchita," said Verdugo.

"All I've got is a blood debt with Colonel Gómez," said Tomás.

"What about the Chinagirl you rescued?"

"Don't take youl coincidences too fal afield, comlade. She's just a pool lonely olphan who managed to escape when the police laided that gambling house whele they had hel like a plisonel. Like a slave. It's the kind of thing you heal about all too often these days, unfoltunately."

"But how can you be sure she's got nothing to do with it?" asked the reporter, playing a blank off the poet's opening domino. "I don't know what to think anymore. Everything seems to be connected. It all fits together too well. Do you all believe in fate?"

"I suppose I ought to. Isn't that what they say: Fatalistic Olientals?"

"Seriously, Tomás," persisted the reporter.

There was a pause in the play as the four friends stopped a minute to think the question over. The rest of the bar was deserted, the swinging doors had been still for over half an hour. The night, the place belonged to the four of them and the bartender. And to the four of them alone, and to the table and the bones, belonged the fragments of a mystery that revolved around the house of the Widow Roldán.

"No, not me. I believe in chance, and when the coincidences stalt to pile up, I believe it's time to do something about it."

"At this point I'm ready to believe in anything," said the poet. "I believe the Archangel Gabriel wants us to get involved in something and he's been sending us messages."

"Why the Archangel Gabriel?"

"Well, I don't believe in God, so I had to pick somebody up there."

"I believe it's going to rain all night long," said the lawyer, and the players turned their attention back to the game.

The Chinaman played a six/three and forced Verdugo to pass.

"What'd you do with her, Tomás?"

"I took hel to my humble home, as my countlymen say in bad novels."

"Do I detect a glimmer of Oriental romance here?" asked the poet. "Without wanting to pry, of course . . ."

"I don't leally know, illustlious bald. Fol now we'le just going to shale loom and boald."

"What'd you say her name was?"

"Losa López."

"Losa López?"

"I think he means Rosa López," clarified Manterola.

"Ah, another enigma for this rain-swept night," said the poet, playing the double-four, and with the last three fours hidden safely in his hand.

20

TACOS FOR DINNER,
GUNPLAY FOR DESSERT

After leaving the taquería where they ate a late dinner the poet lagged behind pissing contentedly against a lamppost. It was time to call it a night. Manterola was only a few blocks from home, Verdugo would head south, and the poet and the Chinaman would walk together as far as Tacubaya where Tomás would catch a streetcar for San Angel.

"Come on, we don't have all night," the Chinaman called to Fermín.

The poet saw the lights of a car turning the corner onto Gante Street and driving slowly toward them, and he hurriedly packed away his valuable instrument and buttoned his fly.

The car passed by Fermín, hidden in the shadows, and stopped a few yards beyond where Manterola stood lighting Verdugo's cigar.

Tomás was the first to react.

"Look out!" he shouted, whipping out his knife and hurling it at the automobile.

Two masked men got out of the backseat. Alerted by the Chinaman's warning, Verdugo clamped the half-lit cigar between his teeth, dropped to his knees, and drew his revolver.

Manterola was slower to react and it wasn't until he heard the shot and felt the burning pain in his leg that he realized what was going on.

From behind his lamppost the poet fired his long-barreled .45, booming like a cannon in the quiet night. The bullet ricocheted off the body of the car and shattered the jaw of one of the masked men. The red blood soaked invisibly into the red kerchief that covered his nose and mouth. The second masked man fired three times at Verdugo. The lawyer returned fire, stepping out a strange ballet as he scurried desperately for cover behind a nearby flower box. The bullets slammed into the wall behind him. A windowpane exploded somewhere in the dark. One bullet passed cleanly through the palm of his left hand and another knocked his hat off his head.

Manterola was thrown backward onto the sidewalk. His glasses were broken, but he pulled out a twenty-five-caliber Browning automatic and fired at the biggest thing he could see, emptying an entire round in the direction of the car.

The masked attacker trading fire with Verdugo glanced out of the corner of his eye at his companion, spread out on the ground and making strange noises through his shattered jaw. With lead raining down on him from all sides he broke into a run, wildly firing his last two bullets and killing a dog that stood anxiously watching the gunfight from a nearby rooftop.

The masked man, pausing at the corner to reload, turned to see if he was being pursued and in that moment Tomás's knife caught up with him. Hurled through the air, it drove home, slicing into his throat. Blood oozed through the kerchief over his face.

One by one the lights came on in the surrounding houses, adding to the glow from the lampposts. The poet approached the car and kicked the man with the bloodied kerchief in the head. The man jerked once and then lay still. Inside the car, a third man lay across the steering wheel, one of Manterola's bullets through his head. The poet reached in and turned off the engine.

The silence was strangely sudden and complete.

Together the reporter and Verdugo assessed their wounds.

"Damn it all to hell, my leg's as good as busted. I'm going to be a gimp for the rest of my days," complained the reporter as he tightened his belt around the upper half of his leg in the form of a tourniquet.

"As for me, it's going to be a while before I can move the dominoes like I used to," Verdugo answered him.

"How's yours, Tomás?" shouted the poet.

"Deceased," said the Chinaman from the end of the block. He wiped his knife on the dead man's trousers.

"This one seems like he's still got some life in him," said the poet, pointing to the man sprawled next to the car.

Two mounted policemen rounded the corner of Gante Street. A pair of hookers, friends of Verdugo, curiously approached the scene of the battle from the other direction.

"Call an ambulance. If it's not too much trouble," Verdugo shouted up to a man in pajamas leaning out to get a look from a third-story window.

A few minutes later they could hear the bells of the approaching ambulance. It reminded the poet of the bells that announced the start of the bullfights in Zacatecas.

By now the street was bright with light, making that little corner of the city seem like just another part of the bigger party.

21

AN UNEVENTFUL WEEK

The following week was absurd enough in its own way. Nothing happened. The poet was asked to prepare an advertising campaign for the Torrelavega Mattress Company (*On a Torrelavega mattress you'll feel like you're riding on a celestial carriage*—rejected; *Even your wife looks better on a Torrelavega mattress*—rejected; *Buy a Mexican mattress for a Mexican mattress massage*—accepted), and he came away with a fat roll of bills in his pocket after several sleepless nights spent poring over different designs, posters, and advertisements in search of the proper slogan.

Tomás the Chinaman got involved in the strike at the Abeja Mill, and he didn't make it home six nights out of the seven. Manterola was taken to a private hospital and the newspaper paid him handsomely for the exclusive eyewitness story of the gunfight (EL DEMÓCRATA REPORTER WOUNDED IN SHOOTOUT). He only wrote one other story the whole rest of the week, a charming little item served up to him on a tray by his friend Verdugo, who in spite of his bandaged hand found a way to get himself mixed up in an interesting bit of bordello intrigue.

There were no domino games and they never got the chance to talk things over all together or retell the story of the shootout.

Verdugo and Manterola managed to talk awhile in the hospital where the reporter was recovering from his wounded leg. The poet went by once to see Manterola, and he ran across Tomás one evening in a streetcar.

Strangely enough, none of the three attackers survived the encounter. The four friends only learned their names from the newspaper reports, confirmed later on when they each appeared before Lieutenant Mazcorro, Chief of Special Investigations for the Mexico City police. Mazcorro interrogated Manterola in his hospital room, and he had the lawyer, the Chinaman, and the poet meet with him in his office at headquarters.

Without having discussed the matter among themselves, they each told the same story and refused to give any additional information. None of them claimed to know who would want to kill them, they denied being involved in any kind of trouble, or having any personal enemies. They didn't need to talk it through to get their story straight. It was a private affair between them and whoever had sent the three men to kill them. And they all were careful to leave out certain details, like the way the poet kicked the wounded man in the head or that he was urinating on a lamppost when the shooting started. Those things were private, too.

Tacitly, they all agreed to postpone further action or comments, and life went on in its own way.

So none of them bothered to try and trace the stolen car their attackers had been driving, or to track down the buddies of "El Gallego" Suárez (the dead driver) or Felipe Tibón (the one who died at the corner with a knife in his throat). The third man went unidentified.

Mazcorro didn't learn anything worth mentioning from his interviews with the four friends. Perhaps the most interesting was his brief session with Manterola, who was under the effects of tranquilizers and craving a cigarette. The reporter, on the other hand, found out from the police lieutenant that the dead Englishman whose suicide wasn't a suicide had a roommate who had since disappeared. The Aguila Petroleum Company was demanding an investigation. Apparently, the two men had come to Mexico to swing an important deal, with a million pesos in stock certificates in their possession. It occurred to the reporter that he ought to make a note of the roommate's name, but at the time the lack of tobacco worried him far more and he ended up forgetting all about it.

All in all it was a pretty stupid week, although both Tomás Wong and the lawyer Verdugo, each in his own way, found themselves with plenty to do.

22

WORKING-MAN BLUES

It might have seemed like a contradiction, but it wasn't. What had started out as a form of self-degradation, the flagrant rejection of his aristocratic past, somewhere along the line had turned itself into a kind of simple appreciation of the ephemeral.

It's enough to say that in a country where over a million dead were witness to ten chaotic years of revolution there was ample room for a lawyer who dedicated himself to the defense of ladies of the evening.

Verdugo's ladies were a motley troupe, dolled up in swirling skirts, fashionable hats, coats, frayed shawls, and Spanish lace mantillas that had seen better days. From the rouged misses who sold their bodies, their time, and their compassion for a few pesos a day, to the gay chorus girls who expected sooner or later to land themselves some young officer or well-to-do merchant, they all availed themselves of the lawyer's professional skills. Verdugo plied his understanding smile and barrister's know-how from within an office whose confines were encompassed by the brim of his hat and a borrowed table in any one of numerous cantinas, cafes, tearooms, brothel sitting rooms, the back rooms of liquor stores, or dance-hall dressing rooms.

Reflecting on the unique nature of his particular contribution to the common good, Verdugo read out loud from his friend Pioquinto Manterola's article concerning his role in the dramatic story of María Luz de García:

She was raised an orphan and an only child in the impoverished home of her aunt, Francisca Jurado. Enduring the

*slow slippage of the hours, a lackluster existence deprived of
the glad affects of a normal childhood and with no one to
share the cornucopia of tenderness that truly belonged only
to her dead mother, in repeated scenes worthy of Toulouse's
macabre palette the child suffered the harpy's beatings without protestation, the aunt begrudging her a corner of her
house and a crust of bread, not out of any heartfelt commis-
eration for the orphan girl, but rather looking forward to
the day when* this heap of flesh and bones *would cease to
merely occupy space and become* productive. *It was thus
that one day the cruel aunt turned her niece over to the care
of one Ema Figueroa, a woman of faded beauty who pre-
sides over a house of ill-gotten pleasures in the heart of the
aristocratic Roma district. The innocent María de Luz was
offered up in sacrifice to the deities of Hedonism during a
party in honor of a certain wealthy personage, and there,
unable to flee, as if hypnotized, a mere child of fifteen
years, she was dressed in silks and served up as the main
course to whomsoever was willing to pay the matron's exor-
bitant price.*

*Is this what we choose to call prostitution? Or is it rather
another example of the perfidy of our society, which abandoned this child, deprived her of her rights, and sank her
into the depths of moral corruption?*

*The story, however, has a happy ending. It was to the
girl's great good fortune that she happened to meet, one day
this week, the lawyer A. Verdugo who, discovering her un-
happy state, and armed only with a single long-barreled revolver, forced his way into the bordello where she was being
held against her will and rescued her from the clutches of
her jailers.*

*But these same individuals, in no way slow to react,
thinking only of protecting their investment, and the influ-
ence they seem to enjoy in the Tenth Police Precinct, accused this well-known barrister of the crime of kidnapping a
minor. Little did they know with whom they were dealing.*

Mr. Verdugo, whom we have had occasion to write about

at other times in the pages of this newspaper, explained the
situation with such vehemence and veracity before Captain
Ponce, that this officer of the public order was moved not
only to dismiss the charges against the lawyer, but ordered
the incarceration of the aforementioned Madame Figueroa,
along with her bodyguard and procurer, a man who goes by
the alias The Snake.

It would be unfitting to end this account without adding
that María de Luz García (obviously a pseudonym adopted
to protect the innocent girl's identity) is now employed in a
reputable commercial establishment in this capital city.

"Well, what do you think, María?"

"They didn't say anything about how you set *doña* Ema's
house on fire."

"That was the work of an anonymous arsonist," replied Verdugo, firing up a long cigar and pouring himself another glass
of mezcal. He gazed dreamily at the afternoon light drifting in
through the open window, painting white splotches across the
elusive form of the naked woman moving languidly by the side
of the bed.

"It's not really like they say. I only wanted to get out of that
place, but that old witch wouldn't let me. I never said I was
going to quit going to bed with whoever I felt like," said the
girl.

"I rather think what we're dealing with here is the twin reality
of a puritanical newspaper establishment, and the fact that our
friend Manterola had to fill up his column . . . Besides which,
yours is simply a problem of independence. And I'm a strong
believer in independence. It is true, however, there isn't a whole
lot of difference between *doña* Ema's place and what Manterola
calls *a respectable commercial establishment* . . . All in all I
prefer it here in your apartment," said Verdugo, cautiously
flexing the fingers of his bandaged hand.

"He didn't put anything in about all that money you took
from behind the painting at *doña* Ema's."

"Let's just call that my honorarium, my dear girl, and a lawyer's fee, like his services, are strictly confidential."

"Confidential my ass. What about sharing some of it with the client?"

"All you had to do was ask, miss," answered the lawyer, smiling. But his smile turned bitter. The man that he's invented, the character he's assumed, the one that answers to his name, wears his suits, his hat, his wound, was all of a sudden not very fond of himself. Verdugo concurred with Manterola's opinion that a man lives during the day the autobiography he writes for himself the night before. But today he had the feeling someone had handed him the wrong book, even as the light slipping through the half-closed venetian blinds sketched beautiful figures over the woman's naked flesh.

CONFUSED ROMEOS

Manterola was about to turn thirty-nine years old in the hospital (La Iluminada, near the streetcar yards), in a room he shared with a moribund construction worker and with the sinking feeling that his leg was never going to be like it used to be, that the bone was never going to mend properly, no matter what the doctors told him.

Manterola turned thirty-nine today, and that sadness washed over him that comes with all birthdays after thirty-five, with the first hours after giving birth, with a man's meaningless victories and overwhelming defeats.

Come that birthday sadness, and crime reporters like this one tend to go transcendental, to look back over their life as if it were a drawerful of old debts, goals unmet, moribund illusions, wasted loves.

He glanced at his bald reflection in a polished chrome tube near the bed and took off his glasses to neutralize the effect. He thought about the cigarettes he'd got stashed under his pillow, and about the manuscript of a novel hidden under his pillow at home. His reflection in the tube was satisfactorily neutralized in a myopic blur, but the sadness stayed with him. A stubborn, sticky sadness, with a good dose of self-pity and idiot melancholy mixed in. A pair of tears rolled down Pioquinto Manterola's cheeks and, with his gaze fixed on the opposite wall, he let them go.

"May I?" she said, already stepping through the door into the room.

Manterola wiped his tears away unhurriedly and looked at her: he had seen her twice before already and held her photo in his hand. Dressed mostly in black, as before, she now wore a broad-brimmed hat that surrounded her face and set off its brilliant whiteness. A short necklace with a single emerald in its center hung around her neck. She wore a tight-fitting long black skirt that nearly touched the floor and a white blouse covered by a knitted shawl embroidered in black.

"Where would you like me to put the flowers?" asked Margarita Herrera, the Widow Roldán. She picked up a glass and filled it with water from a chipped washbasin. The flowers were a half dozen sad-looking magnolias with fragrant open blooms. She took her time arranging the flowers, her back to the journalist. He watched her and she let herself be watched.

"And to what do I owe this visit?" asked Manterola, taking a cigarette out from underneath his pillow. He couldn't think of a better time to have a smoke.

"I told you we'd be seeing each other again," answered the woman, turning to face him.

She glanced around for a place to sit and finally opted for the bed, settling herself at the reporter's feet.

"The left side please," Manterola said quickly. "My right leg's not quite better yet."

The woman did as he asked and, sitting down again, pointed inquiringly at the silent figure in the other bed.

"They tell me he's dying. He's been in a coma for days, ever since they brought him in here. A hod carrier who fell off the fifth floor of a building. They say he's not going to wake up again."

The two of them looked at each other for several long seconds: Manterola trying to find in this woman the signs of another woman he'd lost a long time ago; the Widow Roldán searching for some opening into Pioquinto Manterola's soul, or maybe just looking for some way to start the conversation.

"I know you're not going to believe me, sir, but I want you to know I had absolutely nothing to do with what happened to you and your friends," she said, getting right to the point. She let her shawl slip partway off her shoulders.

"That sounds more like a confession than a denial, ma'am," answered the reporter. He wasn't about to give anything away without getting something in return.

Margarita's eyes shone violet. Her whole face seemed to turn around those eyes and the intensity of her gaze.

"I don't know how much you know about me or my friends, but I can assure you we had nothing to do with this . . . this attempt on your life."

"Are you sure about that?"

"Absolutely. And I came to let you know, so there wouldn't be any doubt. Now, I won't deny that there's been a certain amount of friction. Or that on occasion your presence has been somewhat, shall we say, inopportune. What I mean is that your interest in me has caused a certain amount of suspicion among my friends, but that's far from being a motive for murder . . ."

Manterola sat up in the bed and without taking his eyes off the violet sparks flashing in hers, he reached out for her hand and kissed it.

"We should have met several years ago, sir," said Margarita, letting her eyes wander around the room until they settled stubbornly on the flowers, their sweet odor filling the air.

"That's nothing we can't start to make up for now, Margarita. Do you mind if I call you Margarita?" he said.

"That's what my friends call me."

Manterola remained upright in the bed despite the throbbing pain that shot up his bad leg, holding on to the woman's hand and obliging her to lean toward him to ease the tension between their two bodies.

"You know what's the worst thing about being a reporter?" he said. "It makes a man forget his own preconceived ideas just for the sake of curiosity. The search for the truth takes the place of everything else . . ."

"It's hard to know the truth . . ."

"The search for truth, or anything that looks like the truth, the best approximation, what each of us thinks might have happened . . . You see, it's not that I'm not willing to be flexible . . ."

"I've got the feeling you're leading me into risky territory, sir."

"Your eyes have had me in risky territory for a while now, Margarita."

Manterola was starting to enjoy this melodramatic dialogue, reminiscent of the most tawdry newspaper serials. And he'd read enough Dumas *fils*, Montepin, and Victor Hugo to be able to hold up his end of the conversation without any trouble.

"I read your article. You didn't say who actually killed those men who attacked you . . . Was it you?" she asked, taking away her hand and drawing back slightly.

"I'm sorry to disappoint you, but if I killed anyone it was pure luck. Somehow I lost my glasses when the shooting started and I just fired at the biggest thing I could see, which happened to be the car they were driving . . . By the way, you do own an Exeter, don't you?"

The widow stared at him intently. Then she glanced over at the man in the next bed to assure herself he hadn't moved since she'd gotten there. He lay motionless as before, his face to the wall, and she let her shawl fall completely off her shoulders onto the bed.

The reporter's instincts were highly tuned from so many years of working in out-of-the-ordinary situations, and that apparently casual gesture was all he needed to realize that this woman was about to undress in front of him.

And while the journalist was pulling that unlikely conclusion out of thin air, several miles away in the village of Contreras Tomás Wong the Chinaman sat down to a plateful of eggs and chorizo prepared for him by Rosa López Chang.

The Chinaman lived in a miserable two-room shack, with an outhouse he shared with his next-door neighbors. One room was taken up by a bed, books, photographs, keepsakes, a table and chair, maps on the wall, stacks of newspapers. The other room held his clothes, hung from an old sawed-off broom handle, another slightly larger table, and the stove.

A certain intimacy had grown up between the two of them,

enough for them to share a bed but not enough to overcome their mutual walls of silence. In his own reticent way Tomás had explained to Rosa the basic rules of the game: not to interrupt the meetings of the anarchist affinity group that came together each week in the house, overflowing into both rooms, and occupying the three chairs, the table, the bed, finishing off his meager store of coffee, and filling the whole place with a cloud of smoke. Not to let herself be seen too much in public, in case her former "owners" came looking for her. Not to feel that she owed anything, not to feel that she owed anything to him. Rosa, who was as prone to silence as Tomás himself, listened quietly to his three recommendations and then suggested she be allowed to use a corner of one of the rooms to prepare essences for sale to a local perfumery, bringing in a little extra money to help out with expenses. So far so good. Then there was the problem that there was only one bed which the two of them had to share for four hours every night. Tomás worked from 11 to 7 and they shared the bed from 3 or 4 in the morning until about 7 A.M. when Rosa got up.

It had nothing to do with a lack of imagination. Without having had to work it out beforehand, they'd taken to sleeping in shifts, and on separate halves of the bed, head to toe. The problem was more fundamental, more essentially pragmatic. A foot is capable of provoking as much erotic attraction as a face, and Tomás dreamed he was nibbling on Rosa's tiny toes. For several days now they'd both slept poorly and little during the few hours when they occupied the bed together.

While the journalist was busy thinking that any minute the widow was going to start taking her clothes off in front of him, and while Tomás thought lovingly about Rosa's toes, in nearby Tacubaya, on the outskirts of town, the poet Fermín Valencia lay on his bed and listened ecstatically to the esoteric theories of Celeste the Mysterious.

". . . I'm talking about inner forheth. All around uth. You get it? . . . Do you believe in magnetithm? It'th a thientific fact," Celeste explained to him. She was a different sort of poem, this woman. About thirty years old, speaking with a lisp, slightly cross-eyed, red hair, overflowing breasts (the right one a little bigger than the left? the poet wondered, or was it just a question of perspective?), a superb pair of legs. A run in her right stocking captivated the poet's attention. He nodded his head vehemently as she spoke, lying across his bed on top of the complete works of Voltaire, smoking a cigarette.

"It'th abtholutely thientific. Electric waveth connecting your mind with mine. It all dependth on whothe energy ith thtrongetht."

The woman had appeared unexpectedly at his door, smiling, dragging her lilac-colored shawl over the dust-covered chairs, scattered papers, dirty glasses, finally dropping it over a wash-basin filled with tequila the poet had used to disinfect a cut on his leg where he'd been hit by falling glass the night of the gunfight.

She'd introduced herself as Madame Thuáreth and, after confirming that her host was in fact the poet Fermín Valencia, she'd started in with her story about mysterious electric forces.

"And that'th only part of it. There'th other fortheth that neither of uth will ever be aware of. Do you believe in God?"

The poet shook his head.

"But thertainly you believe in natural fortheth?"

The poet shook his head, trying to look serious, blowing smoke up at the ceiling.

"In thienthe? Do you believe in thientific thinking?"

The poet shook his head again. He looked at her suspiciously.

"Don't you believe in anything at all? What a thilly quethtion . . . everybody believth in thomething."

"You've got a run in your stocking, ma'am," the poet said, tracing his index finger softly along the inside of her leg.

He almost thought he could see her leg vibrate slightly under his touch, and wondered if maybe there wasn't something to all this talk about *magnetic fortheth* after all.

The woman giggled, inching away from the poet's probing finger and brushing back a curl of red hair that had fallen flirtatiously across her face.

Pioquinto Manterola glanced cautiously at the dying hod carrier and confirmed that the man continued his slow slide away from life, eyes glued to the wall seeing nothing, lightless eyes, he thought, looking out onto the other side. Reassured, he returned his attention to the widow, who sat mechanically unbuttoning her blouse, her eyes on his face and her smile blooming like the flowers in the vase. A smile whose tremendous beauty, the inkslinger told himself accustomed as he was in his line of work to making this sort of appraisal, contained a certain aftertaste of cruelty.

"Tomás, we could sleep together, you know. I mean really together, instead of hiding from each other in the same bed . . . Even if there were two beds here I'd say the same thing . . . ," said Rosa, looking straight at the Chinaman chewing slowly on his eggs and sausage.

"Look into my eyeth," Celeste ordered the poet. "Look deep into my eyeth. You will thee a lake, the blue thea."

But the widow Margarita's eyes were violet and her skin under her white blouse was even whiter still.

"Ale you sule?"

"A thtill, calm othean of blue water, with jutht the thoft rocking of the waveth."

"What about your friend there in the other bed?" asked Margarita, demonstrating that she was not only cold but cautious, too.

"Maybe a pair of theagulls floating over the water, thwaying back and forth in the air," murmured the hypnotist.

"Maybe we should get anothel bed."

"You feel thleepy, a thoft thleepineth, a power moving into your body . . ."

"He's been lying there like that in a coma for days, looking at the wall. He never moves. They say it's only a matter of hours now . . ."

"You mean two beds?"

"Are you feeling thleepy now?"

"No, just one, a biggel one."

"How's your leg?" asked the widow, letting her black skirt fall to the floor and revealing a pair of long legs in smoky silk stockings, the latest in German fashion judging from the girlie magazines that arrived occasionally by steamship from Hamburg.

"Very thleepy. You are feeling very thleepy."

"Speaking of legs . . ." said the journalist, who couldn't pass up a chance to mix life and art, "you've got a pretty nice pair there yourself, Margarita."

"You are thinking into my eyeth."

"Which end are we going to put the headboard at, yours or mine?" asked Rosa, shedding a single tear. Tomás abandoned his eggs and sausage and stretched his hand out across the table. Their two hands were more brown than yellow. Their children would be even darker still, and none of them would speak with an accent. It was the effects of the climate. But they could just as well live in Australia, or Vienna, or even China. There was talk about a revolution in China . . . They'd have to learn to speak Chinese . . . But which one, Cantonese or Mandarin?

"What would you think about slipping into something a little more comfortable?" asked the poet, breaking the oceanic enchantment glowing inside the eyes of redheaded Celeste.

"Here, move your leg a little over that way," said Margarita, climbing onto the bed, her hat still on her head.

The next day the poet confessed that he was on the point of succumbing, but he didn't see how anyone could feel sleepy with all those *thh*'s buzzing in his ears. The journalist, on the other hand, kept the fact hidden in some far corner of his memory that his gaze had wandered from the widow's violet eyes down to her white brocaded panties only to discover they had a small perforation sewn into them. It was the first time he'd ever been seduced by a woman with a fly in her underwear. Tomás didn't tell anything because there was nothing to tell.

Perhaps the most transcendental of all these crossed stories was that half an hour later a pair of stretcher bearers walked into the reporter's hospital room, and after discovering the death of the hod carrier, carted him away. They took him down two flights of stairs and deposited him on a slab in the basement.

There the construction worker stood up, took a shiny ten-peso coin out of the pocket of his robe, and handed it to the stretcher bearers. Tugging surreptitiously at his underwear, he did the best he could to conceal the hard-on pushing up from underneath his robe.

24

TOMÁS HAS A RUN-IN WITH THE
GENDARMERY, OBSERVES A COLONEL
FROM A DISTANCE, AND REMEMBERS
THE SAME SONG AS ALWAYS

A small cloud of mist rose up from where the horses stood pissing onto the cobblestones. A pair of gendarmes jousted playfully with their swords.

Tomás walked between the horses toward the factory door where the strikers stood watching the policemen with distrust.

A banner hung over the door denouncing the two foremen whose ouster was demanded by the union: "Pierre's never read a book in his life and Rodríguez is a disgusting satyr who thinks he's handsome."

The Chinaman smiled. Illiteracy and personal vanity hardly seemed like sufficient grounds for firing a pair of foremen and paralyzing a five-hundred-worker factory. But behind the banner there was another story, the story of a bitter struggle with the owner, a Frenchman named Donadieu who with the aid of his two foremen attempted to run his mill with an iron hand, in repeated violation of the workers' contract. So when you took into account the fact that one of the foremen had outlawed newspapers inside the plant (even the reactionary *Excelsior*) and the other one was famous for making passes at the women workers, the spark justified the size of the blaze.

"What's up, *compañelos?*" he greeted the strikers at the gate. There were about forty workers from the Abeja, and another fifteen or so from nearby factories who had come out in solidarity.

"They want us to open the gate, Tomás," said Ciro Mendoza.

The Abeja strike was the first in the history of the Valley of Mexico in which the workers not only walked off the job, but took over the factory itself, closing the doors to scabs and non-union workers. That's what had brought out the half dozen mounted police and given rise to the "red guard" of workers at the gate (inaugurating a grand tradition that was to last throughout the coming years). That's what had attracted the Black Marias and the gendarmery colonel, sitting in his convertible discussing the situation with the mill's manager.

"Who wants you to?"

"Colonel Gómez. He says it's illegal for us to shut the place down. But what's really going on is that Donadieu's been busy recruiting scabs since yesterday, and he's got them all in a house a couple of blocks from here, waiting for his chance to get into the factory."

Tomás looked at the officer, the same man whose name had been circulating around the domino table. He'd changed very little since Tomás had first encountered him three years ago in Tampico: a small dark man dressed in tall riding boots, tight-fitting pants, military jacket, his mouth like a single fine nearly lipless line across his face, short bristly hair fighting to stick out from under his kepi. His small, almost delicate hands toyed absentmindedly with a riding whip.

"Let's tuln the tables on them, what do you say? You go tell the colonel that we'le going to open the dool to the mill, and me and the *compañelos*'ll head over to the house where Dona-dieu's got his scabs and we'll cut them off befole they evel get hele."

"Sounds good. I'll give you ten minutes. They're over in a house on the side street by Satanás's store, a great big place with a red door, you can't miss it. The place belongs to Zacarías the accountant."

Tomás went over to talk with the rest of the workers.

"How many of you men ale almed?" he asked. "Meet me in five minutes in flont of Satanás's stole."

And he sauntered off, staring over at the colonel. Their eyes met for a moment and Tomás remembered the old song about Tampico.

"This time, Gómez, you'le going to get it. And if the bosses aleady paid you off, you'le just going to have to give them theil money back," he thought, grinning at the officer getting out of his car, still playing with the riding whip in his hands.

THE WAY THINGS USED TO BE:
TOMÁS WONG IN TAMPICO

There she was in that pink tulle sundress, a broad-brimmed hat on her head, bare feet playing in the waves, digging her fingers into the sand, the salt water bleaching the bright red from her nails. He remembered how her dress swayed around her hips, how she used to sing to him, how the straps of her tulle dress slipped off her shoulders, how her white breasts danced in the open air. He remembered the palm trees, the evening light, the sun setting behind the refinery towers of the Huasteca Petroleum Company. It was all connected in his mind with that same song everybody was singing back then. He remembered the first time he'd heard it, from some drunk singing in the street: *Oh, Beautiful Tampico, tropical paradise, the glory of the republic, wherever I go, I'll remember you.* He remembered. And he thought that a man's memory was a pointless game created by idle gods.

Her name was Greta. At least that's what she called herself, and she wore a white leghorn hat. She blamed the heat. But Tomás, he liked the sticky heat, the blazing sun that burned their skin, that made them sweat, that dried them off. She killed herself with arsenic. Meticulously distilled from ten sheets of flypaper. Like a good German, disciplined and precise. He wasn't the type for suicide. But hers was another story. And now all that was left was his memory of the woman on the beach in the evening, soaking her feet in the wide ocean, half slipping out of her pink tulle dress so that her huge white breasts glowed in the last rays of the setting sun. And in the middle of all that, a patriotic song about the glories of Tampico.

IN WHICH THE FOUR FRIENDS PLAY DOMINOES IN NEW SURROUNDINGS AND INSTEAD OF DEALING WITH THE MATTER AT HAND TALK ABOUT THE MEXICAN REVOLUTION AND DISCOVER THEY DON'T KNOW WHICH WAY IS UP

"Three masked men try to kill us, the widow says she's got nothing to do with it, the trombonist and his brother are dead, not to mention the Englishman who despite all indications to the contrary didn't commit suicide. Does anybody have any idea what's going on here?" asked the poet as he helped Manterola lean back in the hospital bed.

"No, but that's nothing new, not for me and not for Mexico. You show me one person who understands anything around here. Who the hell knows anything about what's going on in this wonderful country of ours? Everybody pretends like they know, they try and fool everybody else, but they're just as much in the dark as the next guy. How about you, do you understand any of it?"

"Don't look at me, I couldn't agree with you more," said the lawyer Verdugo, throwing the flowers into the wastebasket, and the water back into the washbasin so he could use the vase for an ashtray.

Tomás, sitting on the bed recently vacated by the deceased hod carrier, stared out dreamily at the late-night traffic filling the street below. With his left hand he scratched the fuzz above his upper lip.

"You growing a mustache, Tomás?" asked the journalist.

The Chinaman nodded and flashed the quickest of smiles.

"I didn't think you people could grow a mustache," said the poet, dragging the small night table in between the two beds.

"By this time I think you should have figuled out that I'm a lathel apochlyphal Chinaman. The kind of Chinaman who leads Celvantes, Tolstoi, Blasco Ibáñez, and Balzac. If I wele you, I might stalt asking myself if youl domino paltnel wasn't a spy for Alfonso XIII."

"The fact of the matter is, at this point I'm ready to believe just about anything . . . except that," said the poet.

"Like I said, it's a hell of a country!" sighed Verdugo.

"Now gentlemen, let's not start blaming the country for all our problems. The truth is she's somewhat the worse for wear after so many years of bullets and blood, but it's certainly not her fault."

"The problem isn't too much bullets, but not enough," said the poet. "That's what happens with these halfway revolutions. They're like a tree without any leaves. The country's suffered for it, hell, we all have. When you come right down to it, it's all a matter of hope . . ."

"If that's where this conversation's going, you can count me out. I'm too much of a cynic to be able to handle that rot," said Verdugo, pulling the box of dominoes out of the pocket of his gabardine coat (English made, and purchased at the Correo Español with forty pesos won in a dice game). He spilled the bones out onto the night table, but it was too small to hold them all. Tomás got up, took a picture down from the wall, a Dürer reproduction, and he laid it on top of the bedside table. The bones slid along the glass a fraction of an inch above the surprised faces of the apostles and the leftovers from the Last Supper.

"The winners were the ones with the most resistance, the guys with the thickest skins, the hardest shells," said the reporter, unwilling to leave the poet hanging alone in the Revolutionary balance. "Obregón won in the end because, if you don't count the time he was military governor in Mexico City and had the priests out sweeping the streets, he was always the most adaptable, he was always the one who could find himself a place inside the system."

"Of course. That's what it took to come out on top. The Revolution was lost long before it was over. It was lost as soon as the generals decided it was better to get married to the landlords' daughters than to rape them."

"I'm sorry to say I don't agree," said Verdugo, taking a pack of cigars out of his jacket pocket and offering them around. Only the journalist took one. "Obregón and his officers would much rather have them as their whores and mistresses. That's one of the great moral advances of the Revolution. The aristocracy has taught them how to do business, not how to sit at table. They've simply learned how to turn power into money, not into good manners."

"You really believe that the generals won the Revolution?" asked the poet, slapping the double-six down on top of Dürer's apostles. "Well they didn't, the *licenciados*, the professionals, lawyers and the like, were the ones who won it in the end . . . these newfangled creatures crawling out from under the rocks everywhere you look. Lawyers . . . jolly types, with a little bit of education under their belts . . . but not too much, of course . . . And every one of them's got their own personal little story about the Revolution to whip out just in case . . . field secretary to some general, author of this or that treaty or subparagraph of the constitution; ex-quartermasters, organizing troop trains from who knows where, editing some newspaper somewhere . . ."

The reporter rapped his knuckles on the glass tabletop, passing the hand.

"What are you passing for?" the poet interrupted himself. "Looks like that busted leg of yours has affected your brain."

"Listen, poet, the only bad bones I've got to worry about right now are these ones sitting here on the table in front of me."

Then Tomás knocked on the picture frame, passing to the lawyer Verdugo who laughed out loud.

"Now you've done it, Fermín. That's what you get for bad-mouthing lawyers when you've got one sitting right next to you."

The poet stopped to think. He had two sixes left, meaning that Verdugo had the other four. It was going to take a bit of maneuvering to get out of this one.

"I didn't mean anything personal, you understand," said the poet.

"Of course not. And if I beat your pants off I'm sure you'll understand it's got nothing to do with my professional pride."

"It's all part of the game."

The metallic clatter from the streetcar yard drifted in through the window. Then it started to rain, the soft drops slapping against the glass and muffling the sounds from outside.

"My problem's always been that I never really believed," said the reporter. "I liked Ricardo Flores Magón, but he was always too far away. The Villistas and Zapatistas were my type all right, but they always moved too fast and shot too much, so that I either never had the chance or never wanted to get too close. I suppose it's got something to do with my being a reporter, always too caught up in the details, the little stories, not with the big ideas. Always the observer, always watching from outside. Of course there were individuals I liked well enough, the way they went into the Revolution and when it was over came out the other side without selling out. Colonel Múgica in '17, de la Huerta when he was provisional president, Lucio Blanco in '15, Ramírez Garrido when he was chief of police. Hell, I never thought I'd be partial to a police chief, but Ramírez Garrido's a good man. He made the cops join the union, protected the prostitutes, and organized cooperative kitchens in the jails."

"What's Ramírez Garrido up to now?" asked the poet. After two more rounds, the lawyer had turned the game back to sixes, and he had no choice but to play one of his.

"I think he wants to be governor of Tabasco or something like that. Pass," said Pioquinto Manterola. Besides his abominable hand and the fact that he'd gone and gotten himself thinking about his tangled and foggy relationship with the Mexican Revolution, it suddenly dawned on him that he was in love.

Verdugo watched the Chinaman play a five, blocking off his sixes, and forcing him instead to play a four, giving the poet a brief respite.

"I'm still a Villista at heart," said the poet, setting the four/ two down on the glass. "I'll always remember how the world changed with every charge of Villa's cavalry, how the whole world became undone somehow. We were fury on horseback, the destruction of the old order. What'd they call Attila the Hun? The scourge of God? I used to make up poems on horseback, riding alongside illiterate peons, traveling photographers, ex–cattle rustlers . . . Do you understand? In front of us, the *federales,* the machine guns, the men with their shiny buttons, falling down like toy soldiers.

"A revolution's fought with ideas and violence. We had plenty of violence but not too many ideas. That's what made me doubt all along. I hated things the way they were as much as the next guy, but I didn't know how to turn that hate into something else. Maybe it's just that I didn't really want to change things, I just wanted them to stay the way they were, only with different people running the show."

"Well, if that's what you wanted, Verdugo, that's what you got. All we have today is a sort of modernized version of the same thing as before, full of words, and graves you've got to go visit every Sunday," said the journalist. "But maybe I'm wrong. Maybe what really happened is that we opened the doors of change. Maybe what all those years of war were about was to just open the door a little bit, so the changes could start to happen. They've given land to the *campesinos*, haven't they? We've got a new constitution, don't we? They took the power away from the Church, they outlawed the company store."

"You'le wasting youl bleath, fliends. That levolution did what it had to do. Now comes the second one, the leal one, the wolkel's levolution."

"I'd like to believe you, Tomás," said Verdugo, playing his last six and losing control of the game. "But faith is something you've got to nourish to keep it alive. It's been too long now since I turned into a sort of a beggar of the heart and mind, living like a parasite on borrowed ideas."

"If General Villa rises up again, I might just go and join him for another go-round."

"I suppose that sooner or later a man's got to stop being an observer and take a stand. Although maybe there is such a thing as an active observer, maybe it's not such a bad thing to have somebody around to tell what happened," said the reporter, turning the game to threes, making everybody pass, and then going out with the double-threes and the three/one.

"Well, will you look at that. Maybe you don't know too much about levolution, newsman, but you sule do know how to play dominoes."

"A man's got to be good at something . . ."

27

THE POET WRITES A POEM, EXPLORES
THE MYSTERIES OF MEXICAN INDUSTRY
AND ENDS UP JUMPING THROUGH A
FOURTH-FLOOR WINDOW

In the waiting room outside the company president's office, Fermín Valencia sat and wrote with a pencil stub inside the little notebook he always carried with him: *I stitch my soul to my skin/ overcome with despair/ life bleeds white/ and still/ no Singer was ever made that could mend it/ with fine needlework/ while I lament/ these things in me/ I've lost/ left/ behind.*

Fermín's notebook was filled with short poems, and every now and then some friend would take one and get it published in the newspaper or in one of the many magazines that had begun to appear in Mexico City since the Revolution. It made him proud to receive recognition as a poet and there wasn't anything else he'd rather do with his time than write poetry, but all the same every time he wrote a poem he felt like a poacher, like the perpetrator of some criminal act, an outlaw. So when the secretary came out of the office and told him to go inside, he hid the notebook behind his back in embarrassment, almost as if she'd caught him masturbating.

Henry Peltzer's office was lined with photographs of automobiles and full of shiny new rubber tires on pedestals, reflecting the light with their capricious geometric tread. The German-Gringo-Mexican entrepreneur sat behind an enormous mahogany desk, smoking an oversized cigar and playing with his gold watch chain. Peltzer was a living caricature of the new industrial bourgeoisie. As though he'd modeled his own image on Robinson's drawings of porcine bosses that illustrated John Reed's articles in *Metropolitan Magazine*.

"Mister Valencia, good to see you. I sincerely hope our relationship will bring as prosperous results for both of us as before."

"I sincerely hope so too, mister. What've you got for me?"

"What I have got, Valencia? What I have got? New Mexican tire, very soon, exceptional sales opportunity. Real good, real nice one."

"Well, I'll need more than that to work with. What's so special about it, how's it different, what's it cost?"

"A wonderful tire, just wonderful. Absolutely. Best tire in Mexico. Fits every car, every make, every model, good for all. Peltzer model 96-C. We call it THE ONLY ONE."

"The only one?"

"THE ONLY ONE."

"Okay. So what's the deal? Does it cost less, last longer?"

"No, costs more, lasts less. But very good tire, excellent tire. Imagine a car floating on air . . . Have a cigar."

"No thanks."

"Made in Papantla. Excellent. Just like tire."

"So how do you want to run it? You want to use the same angle as last time? A little cheap nationalism, the only Mexican tire, etc. . . ."

"Not cheap nationalism, expensive nationalism. You leave spaces, we put in prices."

"Speaking of prices, how many lines are we talking about?"

"One, two, three good phrases. We take care of the rest right here, writers, artists. You just give us one, two, three good ones . . ."

"Five hundred pesos, a hundred up front," said the poet, preparing himself for Peltzer's counterattack.

"Pesos . . . Mexican pesos? This is a fortune. Impossible. Mexican industry cannot keep up with foreign competition, terrible situation. Better we do ad work here. No can do, my friend Valencia. Mister Valencia. So what's it going to be?"

"Look, if you ask me to do twenty ads, it'll cost you thirty pesos each. But if you just want me to write the jingles, which is the most work, then my price is fixed, set, solid, good, excellent, the only one, but not cheap, just like your tire. Five hundred pesos."

"Listen to me, poet. I see you do not understand the situation of Mexican industry. We are still suffering the disaster of the Revolution. Any day another one. Instability everywhere, bad for roads, bad for tires. Foreign competition is terrible. From Detroit come tires, many tires, terrible quality, but cheap, very cheap. Cars, there are many cars, five thousand imported last year, but competition terrible. Textile crisis, mining crisis, crisis crisis. No money. Lots of rumors. Rumors everywhere. Less money every day."

"What kind of rumors, Mr. Peltzer?"

"Rumors, problems, United States. Rumors, problems, petroleum. Rumors, army, coup d'état. Again, again. Rumors everywhere, soldiers everywhere, even here."

The industrialist's voice took on a conspiratorial tone. He looked at his watch and pointed with a fat finger toward the door.

"Ten minutes and I have a visitor. You will see. Visitors come, visitors go."

"Five hundred," said the poet.

"Four hundred and not a cent more."

"Five hundred, or I go to work for Detroit for free, out of spite."

"Have a cigar. From Papantla, like tires."

"Five hundred."

"Everywhere rumors. Bad times. Strikes everywhere. Anarchists in the factories. One day yes, one day no, riots, insurrection."

The poet sighed. It figured that the owner of the only tire company in the country would haggle just like the owner of the corner store. Mister Peltzer would never become a millionaire at that rate. Or who knows? Maybe that's what made a man a millionaire. The truth is it was a three-hundred-peso job, but from Peltzer he wouldn't take anything less than four hundred. And whatever he could wangle out of him above that he'd give to the "riot and insurrection" anarchists Peltzer was so worried about. Probably some of Tomás's friends.

"I'll tell you what. Since you gave me a few ideas yourself about the product, I'm going to give you a ten-percent discount. Only I don't want you to get the idea that's the way I usually do business. But seeing as how you're a Mexican company"— the poet bit his lip—"competing with the foreign monopolies, and especially from such a rotten city as Detroit . . ."

"You have been to Detroit?"

"No."

"Okay, four hundred and forty, a nice even number, or better yet, four-fifty. Better, no?"

"Better yet four-sixty," said the poet, helping himself to a Papantla cigar.

Peltzer smiled broadly.

"Good advertisement, good like tire, excellent tire."

"The best, my friend," said the poet, feeling a little bit like Diego de Alvarado selling glass beads to the Tlaxcaltecas.

Peltzer signed a voucher for the cashier and, after ceremoniously shaking hands, led the poet to the door.

Fermín smiled at Peltzer's secretary who he could just see through the partially opened door to the broom closet, adjusting her stockings, and he was heading through the swinging doors that led to the salesroom when he walked smack into a uniform. To be precise, he suddenly found his nose pressed against the upper button of the uniform tunic of a thin young army lieutenant. The poet mumbled an "excuse me," but the officer stood staring at him for a moment and then suddenly went for his gun. Fortunately for the poet he carried a long-barreled Mauser automatic in a showy leather holster, and while the lieutenant wrestled to work the gun free the poet kicked him in the shin and ran back the way he'd come. He had a vague idea of seeing a second man following behind the lieutenant, a blond dandy with a waxed mustache.

As he retreated, Fermín cursed himself for his carelessness

in going out unarmed, but who would have thought that even in the offices of the Peltzer Tire Company . . . He ran through the waiting room, where Peltzer's secretary was just emerging from the broom closet with her stockings perfectly in place, and burst through the door into Peltzer's office. The first gun shot cxplodcd bchind him and the bullet sent splinters flying from Peltzer's mahogany desk. Without taking the time to turn down a Papantla cigar, Fermín ran past the Mexican tire king and threw open the window. "Shit," he thought.

Peltzer's office was on the fourth floor of the Guardiola Building, near the corner of San Juan de Letrán. Without hesitating, the poet stuck his leg through the window and edged along the narrow ledge. A light breeze blew in his face. He could hear shouts from the office behind him, Peltzer arguing with the lieutenant and his companion. Fermín smashed his fist through the window in the next office over. Another shot whizzed by him and he crashed in through the window, splinters of glass cutting into his hand, ripping his trousers, and lodging in his hat. The sight of a stranger bursting into his office amidst a shower of broken glass was almost too much for the already high-strung accountant of a firm that specialized in the sale of contraband Remington rifles and sewing machines. The poor man nearly fainted from the shock. Fermín Valencia filed away for later use the poetic image of the exploding glass and ran like a soul pursued by the devil, out of the accountant's office and into the hall. He didn't catch his breath until he was seated in the bar of the Majestic Hotel, gulping down a double Havana brandy and cleaning his wounds with a napkin dipped into his shot glass.

28

THE JOURNALIST SUMS UP RECENT
EVENTS AND FACES THE FACT THAT HE'S
FALLING IN LOVE. A NUN SAVES HIS LIFE
AND HE WRITES AN ARTICLE ABOUT
A LION TAMER.

Pioquinto Manterola limped over to the sink and lathered his face with a thick coat of shaving cream. His eyes sparkled in the mirror from inside the half circle of white foam. He pulled a German steel razor from the leather kit his father had given him years before, tested it on the hairs of his forearm, and brought the blade to his face.

"You'll be leaving us today, isn't that right, sir?" asked the nun who stood watching him.

"Today or tomorrow, Sister. The doctor said he wanted to take another look at my leg either this afternoon or tomorrow morning, and if everything was all right I could be on my way."

"That's wonderful. I hope you have a speedy recovery."

"By the way, Sister, do you think you could find someone who might like that box of chocolates there? I've never been much of a chocolate fan myself."

"Now isn't that kind of you, brother. I know just the person, too. There's a woman in the next room over who's recovering from a bad case of bronchitis, and hasn't had any visitors since she arrived."

The journalist watched in the mirror as the nun picked up the large box of chocolates tied up with a green silk ribbon and left the room. Manterola drew the keen steel blade across his cheek.

For the reporter, the few minutes he spent each morning in front of the mirror shaving was the best time of the day for getting his thoughts in order, a time when the world and everything in it took on at least a minimum of cohesion. Not too much, of course, but just enough, the absolutely necessary, the indispensable amount. Although there were days when that was so little that he never managed to get past a hazy fog of vague ideas, opinions, impulses, contradictory emotions, black clouds, irrational depression.

But not today. The reporter was determined to concentrate all his deductive powers to figure out just what strange bird of prey had been circling around him and his friends.

His eyes sparkled again in the center of the ring of foam climbing up to his eyebrows.

"One," he said in a low voice as if he were praying, "they shoot a trombonist in the middle of a pasodoble. Or was it a march? In his pockets he's got enough jewels to open up a jewelry store. The dead man is Army Sergeant José Zevada. The killer is left-handed."

Manterola slid the razor carefully over the scar on his neck.

"Two. A man falls out of a window at number twenty-three Humboldt Street two days later. An army colonel named Froilán Zevada . . ."

Numbers three and four went unsaid as he shaved carefully around his upper lip.

"Five. Three thugs try and fill us full of lead in the street. None of them live long enough to tell who sent them . . ."

He was busy considering number six when it suddenly came to him again that he was in love, completely and absurdly in love, with the violet-eyed widow. This sudden realization ruined his concentration and nearly cost him his life, but the razor slipped harmlessly off his throat.

Love and suicide was an old combination for the journalist—he'd tasted it before, familiar and sweet, undesirable but real. People fall in love and later they kill themselves . . . so as not to feel so ridiculous when love goes away.

"Cheggidout, cheggidout. Good to see you up and around,

old man," said Gonzaga, *El Demócrata*'s star illustrator. "Thought you'd still be in bed."

"Gonzaga, what a pleasant surprise," said the inkslinger, silently blessing the man for saving him from his turbulent thoughts.

It had been ten years since anyone had told Gonzaga they were glad to see him, and he stared at the journalist with a look of honest perplexity. He carried his drawing pad in his right hand, and his left arm sagged with the weight of a thirty-pound Smith Corona "portable."

"I, uh . . . ," he said, forgetting his characteristic *cheggidout*. "They sent me over with a story for you."

Gonzaga set the typewriter down and waited for Manterola to finish shaving. The reporter watched him in the mirror.

"That's the sweatshop mentality for you. They can't even wait for a man to get out of the hospital before they saddle him with more work."

"Cheggidout. Was my idea. Figured you'd like the story. Like it was made for you." Gonzaga opened up his drawing pad and stuck it in front of the reporter's face.

Powerful pencil strokes combined with charcoal shadows to create the image of a lion tamer dressed in the uniform of an imperial Hussar from the previous century, cracking his whip in front of a dozen lions. The tall bars of the cage reached skyward in the background. The lions roared aggressively or bared their claws, while the lion tamer stood grandly with his left hand on his hip next to his holstered revolver.

"Yeah? So what's it all about? Cut the telegraphic act and fill me in."

"The Krone Circus, six P.M., got it? German-Spanish lion tamer. Silverius Werner Cañada. Crazy in love with a trapeze artist."

"Female trapeze artist or male trapeze artist? Let's get our facts straight, Gonzaga."

Gonzaga eyed Manterola uneasily.

"Female, kind of a slut."

"There we go. That's a start."

"Tamer goes into cage in the middle of the show . . ."

"As usual?"

"As usual, but instead of going through with his normal routine, he starts to beat the crap out of the animals until they get so mad they attack him and eat him for dinner."

"Holy . . . !"

"Cheggidout. Unforgettable love story. Public saw the whole thing, scared out of their wits."

"And why the hell didn't they pull him out of there?"

"Cheggidout. Locked himself in the cage, threw away the key . . ."

"Pretty efficient. So how'd they get him out in the end?"

"Didn't think to ask. Have to remain unclear."

"What do you mean it'll have to remain unclear? Is he still in there, or what?"

"Cheggidout. Could be. Lions still nibbling over his bones."

"Check it out," mumbled the journalist, not sure whether he should laugh or cry. "Be a good fellow, won't you, and help me put the typewriter on the table over there by the bed. I'm still not a hundred percent with this leg and all."

"Got it," said Gonzaga, lugging the heavy machine over to the bedside table.

"One last favor, Gonzaga. Go out to the reception and ask for a few sheets of paper, will you?"

The illustrator was walking out the door when he collided with the nun rushing back into the room.

"Please, brother, come quick," she shouted, and ran back the way she'd come.

Manterola and Gonzaga glanced at each other and followed the nun's flapping white habit to a room two doors down. A few curious patients had gathered in the hall.

"Look at her, dear God, look at her. I gave her the box of chocolates," wailed the nun, bursting into tears. A woman's body lay on the bed, teeth clenched, eyes bugged out, hands curled in a clawlike grip.

Two hours later the autopsy would reveal that she'd been poisoned by a chocolate bonbon filled with cyanide.

29

THE SHADOW OF THE SHADOW AND A
BULLETPROOF PACKARD

"Hey, you know what? We're like a shadow's shadow. Them, the confabulators there in the widow's house, if there's even any confabulation at all, they're only a shadow, indistinct, without any clear objective, at least as far as we know. And us, following them around haphazardly, erratic, like a bunch of wild kids out on a lark, stumbling across something in the darkness, we're the shadow of the shadow. You get it?"

"A rather lyrical assessment of the situation, my dear poet. That's the least I can say," said Verdugo as they dined on Spanish omelettes and chorizo in the Restaurante Abel (one of the five best restaurants in Mexico City, a little less elegant than the Cosmos and the Bach, and a cut above Sanborns and the Regis). They were finishing off their second bottle of a dry Spanish red wine that had come into Veracruz by steamer less than a week ago, "a bit agitated" according to the proprietor's judgment, but the two friends found it excellent. A bitterly dry wine that stained their lips a dark red.

"It's just that I'm convinced that even if we don't do anything at all and just go on living our absurd lives the same as before, they're going to kill us. Sooner or later we've got to go on the offensive."

"Who's they?"

"The shadow. Or whatever it is that they're the shadow of, or another shadow a little less confused than ours."

"Why the rush all of a sudden? Has something happened since your run-in at Peltzer's?"

"Look, how many times do you think they can miss? In this

town if you want someone dead it isn't too long before they get that way. It's time we started taking things seriously."

"I hate to say it, but it does seem like you're right," said the lawyer, nodding. "I suppose it's not enough to simply return fire and pretend like nothing's going on." He sighed.

The poet pulled his whiskers out of his wineglass and stared the lawyer in the face. His friend was prone to certain suicidal tendencies. And if he thought about it just a little bit, he could see the same thing in Manterola and the Chinaman as well. He couldn't hold it against them, now and again he himself felt a certain nostalgia for death, a yearning for peace deep down inside. All of a sudden he was overcome with the memory of the cavalry charge at Paredón. He felt like a miserable survivor who had lost his chance for glory by not dying along with his comrades in the best cavalry charge in Mexican history. But for him it was always just a passing mood, usually connected to hunger or the flu, not like Verdugo who seemed to live with Marguerite Gauthier's eternal ironic smile fixed across his face, as though suffering from an incurable case of tuberculosis.

"It's time for the shadow's shadow to move into action," said the poet.

"What have you got in mind?"

"I say we take your lottery money and buy ourselves some weapons. If there's one thing I learned from General Villa, it's that whenever you've got a little extra cash on hand you should take advantage of the opportunity to improve your firepower."

The poet's suggestion didn't surprise Verdugo, who understood it fully in both its implications: guns and more Spanish wine. He raised his hand and indicated to the waiter to bring another bottle.

The restaurant was half-empty. It was well past time for lunch and still too early for dinner, but the two friends had come to celebrate with Verdugo's 1,700 pesos in lottery winnings. He'd won in a most curious way. As he was leaving a bordello he'd accidentally picked up another man's topcoat. He found a lottery ticket in the pocket and the next day discovered he'd won third prize. With the winds of fortune smiling on him so openly the lawyer had felt obliged to celebrate, and he'd found Fermín Valencia sitting in Alameda Park writing an impassioned acrostic dedicated to the screen actress Lupe Vélez.

They blissfully started in on their fifth bottle with a feeling of mutual harmony that, on a different occasion, might have seemed like an abuse of confidence. The poet read the lawyer a lengthy poem in open verse he'd submitted to the Milpa Alta Flower Festival poetry contest under the pseudonym Beatrice Flor López, in the hopes of winning a little prize money; and the lawyer was moved to recount in detail the first three chapters of his doctoral thesis in international law: *Territorial Waters and Transoceanic Canals*. If one is to believe the records of the Mexico City tavern archives, a registry carefully maintained in the memories of bartenders, waiters, maître d's, and cops on the beat, this was the first and only drunk shared by the two friends since they'd met many years before. Their motives were obscure. What caused the poet Fermín Valencia and the lawyer Verdugo to pass from moderate inebriation to a full-scale binge? Perhaps it was because they'd both reached bottom in their own way, perhaps their sudden and unexpected wealth had somehow carried them over the edge, or maybe it was simply the tension of those strange times. Whatever it was, the effects of the wine were generous and slow, filling them with a teary but peaceful nostalgia, and they felt themselves capable of anything. By six-thirty they had started in on their seventh bottle.

"We need a tank, that's what we need," declared the poet. "A combat vehicle, like the English had on the Somme in '17. With tracks and a big gun on top, all iron and rusty."

"An armored car, a bulletproof Packard like General Pablo González."

"For all the good it ever did him."

"It was his own fault. The fool went off to Monterrey without the Packard and that was the end of Pablo González."

"So what're we going to do with the Packard?"

"The same thing as with that tank of yours, but without attracting so much attention."

"I don't know," mused the poet, and he hid his head among

the empty wine bottles, surprised by the lawyer's suddenly serious stare. "What if they're really the good guys and we're just sticking our noses in where we don't belong like a bunch of nosy bosybidies?"

"That's a novel way of putting it."

"What is?"

"Do you really think they could be the good guys looking the way they do? If Manterola were here he'd set you straight on that score. This Colonel Gómez looks like the type who'd steal the bottle out of his baby brothers' mouths. Just look at them, the Spic, that crummy little lieutenant, the Frenchman, the hypnotist, the widow . . ."

"I kind of get the feeling the inkslinger's in love with the widow, you know . . . And you're kind of hot on your old friend Conchita, aren't you?"

"You surprise me, poet. I never made you out to be the puritanical type. What the hell do we want a tank for, anyway?"

"Did I say something about a tank?" asked Fermín, and he started to recite the verses of a young poet from Veracruz named Maples Arce, whose poems he'd just discovered that very morning:

> The insurrectional city of luminous signs
> floats in calendars on the wall,
> and there a tramcar bleeds,
> from afternoon to afternoon,
> along the well-pressed street

Verdugo listened attentively to his companion.

"Dammit. I wish I could write like that kid," said the poet. As they uncorked bottle number nine they instinctively returned to the story at hand.

"I saw how they killed the guy with the trombone. Let me tell you, it was ugly. There must've been ten thousand people there. Well, maybe a little less, like five thousand, say, listening to the band, and then, *bam*, they blow the poor guy's brains out. Just like this, *bam*, blew his brains right out of his head."

"Me, I was at the widow's party. Of course I fell asleep, during the picture I mean. But that crowd there, they're just like the Romans, tanked to the balls and screwed to the walls. I mean it, just like the Romans . . . And the bullets, my man, the bullets. Hell, my hand still hurts," said Verdugo, flexing his bandaged left hand.

"Well what about that lieutenant who almost killed me? He had me crawling around the outside of that building like a monkey in a circus. And my face all cut up by the broken glass. Look," and he pointed to the fading cuts all across his face.

"I just wanted to . . . ," said Verdugo, but he hesitated, thought about it for a minute, and by the time he looked back at the poet he'd forgotten what it was he wanted.

The next day after waking up with his stomach all queasy from the Spanish wine, "a bit too agitated" as the proprietor had said, but with the remainder of his lottery money still in his pocket, the lawyer went out and bought himself a used bulletproof Packard.

30

RANDOM EVENTS THE VERY NEXT DAY

Cipriano approached Tomás in the mill shop and took him by the arm.

"Tomás, you think you could put someone up in your house for a few days? I wouldn't ask you if it wasn't important."

Tomás nodded.

"If he doesn't mind being a little clowded. The place is full up these days."

"What's that? You get married or something?"

"It's a long stoly. Bling him by my place in the molning."

"You know the Rialto Movie House in San Angel? Across the street there's a restaurant run by old Magaña's widow, the guy who got killed by scabs at the Carolina. Tomorrow morning at ten-thirty there'll be a guy inside reading *Les Misérables*. If he's wearing a hat keep your distance, but stick around and follow him when he goes out. Watch out, because he might have picked up a tail. If he's not wearing a hat, then it's safe to go ahead and make the contact."

The supervisor walked by and the two men broke off talking and went back to work.

An hour and a half later Pioquinto Manterola, who'd left the hospital the day before sufficiently shaken up by the episode of the poisoned chocolates, went with his friend the lawyer Verdugo to submit his declaration before chief of special services Nacho Montero at the seventh precinct house. According to the police investigation the chocolates had been left at the hospital's front desk by a bellboy from the Bristol Hotel, 316 Jesús María Street. One out of every three was laced with cyanide. The dead woman had been unlucky enough to bite into a poisoned chocolate the first time around. Each poison bonbon had enough cyanide to kill a horse, and in spite of the fact that the confections were made with almond paste it would have been difficult not to have tasted the poison. But by then, of course, it was too late. "Enemies?" the reporter answered the policeman's question. "Who knows? A man in my profession can't help making a few through the years but it would be hard to say just who they might be."

Out in the street a light drizzle had started to fall. A pair of horsemen spurred past a limping Ford. Verdugo opened the door of his bulletproof Packard and helped the journalist inside.

"I've about had enough of this. It's time we did something."

"The widow swore to me the whole thing's got nothing to do with her or her friends . . ."

"Who's it got to do with, then?"

"Beats me. But you're right about one thing. It's time we did something."

"No one comes and says they're not guilty if there isn't some reason to suspect they are. No one comes around giving answers if there isn't somebody asking questions."

"I suppose you're right. And anyway, it's the only lead we've got."

"Two days ago some guy started taking potshots at the poet and nearly killed him. I say it's time we tighten the screws and see if the shadow comes out of the darkness and shows itself."

"What shadow?"

"Them, the enemy. That's what the poet calls them. And he says our little domino club's the shadow of the shadow. Lyrical, isn't it?"

"Not bad. Valencia ought to come and work with me at the newspaper."

While the lawyer and the reporter talked, the poet stood outside the delivery entrance of the Hotel Regis trying to sell the head cook six grade-A Toluca hams he swore could easily pass for Spanish Santanders. The poet had received the hams, which were really from Tlaxcala and not from Toluca at all, as payment for a poem he'd written for the fifteenth birthday of a rancher's daughter from Santa Inés. After a fair amount of wrangling he managed to trade them for seventeen pesos and a coupon good for six meals in the hotel restaurant.

A little while later, as he was trying to exchange the meal tickets for an equivalent amount of drinks at the bar, he ran into the North American Bertram Wolfe arguing with a reporter from the Hearst chain in one of the booths. The poet had met Wolfe before, an English teacher at the National Preparatory School and a friend of the muralists who were then decorating the school with their enormous paintings. The poet had taken a liking to the gringo from the very first time they'd met. His Spanish had improved considerably in the last few months and he talked about his experiences in the country with a passionate affection. He worked for a leftist news agency out of New York, wrote for the American Communist party newspaper, drank with moderation, and had a beautiful wife named Ella. All the same, the poet would have gone on and sat alone in a booth at the back to work out a poem he'd been carrying around in his head, if he hadn't overheard the pair of gringos talking about the dead man Manterola had been investigating a week ago in the same hotel. He was getting used to the way the threads of this strange story kept crossing and recrossing without the slightest respect, so he pulled up a chair and joined them.

There's not much else to say about that day's events except that, while the Chinaman worked at the mill, Rosa looked out the window of the tiny house in Contreras to see a pair of shadows keeping watch from down the street; Pioquinto Manterola slept restlessly through a series of nightmares in which a naked woman in a leghorn hat crawled on top of him to embrace him, with a pair of huge meat cleavers in her hands; and General Pancho Murguía crossed the border from the United States to head up yet another unsuccessful rebellion against Obregón's government.

31

IN WHICH THE FOUR FRIENDS START A
GAME OF DOMINOES THEY NEVER
FINISH, THANKS TO THE REPORTER AND
HIS FIFTEEN QUESTIONS

The poet walked through the Majestic's swinging doors. Tomás, standing at the bar, didn't seem to notice the breeze blowing in from the street, but Manterola and Verdugo, seated at
the customary table, smiled in greeting.

It was time for another game of dominoes, a game that
doesn't matter so much for the bones and the way they fell.
But somehow they had to take control of the strange story that'd
woven itself around them like a play where some absentminded
director forgot to hand out the scripts and the actors found
themselves caught up in the middle of dialogues, murders, parties, orgies, and songs without any clear idea of what part they
were supposed to play. The poet knew it, and he walked straight
to the table and sat down. Even Tomás felt strangely attracted
by this new urgency and he left his glass half-drunk on the bar
and went over to join his friends.

This new change in the rules hung subtly in the air and the
bartender, unable to understand, sensed it as some kind of
threatening presence. He kept his distance from the marble
table where the dominoes, black side up, mixed and turned
under Pioquinto Manterola's agile hands.

They wouldn't like to admit it, but tonight for the first time
ever they sat down without choosing partners, drawing their
chairs up to the table without any particular order.

"Hele we go, gentlemen," said Tomás as he set the double-six, and with that as the signal the reporter pulled a sheet of paper from his vest pocket and unfolded it slowly.

"I made up a list of questions to see if we can start to figure out this mess we've gotten ourselves into."

"It's time we went on the offensive," said the lawyer Verdugo, playing the six/four.

"If those fouls thele ale youl idea of an offense, then you'le in tlouble, fliend," said Tomás, taking a strange pleasure from the others' uneasiness. By now his mask was like a part of his own skin and it amused him to see how his "inscrutable Oriental bearing" threw his companions off their guard.

"Double-fours," said the poet.

"Double trouble," said Manterola.

"No, I wasn't referring to the fours, Tomás," said Verdugo. Then turning to the reporter, "Let's get on with it, Manterola. This whole thing's gone and woken me out of the sleep I've been in ever since November 1887."

"What happened in November 1887?" asked the poet. "Oh, that's your birthday, isn't it? I guess I'm a little slow on the uptake tonight."

"Well, I didn't put them in any particular order, but here we go. Number one: What's Margarita the Widow Roldán got to do with Colonel Gómez, Conchita, Celeste the hypnotist, Ramón the Spic and long-distance ejaculator, the lieutenant whose name we don't know, and the French aristocrat about whom we know even less? And after that, what have they all got to do with one another? What brings them together? Who else frequents the widow's house, and why?"

"Not bad for starters, inkslinger," said the poet. He eyed the five the Chinaman set down on the table, and concluded that his partner's opening sixes were merely the luck of the draw. Following his instincts he rearranged his hand, separating the two sixes he'd been holding in reserve, placing one in line next to the blanks and the other upside down with the rest of his threes.

"Do you want answers or have you got more questions?" inquired Verdugo with an embarrassed smile, both wanting and not wanting to go deeper into this strange story that had taken them prisoner.

"We'll do the answers later," said the reporter. He played another four, leaving the original six still open at the other end of the row of dominoes. Then he returned to his sheet of paper and read in a dull, even voice: "Number two: Who killed Sergeant Zevada? Who killed Colonel Zevada? Let's assume for the time being the murderer or murderers were the same, which brings us, of course, to *why?* Next we have to ask ourselves what connects the Zevada brothers to the widow, Gómez, and the others. Are they connected, how are they connected, and to which ones? All of them or just some? We know the Zevada brothers knew Margarita, or at least one of them had her picture in his pocket and that's how we found the widow and her friends, by tracing the photograph. And we also know the widow was in the building on Humboldt Street when Colonel Zevada fell out of the window. That's all we know."

"Bravo," said the poet. "A hell of a question." The Chinaman sat in silence, caught between the game and the conversation, debating whether or not to try and turn the game back to sixes. He sensed that his partner the poet had misinterpreted his strategy of holding out with the rest of the sixes in his hand, although the poet certainly hadn't done much to open the way for him either.

"Go on," said Verdugo with a wide smile. "At the moment we seem to have more questions than answers."

"Double-twos," said the journalist, setting his domino down with the rest.

"Sixes," said the Chinaman, breathing an inaudible and private sigh of relief. He played the six/two.

"Well that's one mystery solved," said Verdugo.

"Number three," said the reporter. "Why did the dumber of the Zevada brothers have his pockets full of jewels?"

"All right," said the poet, "all right. Twos, sixes, jewels. It all goes to show that when you don't understand anything there's nothing you can do but let the water run under the bridge."

"Four: How many left-handers are there in this story?"

"Before we go on to number five," said Verdugo, "I suggest that instead of classifying the Zevada brothers as the smart one and the dumb one, unless you know something the rest of us don't, we just call them the trombonist and the colonel," and he lightly tapped one of his dominoes on the tabletop, passing the hand.

"Five: What was the Widow Roldán doing in the building on Humboldt Street? What was Colonel Zevada doing there? Maybe I'm an idiot, but I have to confess I was so taken up with the woman that I didn't really notice anything else. I apologize, gentlemen, for my complete lack of professionalism. I didn't even read the story in the paper the next day."

"No problem there," said Verdugo. "I read it. He fell, or was thrown, out of the window of the waiting room of Weiss's jewelry shop."

"But, if I remember correctly, the colonel didn't have any jewels on him."

"And to complicate things further, the jeweler said he'd never seen the man before."

"Excuse me, gentlemen, but, seeing as how the lepoltel hasn't gotten alound to taking his tuln, I suggest that you all go and lead the books of an Englishman named Althul Conan Doyle."

"Have they been translated?"

"No," said Verdugo, "but it wouldn't be a bad idea to get ahold of a copy. He wrote a whole series of detective stories in *Strand Magazine.* It's been a big hit in the United States, too. He's got this detective that always goes around with a doctor."

"I suppose a detective needs a good doctor. We could use one, that's for sure."

"Sorry, friends, but I think that things are complicated enough with the Brits and the Frenchman we've already got to deal with. What's this Frenchman's name, by the way?"

"Michel Simon, something like that. I don't know if he's left-handed, but he carries his gun on the left side, in his boot, a little number, a Derringer or some piece of trash like that."

"Derringers are what they use to make those little holes in Swiss cheese," said the poet.

"At three yards it'll kill you just as well as a Colt .45," said Verdugo, who knew about that sort of thing.

"Six: How did Gómez get to be Colonel of the Gendarmery when he used to be buddy buddy with Pablo González? How did he survive the purge of the Gonzalistas in 1920?"

"Now there's a good question. Do you know anything about that, Tomás?" asked the poet.

The Chinaman shook his head.

"Seven: How did Mr. Roldán, the widow's deceased husband, die? That is to say, is Margarita a widow by natural causes?"

The game had come to a standstill. Tonight the four friends were unable to interlace the conversation with the play of the bones. None of the other regulars came over to watch the game, as sometimes happened, and not even the bartender came by with the usual bottle of Havana brandy.

"Eight: Does the Shadow Club, as our friend the poet has been inspired to call it, have anything to do with the Englishman murdered at the Hotel Regis? Is it just a coincidence that Colonel Gómez happened to be there, and what about his little trick with the keys? Who is the dead Englishman? What was he doing in Mexico City? Who's his disappeared friend? What happened to the million pesos' worth of stock certificates?"

"I've got some information there," said the poet. "I ran into Bertram Wolfe and Williams, that patsy working for the Hearst chain, yesterday."

"What's Wolfe say?" asked Pioquinto Manterola, who also knew the North American journalist.

"Apparently the guy was representing the English-Dutch oil companies. They sent him to Mexico to talk with the government about export rights. Wolfe's got a whole theory about it. He says that since the Lamont–de la Huerta treaty was negotiated in New York, and since President Obregón acknowledged a billion-peso debt to the foreign bankers, with the railroads and oil-export rights as collateral, the oil barons are afraid the government's going to try and apply Article Twenty-seven of the constitution, which would make all mineral and oil deposits public property. In other words, the oil companies may be in for some tough negotiating. He says that this guy Blinkman was sent in secret by Aguila Petroleum to try and work out a separate deal with the government, separate from the gringos that is, before everything blows up in Obregón's face. Williams says that Blinkman had strange habits and that they shoved a pistol in his mouth instead of putting something else there, if you know what I mean. Wolfe swears up and down the whole thing's got to do with some hanky-panky of the oil companies, and he thinks that the hired guns of the American companies, Huasteca Petroleum or Texas Oil, were the ones who worked Blinkman over. He says there's going to be a lot of dead men without a name to put on their tombstones if the companies start to play roulette with one another like that. Williams says that Van Horn killed him—he's the guy who shared Blinkman's room and has since disappeared."

"That brings me to number nine: What's Tampico got to do with all this? Both Zevada and Gómez were promoted to colonel while stationed in Tampico, and that's where the oil companies have their headquarters. Does this whole thing have something to do with Tampico?"

"Tomás?" asked Verdugo.

"When I was in Tampico I was wolking fist in a laundly and latel on as a calpintel. These two guys wele famous in Tampico back then. Ol maybe infamous is a bettel wold. In the big stlike back in '19, they wele both thele with oldels to splead a little lead among the wolkels. That's all I know. Back then Tampico was a dilty little city with a ton of dough going flom hand to hand. You could buy a colonel ol a genelal just as easy as a piece of land, if you had the sclatch. Life wasn't wolth too much in Tampico. An oil well is like a big hole in the glound full of black shit. That's all I know."

"Number ten: What's Tomás's Chinawoman go to do with all of this?"

"Nothing," said Tomás, and he smiled as Tampico slipped momentarily from his thoughts.

"Sorry to say it, Tomás, but there just aren't any chance encounters in this story. So when a young woman runs out of a gambling joint in the middle of a gunfight and asks you to take her away, I can't help but wonder."

"Nothing," said Tomás again.

"All right then, eleven: Who hired Suárez and Felipe Tibón to kill us? Who was the other guy that was with them? Which one of us were they gunning for? Was it me because I'd gone after the widow and said too much? Or the poet because he'd witnessed the trombonist's murder? Or Tomás because he'd saved Rosa López and taken her away? Or me again because I wrote in the paper that Blinkman had been killed instead of committed suicide? Or were they going for all of us? And does it have anything to do with the rest of the story?"

"That's too many questions for one night," said the poet.

"Hold your horses, Fermín, here comes another one. Number twelve: What did Margarita Roldán want from me when she came to visit in the hospital?"

"And what did Celeste the hypnotist want from me, apart from that little chat about magnetic forces? It's the same question. I never did figure it out."

"One more. Thirteen: Who's this officer that suddenly starts taking shots at our friend the poet, and why?"

"Hell, that's an easy one," said Verdugo. "If we hadn't had so much wine in us the other day we could have figured it out sooner. Was he a guy about five-seven, long sideburns, sort of bug-eyed, thick eyebrows, in his late twenties?"

"Sorry, that's not him. If I remember right, and you've got to understand as soon as he saw me he went for his gun, he was a skinny guy, plenty taller than me, clean shaven, light haired. One of these dark-skinned guys who's hair's gone blond from too much time in the sun or cold."

"Who's your man?" Manterola asked the lawyer.

"I thought it might be Gómez's aide-de-camp, this little lieutenant that was hovering around him and the hypnotist the whole time the night of the party at the widow's. But the poet's man still sounds familiar to me. Maybe it's some other officer in Gómez's entourage."

"Well if he isn't, then it's even more complicated. Did he say anything before he started shooting? Not very Mexican of him, if you ask me, to shoot first and ask questions later."

"He didn't even say *buenos días*. He looked at me, gave a double-take, and went for his gun."

"Fourteen: Who sent the poisoned chocolates to me at the hospital and why? Fifteen: What do we know? Are we getting in somebody's way, and who is it? What did we do?"

"That's the best one of the bunch, inkslingel."

"And the last one, too."

"That's enough," said the lawyer Verdugo. "What do you say we cut your sheet of paper there into pieces and divide up the questions? I think it's about time we had some answers. At any rate, the game's gone cold."

"And just when Tomás and I were about to win, too."

"My father always said that dominoes and talk don't mix," said Verdugo, carefully tearing Manterola's list into four equal pieces.

"What'd he say that for?"

"Who?"

"Your dad."

"My father never said anything to me in his whole life," answered Verdugo.

The poet smiled. Tomás got up from his chair and headed over to the bar of the Majestic Hotel.

ENCOUNTERS WITH OLD FRIENDS
ON A RAINY DAY

Mexico City stretches out toward the south into that prole-
tarian world of San Angel, Puente Sierra, Tizapán, and Contreras, towns connected to the city by the thin umbilical cord
of the Tacubaya streetcar line. Labyrinthine cobbled side streets
invariably lead to the doors of the great textile mills in the
converted shells of old haciendas: the Abeja, the Carolina, the
Eureka, the Magdalena, the Alpina, the Santa Teresa, with
their French, English, or Spanish owners; sweaty mills reeking
with the stink of the dyes, surrounded by hundreds of ramshackle hovels the companies let out to their workers and small
vegetable gardens where the men and women from the factories
spend a few hours each week trying not to lose touch with their
country roots.

It was raining in the south. But the rain was too much for
this city that was born in the rain, for the rain. The rain drives
it crazy. The streets turn into rivers that run down toward the
little plaza at the center of San Angel, rivers of mud swirl around
the autos and horse carts, wash out bicycles and spook the
horses of the mounted police that regularly patrol the town.

Covered with a gray rubber poncho Tomás jumped across
the puddles from cobblestone to cobblestone, slipping con-
stantly but somehow managing to keep his balance. Finally he
stopped in front of a small cafe where three or four workers
sat eating at the tables farthest from the door. One of them, a
thin man with a narrow nose topped by thick eyebrows that
practically grew together in a single line, sat reading volume

two of *Les Misérables*. His railroad hat lay on the table next to an untouched bowl of soup.

"Sebastián," said the Chinaman as he approached the man.

"Well hell, Tomás, they didn't tell me it was going to be you," the man answered with a big horselike grin.

"What's it been? A yeal at least . . ."

"Something like that," said Sebastián, motioning for the Chinaman to take a seat. "Since May 1921."

"Did it take you long to get back in?"

"I was in Guatemala six months, doing some organizing down there, and then I just walked back over the border. Shit, down there the mosquitoes're thicker than the trees. I spent the rest of the year in Atlixco under another name. The scabs were playing for keeps, and I got mixed up in a hell of a gunfight. So I had to get out of there and I went back on up to Tampico. But things there just aren't the same anymore, not like when you and me were there. You got to keep in the shadows all the time, can't work out in the open. I'd give a speech and then have to spend the next two weeks hiding out. But all the same, things are heating up just fine. Every day there's more men catching on to the idea out in the oil fields. It won't be long before they've got a union going. It's a matter of months or a year at most, my friend."

"What blings you to Mexico City?"

Sebastián stood up and gave the Chinaman a big hug. Other people's emotions always made Tomás nervous, but in spite of his uneasiness he returned Sebastián's embrace.

"You'le awful thin. Don't you evel eat?"

"Hell's bells, man, after I left Tampico I stayed a couple of days in San Luis Potosí with some comrades and there wasn't a crumb in the cupboard. What was I supposed to do?"

"Ale they after you hele?"

"I don't think they know I'm in Mexico. But if anyone recognizes me and tells the law, I'm done for. I was in touch with Huitron and Rodolfo Aguirre and they told me to stick to the south and not make the city. Any chance of getting work as a mechanic around here?"

"Thele's always wolk alound fol a good mechanic, boilel loom wolk mole than anything else. But unless you've got a lecommendation the pay's pletty bad. That's the way they wolk it."

"No problem there, buddy. I've got the best fake recommendations in all of Mexico. Papers are the least of my worries right now."

"Ought to be easy enough to find you a gig, then. We'll just have to find someplace whele they don't know youl face. Maybe the Plovidencia ol the Aulelá. You going to wolk in the union?"

"No, just with affinity groups. I asked them for somebody to connect me with the ballsiest group around. I've got a couple of ideas I want to try out."

"You talking about some kind of dilect action? We've got a good tough gloup, but it's stlictly fol plopaganda wolk. Sometimes thele's nothing fol it but to hit the stleets, but we'le not in fol any individual actions."

"Well you can at least hear me out before you say no, eh?" asked Sebastián San Vicente, looking steadily at the Chinaman.

"Of coulse."

"That's the way. You got a place I can stay until I cash in?"

"Sule, you can stay at my place, but thele's only one bed between the thlee of us," said Tomás. The bed was going to be awfully narrow with three of them, he thought, and they'd have to work out another head-to-foot rotation. Rosa wasn't going to be any too thrilled about it.

"Don't worry, brother, I can sleep on the floor. It won't be the first time. You get married or what?"

"I've got myself a paltnel. It's a long stoly, I'll tell you about it some othel time."

"You think you can find a place for another comrade who's coming in from Puebla? He can be trusted, you've got my guarantee."

"I don't think it'll be any ploblem. Let me talk to the comlades this Satulday."

Tomás sat and looked at Sebastián San Vicente, the Spanish anarchist deported from Mexico in May 1921. He was a true comrade if there ever was one, a man who could be trusted without reservation, but prone to respond to the violence of the system with violence of his own. Still smiling, San Vicente looked out onto the rain-drenched street.

It was also raining heavily outside the Cafe Paris where a flower seller had taken shelter in the doorway, blocking Pioquinto Manterola's view of the street. The rain usually left Manterola feeling blue, but now he could feel it in his recently mended leg as well, a subtle diffuse ache in the muscles around the bullet wound. Whether it was from the sadness or the pain, he couldn't seem to concentrate. It was that way with almost all journalists in their late thirties, the rain reminded them of old love stories, romances ruined by the impatience and possessiveness that come with love.

"Have another one, sir?" asked the waiter, with the bottle of Spanish brandy in his hand.

"No thanks, Marcial, I think that two is just about enough for a rainy day. But pour a glass for my friend, will you? In another minute she's going to be crossing the street, step in that puddle there, and walk in the door."

"How do you know that?"

"Because ever since I've known her she always comes half an hour late," said the reporter, pulling a Swiss watch from his vest pocket. The watch was inlaid with mother-of-pearl. He'd had to have it repaired once after it was damaged in the line of duty, and it bore a pair of deep scratches across its silver cover.

The reporter looked up toward the door. The flower seller leaned to one side, and he caught a glimpse of Elena Torres getting out of a taxi and running across the street between the puddles.

They'd first met in 1919 when the Yucatecan school teacher came to Mexico City as the personal representative of Carrillo Puerto and the Socialist Party of the Southeast. She was the only woman delegate to the Yucatán socialist congress but she'd left her mark in the formation of decrees on divorce, working women, and women's suffrage. Once she came to Mexico City she'd worked alongside such figures as Evelyn Roy, editor of the newspaper *Woman* and one of the foremost leaders of the first Mexican Communist party, who at one time had run *El Comunista,* one of the party's first newspapers. The Agua Prieta Revolt had ended with both Elena and Carrillo Puerto on the winning side and she'd worked for a time as an aide to Mexico City Police Chief Ramírez Garrido, during his brief tenure in office. Later on she'd joined the feminist bloc inside the Revolutionary Confederation of Mexican Workers (CROM). She'd broken with the CROM only recently over disagreements with the sinister Napoleon "The Pig" Morones, the Mexican Sam Gompers. She still had strong connections with the Socialist Party of the Southeast and now worked as chief of staff for the Yucatán congressional delegation.

Shaking a boot filled with water from the puddle in front of the door, she stepped into the cafe, headed straight for Manterola's table, and downed the glass of cognac in a single gulp as though she were in a great hurry.

"Hello there, reporter, what can I do for you?"

She was a short blond woman with a memorable deeply carved face and a heavy voice. She almost never smiled, and when she did, watch out.

"Take a seat, Elena. I need some information," said the journalist, standing up and waiting for the small woman to sit down.

"That I take for granted, Manterola, what I want to know is what do I get in return?"

"I don't have anything to trade, Elena. You'll just have to put it on my tab."

"If you owed everyone in this town as much as you owe me, you wouldn't dare show your face in the street."

"What do you know about Colonel Gómez? How did he get from being one of Pablo González's cronies to commander of the Mexico City gendarmery?"

"Is Gómez the saint you're praying to these days?"

"A week ago someone shot a hole in my leg, Elena. I need to know if Gómez had something to do with it."

"You picked a hell of an enemy, I'll tell you that much. The man's a snake, I don't even think his friends like him. Have you ever met him?"

"One time in Pachuca he gave the order to have me shot by a firing squad, but I don't think I've ever been any closer to him than maybe about ten yards."

"And the firing squad?"

"Let's just say I was lucky," answered the reporter, and his hand rose unconsciously to his chest to finger yet another ancient scar.

Elena laughed, her blond curls falling in front of her face. She brushed them aside with a flick of her hand.

"They say that before Gómez went into the army he was a foreman in an American-owned mine in Coahuila. He took up arms late in the game and that's why he never made general under Carranza, who always sent him out to do his dirty work. Then he was part of Pablo González's inner circle. Paymaster of the Northwest Division. Military governor in the oil country. The truth is that if he ever fought in a battle I don't remember it. That's something you'd have to ask a soldier. I do know that he was in Tampico in 1919 and that he was the one who gave the order for the troops to fire on the strikers. That's his specialty: executioner, firing squad commander. But I guess you know about that firsthand. With the Agua Prieta uprising he climbed on the donkey with the rest of the insurrectionary generals. At first he stuck with his old protector González but once he saw which way the wind was blowing and that Obregón's troops were going to get to Mexico City first, he buddied up with Benjamín Hill, turning over the garrisons under his command in the Huasteca. The word is that his wife died somewhere around then, under rather suspicious circumstances. I heard someone say once that he shot her because she nagged him too much. I wasn't ever sure whether it was a joke or what. He's a tight-lipped sort, always got some scam going, too. The man's got a dirty look and a dirty mind."

"You're starting to sound a bit puritanical, Elena." The reporter laughed.

"What do you want? The guy makes me sick. Once at a party he asked me to dance and I didn't last more than half a polka. When Obregón became president he was looking for just that sort of man to run the gendarmery here in the city, so he installed Gómez under General Cruz. Birds of a feather, you know. A few months back a friend of mine told me Gómez's got some shady deal going with the government, something to do with fodder for the army's horses in the Valley of Mexico, he's got the concession wired, something like that. But that wouldn't be anything new."

"How much money'd be involved in something like that?"

"Probably six or seven thousand pesos, after he pays off the other five or six people he's got down the line. Is any of this what you're looking for?"

"Gómez and oil, Gómez and jewels, Colonel Zevada and Colonel Gómez. Do any of those combinations ring any bells?"

"You do ask a lot, don't you? No bells there. Back a couple of years ago when I was working with the police I could have gotten you more information, but today I'm just a harmless provincial schoolteacher serving her country in the Chamber of Deputies."

"Provincial maybe, but harmless never, Elena . . . even your own mother wouldn't go for that one. I heard you kicked some poor bastard in a restaurant the other day and broke his leg."

"The idiot slapped his wife in public."

"Maybe you and I should get married, Elena."

"Me marry a journalist? Never, Manterola."

"Well, at least I tried," said the reporter. He looked out at the rain still falling hard against the window, the words CAFE PARIS spelled out in reverse.

THE WAY THINGS USED TO BE:
ROSA IN THE MIRROR

I look at myself in this broken mirror and think about another mirror, tall and set in a white scented wooden frame. I'm a different person and I'm not. My body lies to me, tries to fool me, forgets about me, hides itself. It's almost like this memory of the mirror belongs to someone else. Other eyes looking at me naked, admiring this pale skin and the breasts pointing up at the sky as if they were hunting for birds and ready to shoot. Birds painted on paper screens in Chinese houses in exile.

I look at myself in the mirror and think that nobody wants to be different. Nobody. I never asked to belong to a place I never knew, this naked body of mine never lived in Canton, Shanghai, Hangchow, Peking. Two-syllable words without any memories, but with plenty of rules of their own.

I look at myself in this new mirror and I remember the other one, the other woman, and even though I don't want to I can't help remembering that the mirror doesn't only reflect a naked body but also a naked face, another face that doesn't belong to me. A face looking at this body as if it owns it, and it does. Owner by right of sale, one woman for three IOU's signed with the name of that wrinkled old man who was my father.

And I break this mirror in front of me into pieces, but the other one I can't destroy and it remains shaken but in one piece in my imagination, in my memory.

MORE RAIN AND MORE QUESTIONS,
ALL ON THE SAME DAY

Fermín Valencia and the lawyer Verdugo had agreed to combine both their business and their investigations. The poet had gone along with the lawyer to the seventh-district court house to file a complaint against a bullfighter for the rape of a chorus girl. And the lawyer had accompanied the poet to the offices of the Peltzer Tire Company, so that his friend could draw his pay and protest his treatment at the hands of the lieutenant with the itchy trigger finger.

In between they made a stop at the "National Armory" gun shop, following the advice Pancho Villa had once given the poet, expanding their arsenal to the tune of a pair of shotguns, ammunition, and a German-made Walter repeating pistol.

Now they motored through the rain down San Juan de Letrán in the lawyer's bulletproof Packard, without any particular destination in mind.

"The lieutenant's name's Estrada," said the poet. "Juan Carlos Estrada. They said he was there to buy tires for the gendarmery fleet."

"Gómez."

"That's right. And besides that, I've got the idea there was more to his visit than just tires."

"What'd he tell Peltzer about why he was trying to pick you off?"

"He said I'd insulted him."

"Dammit, poet, this thing gets more confusing all the time. Are you sure you've never seen the guy before? Maybe you killed his dad or laid his sister or something."

"Well, I couldn't swear one way or the other about his dad, but I'm sure no Estrada's ever gotten between my sheets, or me between hers, for that matter."

"So what's next?"

"Let's try the jewelry store. I've got the feeling there's a thread there that'll lead us to something more solid."

With the windows closed the Packard started to fill up with steam and cigar smoke, until it finally pulled to a stop, casting up a silent curtain of spray in front of the *El Demócrata* offices on Humboldt Street.

The poet and the lawyer paused in the waiting room of Weiss Bros. Jewelers and automatically turned to stare at the window over the street. A new pane had replaced the one through which Colonel Zevada had taken his fatal fall. The rain tapped placidly against the glass.

"I don't ask too many questions these days. It's the Revolution. Everything's gone shady, strange, unpredictable. One guy sells a gem for train fare, the next guy trades it for three horses and a suitcase. A house burns down and a child saves his mother's jewelry from the fire. A soldier steals the ring off a dead man who stole it off another corpse the day before. A maid sells off her former employer's jewels. Nothing's like it used to be. These aren't normal times. It's been ten years now since I asked to see a sales receipt or certificate of ownership. I buy and don't ask any questions. Possession is ownership these days, I give the seller a receipt and a fair price. You shouldn't be surprised. Nothing's the same anymore. I run a straight business, above board, it's just that these are strange times for a man in my trade," announced the wrinkled jeweler in one long paragraph.

Except for the enormous strongbox sitting on four stout iron legs, with the words STENDHAL AND COMPANY scrolled across the front, the office could easily have belonged to any type of business at all. The walls were bare, the oak desk empty, the many grooves in its worn surface poorly covered by a coat of glistening varnish. There wasn't even a jeweler's glass or a velvet pouch, a pair of pliers or a hand lens in sight. Weiss, a little man with white hair that stood straight up off his head, sat behind the desk smiling at our two friends. They stood in the middle of the room, there being nowhere to sit except for a ridiculous pink velvet love seat pushed up against the far wall.

"What about Zevada?"

"I'd never seen him before. It would have been the first time he came to do business with me."

"The name doesn't ring any bells?"

"None at all. The second time the police came they showed me a photograph of his brother. I didn't know him either. They showed me some jewelry, too. I'd never seen those pieces before."

"How about Margarita Roldán, the widow of the fellow who used to run the Industrial Printworks."

"Margarita Herrera, the Widow Roldán. Yes, yes, of course."

"She buy or sell?"

"Both. But she's bought more than she's sold. Nothing out of this world, really. A very nice sapphire once. A Russian pearl tiara, a pair of diamonds in the rough, a topaz necklace. All gifts, I suppose . . . Nothing out of this world, like I said . . . I'm afraid you're mistaken, gentlemen. The only thing I have to do with this whole story is that I'm the one who had to pay for the broken window."

They left the car in front of the Bank of London and walked along, covering their cigars with their hats to keep them out of the rain. Verdugo had insisted they arrive on foot at the Araña Cantina on Netzahualcóyotl Street, one door down from the bakers' union local. "A bulletproof Packard'd be in bad taste around a place like that," he'd said.

In the Araña the poet discovered the remarkable popularity his streetwise friend enjoyed in certain quarters of the city. Grifters, hookers, rumrunners, small-time hoods all greeted him with affection, or at least with respect. A player piano stood abandoned in one corner of the room and the shouts of the customers and the tobacco smoke were all the atmosphere there was to the joint. The Araña was the kind of place where you could just as easily be served rubbing alcohol cut with sugarcane juice, as a glass of authentic Napoleon brandy.

Verdugo greeted the proprietress with a kiss on the cheek, a disfigured paralytic woman serving drinks from behind the bar, and then glanced around for his source of information.

"What's the haps, *licenciado?* You buying or selling?"

"Neither, One-eye. I'm looking for someone mourning the loss of a couple of dead friends. We can talk price later."

"I don't give nothing for free, not even to my own mother."

"I'm sure we can work out a fair exchange. How about some information today in exchange for future legal services? You get the best lawyer in Mexico City free at your disposal the next time you need him."

"Two for one."

"Two for one it is, One-eye . . . The dead men I referred to are Gallego Suárez and Felipe Tibón."

"You want a name or you want the man in person?"

"In person'd be better, One-eye."

"Stick around half an hour and I'll have him for you," said the serape'd One-eye, and without another word he walked out of the dive and hurried down the street. The two friends leaned back in their chairs and called for a bottle of English gin, lemons, and a pitcher of water, and settled down to wait. But fifteen minutes hadn't gone by before the one-eyed man reappeared, dragging along a soaking-wet and sickly-looking fellow dressed in a suit that hung limply off his shoulders, the rain dripping off the sleeves and forming a puddle on the ground at his feet. He was about forty years old, with his forehead wrinkled into a permanent frown, his shiny black hair plastered just above his eyes, and a dirty black tie that danced across his shirt, now and then brushing against the bulge of his gun.

"The Gypsy, at your service, lawyer," said the one-eyed man, gesturing toward his companion. Then he disappeared into the surrounding hubbub.

The new arrival set his wide-brimmed black hat down on the table next to the bottle of gin and, dragging over a chair, sat down with his elbows resting on the chair back.

"What can I do for you, *licenciado* Verdugo?"

"Do we know each other?"

"Not personally, but once a while back you defended a cousin of mine in court."

"In other words, I've already worked for the family."

"You could say that," said The Gypsy and, after glancing at the lawyer for permission, poured himself a shot of gin.

"About a week ago Gallego Suárez, Felipe Tibón, and another man whose name I don't know tried to kill me and three friends of mine. We'd never had anything to do with them before, so it stands to reason that someone else paid them to do the job. I want to know who."

The Gypsy looked from the poet to the lawyer and then spoke in a low voice that could only just be heard over the noise from the nearby tables.

"They weren't gunning for you, *licenciado*. They were after your friend the reporter. It wasn't you they wanted."

"How do you know?"

"What's it matter? Maybe I was the one who fixed them up. Maybe the third stiff was another cousin of mine. What difference does it make? You know how much a man's life is worth in this town? Now I don't mean any offense by it, but it costs three hundred bills to off a gentleman like yourself. You just put six hundred pesos on the table there and I'll personally take care of the man who hired Gallego and Felipe. I'd enjoy it, too, because the man in question never even bothered to tell those poor boys that you fellows knew how to shoot. They went off to hunt rabbits and ended up with a bunch of Apaches."

"Why six hundred, friend?" asked the poet with a smile.

"Because the guy what hired them isn't any John Doe, and he's no fool either. He can shoot as good as you, maybe better. Oɪ maybe we should just say that the rates are going up."

"I'll give you the six hundred just for the name," said Verdugo.

The Gypsy thought for a minute. Then he glanced nervously around the bar.

"Six hundred and a promise, *licenciado*."

"Sure, if I can."

"Promise me you won't miss, because if you do I'm not going to be around long enough to enjoy all that money."

Verdugo and the poet exchanged glances. The lawyer took out his wallet and drew out six hundred-peso notes from what was left of his lottery money.

"I'm all ears."

"Hell, if it wasn't so hard for a man to make a living out there I'd beat it for Zacatecas or San Luis Potosí."

Verdugo folded the bills and slid them across the table toward The Gypsy.

"You don't have to hide it, lawyer. There's more eyes in this joint than in a movie theater. More than one of these stiffs's already heard everything's been said without hearing nothing at all." The Gypsy poured out another glass of gin, tossed it down, and said, "You all want to have a chat with Colonel Martínez Fierro."

35

WORKING-MAN BLUES

Manterola lowered his eyes from the Virgin, with her lilac-and-yellow mantle, to the nineteen-year-old painter standing beside the figure, and it dawned on him that he was looking at a man in possession of the truth. How could he describe to his readers this sudden realization of another man's absolute conviction? This young man, dressed in shirt and tie, with thick lips, a pale face, interrogative eyebrows, who seemed to concentrate all his energy into a pair of intense black eyes . . .

"Señor Revueltas . . ."

"Call me Fermín."

"What's an atheist doing painting the Virgin of Guadalupe?"

"You think she's a virgin? Look at the colors. Maybe she's not a virgin at all. She is very Mexican, though. Isn't she? And she's dressed for a party, her and the people worshiping her, too. And the worshipers are the people. I'm sorry, but I'm not explaining myself very well am I?"

"No, you explain it just fine. I'm just not so sure I can explain it to my readers that clearly. I'm really an action writer at heart. I write about accidents, gunfights, crimes of passion. I didn't really come here to talk about murals."

"Do you like Tintoretto's virgins, Botticelli's winged women? What would you think if we erected the Eiffel Tower in Alameda Park?"

"Is it true that Rivera's painting the Creation in the amphitheater?"

"Don't let the title fool you. Just take a look at his women's thighs. There's more than one road that leads to Rome. Mine is color."

"I understand you studied painting in Chicago."

"For all the good it did me," said the young artist, contemplating his brightly colored Virgin of Guadalupe, for which the Ministry of Education would pay him four hundred pesos when the mural was finished.

"I hear there's been some shooting in the halls."

"There's been more insults than bullets. The students get all upset because we're covering the walls with ideas. They paint over our work, throw gum, spitballs, that sort of thing. And sometimes we've exchanged more than words, if you know what I mean . . . Do you like it?" asked the painter, motioning toward his work.

"Very much," said Pioquinto Manterola who, say what you will, was highly receptive to any act of passion, not just the day's sanguinary headlines.

Manterola left the young painter gazing at his Virgin from a scaffold buttressed to protect him from the students' attacks.

He wandered through the halls of the National Preparatory School. Charlot, the Frenchman, was working on a group of Spanish conquistadors looking like metallic monsters in a fight against Aztec warriors. Rivera wasn't on the scaffolds today. Stomachaches, romantic troubles, back pain kept him shut in at home.

When the reporter circled back he found Revueltas armed with an enormous brush dripping yellow paint, fighting off a pair of dandily dressed but rather effeminate-looking students.

"If you don't like it, you've got your ass to look at instead, gentlemen," shouted the muralist.

"Instead of painting that kind of crap, you should leave the wall painted white. This is a house of study. And that's the way it ought to be," said one of the students whom the reporter recognized as a certain Salvador Novo who brought his ingenuous poems by the newspaper every now and then.

"Need a hand, painter?"

"No, I can hold them off, thanks. Come on by some evening after the light's gone and we'll go have a drink."

"Have you wounded any students yet?"

"Three so far, scratches, nothing much, but these two jack-anapes are going to make it five," said the painter, advancing on his attackers. A small dark-skinned helper came to his aid armed with a spatula instead of a dripping brush.

The reporter smiled.

36

AN ABDUCTION AND A RESCUE THAT
DOESN'T CORRESPOND

Although the affinity group Fraternity was small, its members
filled Tomás's tiny house to the seams, occupying the bed and
the few chairs, leaving no room for them to pace up and down
as they talked. Each man took his place and stayed there until
the meeting was over. The group had no rules, no affinity group
did. They were drawn together by chance and sympathy of
ideas, and they took an active part in the movement according
to agreements arrived at during their interminable meetings.
There were groups dedicated to promoting the idea of free love,
the concept of rational education, violent direct action, groups
dedicated to propagating the classic anarchist texts, and simple
discussion groups.

Six men made up the group Fraternity. They made no effort
to recruit more members but if someone else happened to join
it was fine with them, the same as if one of their members left
the group due to a conflict of ideas, travel, or boredom. Their
main concern was propaganda work to further the cause of
radical unionism. Besides printing an occasional pamphlet,
they'd taken on responsibility for the distribution of the CGT
newspapers in the southern part of the city, the tabloids *Our
Ideals*, and *Solidarity*. But the group had another distinguishing
feature. Its members were widely recognized in union circles
as "men of action," they were armed and always ready for a
fight, and they'd taken to the front lines in the growing conflict
between the anarchist-led unions and the police and the
CROM's hired gunmen. If you were to ask them their position
on violence, each of these men—Varela (who hailed from Ve-

racruz), the gimp-legged Paulino Martínez, the pastry cook Hidalgo (born in Badajoz, Spain), Hector (a sixteen-year-old black from Tabasco), Manuel Bourdillon (the bastard son of a French mill foreman who worked as a machinist at the Santa Teresa Mill) and Tomás Wong—would tell you that violence on the part of the workers had to be a function of the masses, a defensive weapon—a protective shield for mass demonstrations and strikes, a righteous and just violence that would allow the movement to spread by protecting its flanks from the violence of the system. There was a time when they'd debated the need for individual acts of violence, especially in the summer of 1920 following Gómez's bombing of the archbishopric and the Recuerdo costume jewelry factory. The group had unanimously agreed that this sort of action could never help to advance the movement, its ideas, and the organization of anarchist unions—and that it would only serve to scare off the weaker segments of a movement that was just then gaining strength and which, a few months later, would bring about the creation of the CGT. So Tomás regarded the presence of San Vicente and his friend Lefty, just in from Puebla for the meeting, with cautious skepticism.

"Hell, Tomás, you know me well enough . . . I'm not crazy," said San Vicente without wasting time. "I'm not the kind of guy who preaches individual action and propaganda of ideas just for its own sake. I'm against assassination as a basic tool in the struggle. I'm a union organizer, you know that, but everywhere I go I see that what we need's a real newspaper, a daily newspaper, and that's something we'll never be able to pull off without a full staff of writers earning a decent wage, and without buying our own printing press. What happened during the railroad strike last year? They shut us out of the presses. What happened in Atlixco a few months ago? Every time we need our own propaganda the most we don't have the money to make it fly. Now Lefty and I made up some figures . . ."

Lefty carefully unfolded a single sheet of paper and read out loud in a mechanical voice.

"Two-year budget for organization newspaper. Wages for

three reporters, one typesetter, one compositor, one pressman, two distribution men, one administrator: nineteen thousand six hundred pesos. Two used German Stein linotypes, type, lead, paper, ink, typewriters, telephone, furniture: one hundred and eighty-two thousand pesos. Mailing costs for two years: six thousand pesos. We'll start out with a run of five thousand copies and expand to twenty thousand. Also one pamphlet per month, and a weekly magazine like *La Protesta* puts out in Argentina. For office space we could use the ground floor of a union local, the upstairs can be used for meetings: five thousand pesos. Total expenses: two hundred thirteen thousand pesos, give or take a few."

San Vicente looked out at his listeners, their shining eyes.

"Where are you going to get the dough, San Vicente, and how are you going to explain where it came from?" asked Bourdillon.

"We'll say it comes from the inheritance of a Turkish millionaire, distant relative of some imaginary comrade who gave it all over to the movement. That's not the problem, we'll work the cover so it'll stick."

"Yeah, but whele's the money going to come flom, Sebastián?"

"Lefty, the other paper," he said with a smile, lighting up a filterless cigarette.

Lefty took another sheet of paper out of the pocket of his patched vest and read to the group.

"Mail train from Puebla, stopped at kilometer eleven in Apizaco. Three men make the hit, we need one more at the Apizaco station, one driver, and a man for the horses. Six comrades in all. Estimated take: eighteen thousand six hundred to twenty-one thousand pesos. The American Smelting Company payroll in Aguascalientes. Paymaster collects the money from the bank every Friday along with two armed bodyguards. Four men make the hit, one more drives the car. Estimated take: nineteen to twenty-three thousand, depending on the time of the month. Mexico City Central Post and Telegraph Office . . ."

"We get the idea. How many more are there?"

"Nine," said Lefty. "I've got another sheet with details for each operation. We can pull off all the jobs inside of two months. All of them in different towns, no dead or injured, nice and clean. Isn't that right, Sebastián?"

"Hell, man, that's how we want it. I'm not too hot on the idea of taking out some paymaster or innocent bystander, myself. You always hope that things'll go the way you plan them."

"Yeah, but if for some reason we get caught and they can connect the robberies to the organization, that's all the government needs to declare the CGT illegal and sink the movement."

"It's a risk we'd have to take. I'm not trying to fool anyone. I've thought about that myself," said San Vicente, losing his smile.

"I don't like it," said Tomás, with his head propped between his hands. "I don't like any of it. This newspapel idea is like a favol we'd be doing fol the wolkels. But it's not the kind of thing we need to move things ahead any fastel. Don't get me long, I'm not aflaid of violence, and it's not like I think the money, the mail tlain, the payloll, leally belongs to them. It's just as much ouls as anybody else's, they lobbed it off the wolkels in the filst place. It's not that, but I still don't like it."

"I don't like it either," said Hector.

"Me neither," said Paulino Martínez.

"I'm not so sure," said Hidalgo. "Seems like they've got it pretty well thought out."

"I think it's a good plan," said Varela.

"If the majority says no, will you abide by our decision?" Bourdillon asked San Vicente.

"And if the majority says yes, does that mean all of you will come in?"

"Thele's eight of us. We'll go along with the majolity, but I don't think we should decide light now," said Tomás. "Let's take a week to think it ovel."

The other men agreed. After that they spent a while talking about propaganda distribution around the Abeja Mill, which was still on strike and surrounded by marauding gangs of CROM gunmen. Finally the meeting ended just as it had begun, without any kind of ceremony or ritual.

"Hell, man, I'm not going to offend you by trying to convince you if you're dead set against it. I said what I needed to say already. Here, I'll help you clean up a little bit," said San Vicente. "What happened to your lady friend? Did you tell her not to hang around while the meeting was going on?"

"I told hel to go out fol a while. She said she was going to see a pictule show," said Tomás, emptying the ashes off a plate into a garbage tin.

After a few minutes San Vicente stretched out on the bed with a sigh.

"Looks like I got myself a gig at the Providencia. I used the name Arturo Reyes. I think it would be better if the rest of the comrades called me Arturo from now on. It wouldn't do for it to get around that I was in town."

Tomás nodded, putting away a pitcher of water.

"They got her, Tomás! They got her!" shouted a young boy bursting into the house. The open door swung back and forth on its hinges.

"Who'd they get, boy?" asked San Vicente.

"His Chinawoman, mister. Tomás's Chinawoman. They took her away."

"Where? Who?" asked Tomás, his face suddenly tense.

"In front of the Aurora Theater, Tomás. When she was leaving the show. They took her and put her in a car. There was three of them in all, in a white car with wooden strips on the side. I was with her, Tomás, she took me to the movies and when we were coming out they got her. She was holding me by the hand, and one of them kicked me so's I'd let her go. I grabbed on to her but then her dress ripped. I did what I could. Honest, Tomás."

"Shit." Tomás spat out the word.

"They were Chinese, too, Tomás. Just like you, but bad ones."

San Vicente opened the upper drawer of the dresser and took

out a .38 revolver. Flipping back the cylinder, he checked to see that it was loaded.

"I guess you know where," he said to the Chinaman.

"Shit," Tomás said again, and took his knife out of another drawer.

It was a Saturday evening and the pairs of soldiers and maidservants, the most common couples in Mexico City in those days, strolled contentedly through the streets of San Rafael. Pair after pair ambled past the house of the Widow Roldán, under the watchful gaze of the poet and the lawyer who sat parked in the bulletproof Packard twenty yards beyond the widow's front gate, on Rosas Moreno.

"Tell me the part about electricity again, poet."

"Okay, but then you tell me that poem by Verlaine you translated."

"If you want, but I'm no poet to go translating someone like Verlaine. It's strictly an amateur job. You're right about that Maples Arce kid, he's the poet of our times."

"*The insurrectional city of luminous signs/ floats in calendars on the wall,/ and there a tramcar bleeds,/ from afternoon to afternoon,/ along the well-pressed street,*" the poet recited in a soft, even voice.

"*We walked at the mercy of the night and the road,/ like infamous men and murderers,/ Widowers, orphans, roofless, childless, with no tomorrow,/ In the light of familiar forests in flames,*" quoted the lawyer Verdugo in return, giving the poet a glimpse of the esoteric knowledge he'd gleaned throughout so many years of solitary abandonment.

They'd passed the afternoon in this way, their attention drawn occasionally by some movement around the widow's mansion. Around five-fifteen the widow and Conchita had arrived, and the lawyer had to duck down in the driver's seat to keep from being seen. An hour and a half later, Ramón the Spic drove off in a ramshackle Ford. Shortly thereafter, Celeste the hypnotist appeared in front of the house in an ornate cocktail dress and boarded a waiting taxi. After that, nothing.

Seen from the outside, the mansion looked like a pile of gray stone, surrounded by a large garden built no more than five years earlier. There was a double entrance with a black iron gate. An imposing tier of stone steps led up to the house, with pink stone balustrades crowned by flower boxes full of mallow flowers. From the street and through the railing of the gate the two watchers could see the main hall, its brightly lit windows.

It was the poet's idea to set up watch outside the widow's house, a way to bide time until they could get together with their other two friends at the Majestic later on that night and report on the unexpected entrance of Martínez Fierro into the story. They'd already tried unsuccessfully to find the reporter at *El Demócrata,* and they had no way of getting ahold of Tomás. The poet practically had to drag the lawyer along with him, since Verdugo wanted to go home, change his clothes, and read over some papers for a court hearing scheduled for the following Monday. In spite of his insistence, not even the poet really expected anything out of the ordinary to happen. But life often does its best to make sure that things turn out exactly the opposite from what we expect.

"Here comes the Spic in the Ford again," said the poet all of a sudden, elbowing his companion and staring intently into the rearview mirror. The Ford's horn beeped twice and the garage door swung open. Ramón got out of the car and walked toward the garage. The poet realized that something unusual was in the works when he saw the Spic look cautiously up and down the street. The Frenchmen stepped out of the garage dressed in a gray suit and derby hat, dragging the struggling figure of a man across the pavement toward the waiting car.

"What's going on?" asked the poet.

"Grab your shotgun, man!" yelled the lawyer as he opened the car door. The poet wasted a few seconds fumbling for his glasses in the pockets of his coat, then scrambled for the shotgun in the backseat and ran after the lawyer, jamming a shell into the barrel as he went.

"Hands up, you clowns!" shouted Verdugo at the two men.

In their surprise they dropped the man they'd been carrying onto the ground. The man was in a sorry state, bloody scratches all over his face, his shirt tattered and soaked with blood, his pants torn. He made a feeble effort to haul himself up, grabbing onto Ramón's pants leg.

"This is inadmissible, a violation of public order, dammit," protested the Spic.

"And what do you call what you've done to this poor fellow?" answered the poet, training his gun on the Frenchman who was slowly moving his hand down toward his left boot. The poet might have been a little slow to react, but he had a quick memory.

"*Qu'est-ce qui se passe?*" said the Frenchman, just to say anything at all. But the fact of the matter was that the situation was perfectly clear.

"It's time to pray, gentlemen, because we're going to fill you full of holes," said the lawyer, cradling his shotgun in one arm and pointing alternately at the two men.

"I won't forget this," said Ramón.

"You don't even know where to stick your dick, mister," answered Verdugo. The poet let out a brusque laugh and glanced nervously toward the mansion beyond the iron railing.

Under the surprised stare of a maid out walking the dog, the two friends made off toward the Packard, with the lawyer carrying the wounded man like a sack over his shoulder. The poet covered Ramón and the Frenchman with his gun while Verdugo started up the engine. Then he jumped onto the running board, steadying himself with his free hand.

"Let her rip, lawyer, I always wanted to be part of a fancy getaway," he shouted.

The Packard roared into gear, burning rubber. From his place on the running board, the poet discharged his shotgun only yards from the terrified enemy, shattering one of the flower boxes on the mansion's front steps.

"Viva Villa, you sissy bastards!" he shouted happily as they roared past.

Perhaps at that very moment Tomás and his friend Sebastián San Vicente were getting out of a taxicab in front of the Alameda and heading off toward Dolores Street.

In the late-evening hours with the first shadows devouring the light of day, Chinatown began to change its face. The shops and restaurants were abandoned by their non-Chinese customers and the Chinese residents retook the streets. The opium trade, hidden away during daylight hours in elegant salons and lowly dives, moved out timidly onto the sidewalks. Beggars turned into opium freaks, family men, moon-eyed lovers. Human relics collapsed unconscious in the middle of the street, where passersby nimbly stepped over them without a backward glance.

The recent rain had left the ill-lit cobblestones covered with mud. Tomás shook off a medicinal herb vendor who followed stubbornly along brandishing a wooden tray full of samples. San Vicente stuck to his friend like a shadow until they stopped in front of the Peking Duck Restaurant, where Tomás stood silently considering his next move. Their faces were lit up now and then by the light from inside the restaurant as groups of customers went in or out.

"What are we waiting for, Tomás?"

"This is the place, whele she came out of. Eithel this one, ol that place next dool."

During the cab drive, Tomás had forced himself not to think about how much the girl really mattered to him. He didn't want his emotions clouding his thoughts. But he had so little to go on. All he knew was that Rosa had been sold to a Chinese restaurant owner in exchange for gambling debts acquired by her father, the owner of a laundry on López Street. And when the police raided the gambling house in back of the restaurant she'd taken advantage of the chaos and escaped.

He finally made up his mind and pushed in through the beaded curtain.

"I want to talk to the ownel," he said to a Chinaman in a white waiter's jacket.

"Ta'i Lu." The Chinaman spoke his employer's name.

"I don't speak Chinese, comlade," answered Tomás. The waiter stared at them darkly and motioned them to a booth at the back of the restaurant.

Two couples sat eating dinner at the tables, and a pair of Westerners were drinking tea and talking business with a Chinaman at the red lacquer bar. The place seemed too desolate for that time of night. San Vicente cautiously eyed the door through which the waiter had disappeared, then lit up a cigarette and settled down to wait. Tomás felt as much of a stranger there as his Spanish friend. When it came right down to it, he was a Chinaman only by chance.

"Come right this way, mister," the waiter said, returning almost instantly.

Tomás listened admiringly to the way he pronounced his *r*'s.

The waiter led them along with a Coleman lantern through dark and narrow corridors, behind the kitchen, through a store-room full of grains and vegetables, along a hall covered with paintings and tapestries several layers thick, past a coop full of chickens and ducks and through other rooms piled high with boxes. They followed a strange, circuitous route, turning left, then right, then left again, occasionally doubling back the way they'd come. After they'd walked more than a quarter mile the passageway came to a dead end. The Chinese waiter opened a door and stepped to one side for Tomás and San Vicente to go through. Our two friends found themselves in a large deserted room, decorated like a variety theater and dominated by a huge bamboo throne surrounded by a set of bronze spittoons. The door closed behind them.

"What the hell is this? Where the hell are we?" asked San Vicente, walking toward the center of the room.

"Youl guess is as good as mine," answered Tomás at his heels.

That's when the floor gave way under their feet.

37

LOOK IN HIS SOCKS

Throughout his long career as a police reporter, Manterola had developed some very definite opinions about the limitations and possibilities of the police force that had evolved out of the Revolution. His basic impression could be summarized very precisely in a single sentence: It was good for nothing. The police only discovered crimes by absolute chance. And the force's contacts with organized crime in the city were so intimate and extensive that the shadowy zone that separated them had turned into a practically limitless territory where the police and the criminal element cohabited, dedicating themselves to the same activities. And what was worse, while the police were good for nothing, the Mexico City mafia had managed to develop a remarkable sophistication in the years since 1916, when the Revolution finally left the capital city in peace. On the one hand, a tremendous army of specialists in the various sectors of criminal activity had found their way to Mexican shores, fleeing the war in Europe. On the other hand, all sorts of easy money, stocks, jewels, gold, and silver had floated to the top on the Revolution's chaotic tide, where many an anxious hand groped for advantage. The violent world of kidnappers, bandits, and murderers was buffered by a feather mattress of confidence men, pickpockets, swindlers, opportunists, grifters, procurers, ladies of the night (or the afternoon, time willing), quack doctors, and bogus inventors. The criminal underworld's sophistication was visible not only in the quality of its work but also in the exotic names that adorned the principal gangs: The Hand That Squeezes, The Murderer's Legion, The Red Mark; and their leaders: Mario Lombardi, The Black Hat, The Silk-

Fingered Frenchman, The Apache Turk, Shitkicker, Won-Li, Fingers Eufrasio.

Manterola admitted a certain responsibility for this new sophistication, shared in part by his colleague at *El Heraldo*. The power of the press and a well-turned phrase were capable of converting a miserable rat like Ranulfo Torres into the legendary Invisible Man, or an undistinguished streetwalker like María Juárez into The Woman with the Fatal Bite, on account of her bad aim.

Never before had the city seen such an underworld, so many outcasts, such an extensive sewer system. So when Manterola decided to try to trace the jewels found in Sergeant Zevada's pockets, he had plenty of material to work with. He started out by reading clippings from his own paper, *El Heraldo*, and *Excelsior* which he'd been storing in a box in his office over the last three years. The key word was *jewels,* and with a little bit of patience he dug out six or seven articles in only half an hour of leafing through the first of three fat notebooks. But the newsroom was too quiet for him that early in the day. He went and asked his boss for the morning off, saying he was in the middle of an important investigation, and went out to read somewhere else.

Just two minutes after Pioquinto Manterola walked out the door the phone rang in the newsroom.

"What'd they say?" asked the poet.

"He just went out," answered the lawyer Verdugo.

They'd spent the night at the Red Cross waiting for the sawbones to patch up their battered foundling. But the man had taken a brutal beating and there was only so much the doctors could do.

"He's in shock and likely to say any sort of craziness," the doctors told them. "I wouldn't pay much attention to anything he says for the next couple of days at least. Make sure he gets a lot of rest. Feed him soup and chicken broth. Once he comes around bring him in again and we'll see that you get him back just like new."

They spent half the morning driving around town with the

unconscious man in the backseat of the Packard, wrapped in an English wool blanket.

First they went and made a court appearance, where the lawyer demonstrated his ample abilities by sending a professional soccer player up the river for rape. The fellow, who played for Pachuca, had the gall to claim that his talents on the field (quite inferior in the poet's opinion) justified the violent seduction of a chorus girl from the Eden Theater (her stage name was Iris but back in Puebla where she came from everybody called her Magdalena). Afterward, they'd made their way over to the lawyer's empty house to rest up and kill time until they could find Manterola and bring him up to date.

They deposited the unconscious man on the lawyer's bed, Verdugo dropped exhausted into his armchair, and the poet stretched out on the floor cradling his new shotgun in his arms.

"You know what, that Frenchman looked a lot like the guy who was with that trigger-happy lieutenant who tried to kill me the other day."

"Wouldn't surprise me if it was the same guy," said Verdugo, stifling a yawn.

"Did you know your shotgun was unloaded back there at the widow's place?"

"Damn, I think you're right. My father always said I was totally irresponsible," said Verdugo with a smile.

"It just goes to show that style is what matters the most," said the poet, lighting a cigarette. "You know, we really ought to search this guy here. Maybe he's got something on him that'll tell us something."

Verdugo slowly detached himself from the armchair and walked over to the bed.

"Let's see. Nothing in his pants pockets . . . Nothing in his vest. Hey, look at this, a receipt from the Hotel Regis."

"It's the missing Dutchman!"

"What'd they say his name was? Van Horn, isn't it? . . . Nothing in his left jacket pocket, a blank picture postcard of Toluca in the right pocket, and another one with a photo of my friend Inés Torres."

"Let me see."

"You want it autographed? I can have her sign it for you free of charge."

"No, I'm just curious, that's all. Look in his socks. These Europeans are pretty stupid, chances are some chump from the British foreign office told him that'd be the best place to hide something in Mexico."

"All right . . . hey, you were right."

"What'd I tell you?"

"It's a certificate for a safe-deposit box in the Bank of London."

"Let me see that."

The lawyer handed the stiff green paper to the poet, who pulled a pencil stub from his pocket and started to write a poem about socks on the back side.

"I'm going out to buy us some cigarettes," said the lawyer after a while. "If anyone tries to get in this door without knocking three times, shoot to kill, but just make sure you shoot high. You never know when some young lady might drop by for a visit."

"Yessir," answered the poet, reloading his shotgun and taking up position in the armchair. Verdugo straightened his pearl gray hat and walked sluggishly out the door.

Pioquinto Manterola had always wished he were a more methodical sort and he often told himself that now, today, was as good a time as any to begin. So he carefully compiled the relevant clippings, made a list of all the jewels mentioned, with an accompanying description of each one, wrote down the names of the various gangs reputedly involved in each of the holdups, robberies, embezzlements, swindles, confidence jobs, and the corresponding convictions, confessions, arrests, and cases pending. Then he went through his list again, crossing off the jewels that had already been recovered. In the process he ran across the names of a pair of fences but, if his information was correct, both of them were currently resting their bones in the Belén Federal Penitentiary.

All that effort made the reporter nervous. Too many jewels, too many cases of old ladies tortured until they told where the family fortune was hidden. Too many officers implicated in robberies, with the booty ending up decorating the necks or ears of their high-class mistresses, shining in the candlelight at some fancy reception. The words he read propelled him back into his memory: he remembered the color of the rug, the bugged-out eyes of the strangled women, the stuttering voice of the captured fence, the cold night air in the garage with the bodies of the couple who'd committed suicide.

"Why'd you ever go and become a crime reporter, in the first place, Manterola? Because that's where you find the real literature of life, my friend," he asked and answered himself, absolutely convinced he was right.

Every now and then the music from the Ferris wheel quit and the reporter would look up from the thick hardcover notebooks with their brass-lined edges. The sun was getting high in the sky.

38

PLENTY OF FIREWORKS AND AN EX–HOD CARRIER WITHOUT AN ERECTION

The light filtering through the half-open venetian blinds was fading steadily. The poet had taken off his boots and now crouched inside the armchair like a cat, glancing back and forth from the unconscious Dutchman to the door through which his friend the lawyer had gone over six hours ago. He was hungry, but there wasn't so much as a scrap of food in Verdugo's house and he didn't dare go out onto the street for a bite to eat. Occasionally he went and looked out the window, hoping to see some sign of the lawyer, but all he saw was an old organ-grinder playing for a circle of children, and a couple of construction workers heading home from work. Now and then the Dutchman murmured something and Fermín, who'd picked up a little English in his years with Pancho Villa when he'd crossed the border to take on arms or supplies, carefully jotted down the man's incoherent ravings. The sum total of his efforts throughout the course of the afternoon was a mixture of random sentences in English and Dutch and a few lines of poetry all written down on the back of a piece of sheet music. Did the lawyer play music, did he compose? There wasn't a piano, a guitar, or even a penny whistle in the lawyer's house, but the sheet of paper the poet had been using was covered with hand-written notes and bore the title *Carmen,* a bolero.

The poet was returning from the bathroom with a vase full of water for the comatose Dutchman when a faint knock sounded on the door. The poet dropped the vase onto the rug and grabbed his shotgun. "Who's there?" he called out, masking the metallic click as he cocked the twin hammers.

"Milkman," said a man's voice that was immediately drowned out by the massive double-barreled blast.

Fermín Valencia aimed high, following the lawyer's advice, although high for him was only about five feet seven inches off the ground. The result was a fifteen-inch hole in the middle of the door, pocked all over with buckshot. He reloaded and crept forward, careful to stay out of line of the smoking hole. Kneeling down, he turned the knob with his left hand and cautiously pulled the door open. A bloody corpse lay on the floor in front of him but he couldn't afford more than a quick glance, as three pistol shots suddenly rang out from the landing, the bullets whizzing by inches from his head. The poet let go with another blast from the shotgun and, without taking time to reload, threw the weapon to one side and drew his Colt. Leaping over the dead man he ran down the stairs, yelling at the top of his lungs and firing away as he went. Another corpse lay hunched up on the stairs between landings. The poet had no time to react. He tripped over the body and tumbled crazily down the stairwell finally coming to rest against the door of a dentist's office on the floor below. Taking advantage of this involuntary pause, he reloaded the Colt then continued down the stairs, more cautiously this time, until he came out onto the street. There was no one in sight. The poet made a vengeful figure, standing in the doorway in his stocking feet, his hair sticking out in all directions, and a Colt .45 smoking in his fist. Suddenly a car roared into gear. Without hesitating, the poet fired on the accelerating vehicle, perforating its rear window and picking off one of the side mirrors.

He was left alone in the empty street, one stockinged foot ankle deep in a puddle of rainwater, deafened by the gunfire, his teeth clenched, his throat dry, possessed by a slow shaking that started in his legs, turned into a nervous ache around his kidneys and climbed in a subtle shiver up the back of his neck. He dropped down onto his knees and mumbled under his breath as though he were praying:

"Fermín, what a man you are. Fermín, what a hell of a

tough guy. Fermín, don't shoot anymore, Fermín. Fermín, forgive me."

All of a sudden he felt someone watching him, and turned his head to see the lawyer Verdugo sitting against the wall a few yards to his left, his head dropped listlessly onto one shoulder, his eyes glazed over, his shirt unbuttoned, and his sleeves rolled up.

"Verdugo, what's wrong? What've they done to you?" asked the poet in desperation, scrambling hurriedly to his feet.

When Manterola got back to the newspaper he had two routine assignments waiting for him. One was the story of a Guadalajara bank robbery in which the holdup men's trail led to Mexico City, where the police had run out of clues. The other was the story of a single mother who had turned on the gas and stuck her head in the oven. The two together took him only a couple of hours and he handed in the work before deadline just as the rumbling inside his stomach reminded him he hadn't had a bite to eat all day.

He tracked down his editor, told him he was going to keep working on the story of the stolen jewels, and got himself out of a few pieces of minor work. It was eight o'clock by the time he left *El Demócrata*. He stopped first on Puente de Alvarado for a plate of chilaquiles then headed over to Guerrero to look up the manager of the Industrial Printworks, having gotten the address from a friend at the paper who used to work there. After talking with the manager for half an hour, he limped his way toward the Majestic Hotel.

A baseball team was celebrating its latest victory at the bar. There was some small action at the pool tables in the back, and a group of Galician swindlers and cardsharps sat scheming at the strategic table by the door.

Manterola took his seat at the normal place, joined shortly by Eustaquio with a bottle of Havana brandy and a dirty rag he passed a couple of times over the marble tabletop.

"My friends haven't been by yet?"

"Haven't seen hide nor hair of them, no messages, no telephone calls. But that gentleman over there says he wants to talk to you."

Manterola followed the bartender's pointing finger and found himself contemplating an elegantly dressed officer, his military jacket and pants impeccably pressed, his stripes shining in the dim light. It was the same man he'd known only a week earlier in the form of a comatose hod carrier. The journalist smiled. If Jesus of Nazareth had come back from the dead, why not a Mexico City construction worker? He waved the man over to his table and asked Eustaquio for another glass.

"Major Martínez, secret service," the man introduced himself. "I'm sorry if I gave you a bit of a start."

"Not at all, Major. My only regret is that you were unconscious the last time we met. A little bit of conversation would have done me good."

"My apologies, Manterola. You know, when duty calls . . ."

"Who do you work for, Major, if I may be so blunt?"

"I report directly to the President of the Republic, General Obregón, through his secretary Mr. Alessio Robles."

The barman set another glass on the table and Manterola poured it full of brandy, but the officer declined with a wave of his finger.

"You'll have to excuse me. I don't drink when I'm on duty."

"I'm all ears, Major."

"I think it's the other way around, Mr. Manterola."

"What do you want me to tell you?"

"Everything you know about Colonels Martínez Fierro, Zevada, and Gómez. Everything you know about the Mata Redonda Plan."

"The what?"

"Let's start with the colonels."

"Well, this is the first I've ever heard anything about Martínez Fierro. Zevada is dead, he either fell or got thrown out of a window in the building across from the newspaper. Gómez is chief of the gendarmery. That about sums it up. If you want my personal opinion I'd say that Gómez is corrupt, a thief and a murderer."

"What would you think if I told you that on separate occasions, both Gómez and Martínez Fierro tried to have you killed?"

"Listen, Major, let's quit beating around the bush. You tell me what you know and I'll see if I can't fit the pieces of my puzzle into the frame you give me."

"I'm sorry, Mr. Manterola, I can't do that. However, I do have an important message for you: the President of the Republic personally urges you to continue with your investigation. I myself second the president's wishes, and furthermore, I suggest you proceed with great caution. That's all I'm at liberty to tell you for the time being. Take this telephone number. If something important happens or if you need my help, don't hesitate to call."

The officer handed Manterola a card with the number 42-38 written on one side.

"Is this an Ericsson number or a Mexican number?"

"Mexican. When they answer, ask for the 'red line,' " said the major, getting to his feet.

Manterola raised the card to his temple as a sort of goodbye, then watched as the man walked out the door. Left alone, he let out a sigh.

" 'General Obregón personally urges you . . .' Damn. What kind of a chump does he think I am that he figures he can come along and give me orders just like that?"

39

THE WAY THINGS USED TO BE:
FERMÍN VALENCIA IN ZACATECAS

In the middle of June 1914, General Villa ordered the entire Northern Division to advance on Zacatecas, despite General Carranza's objections. The horses rode inside the train cars, and the cavalry rode on top making up songs about how they were going to break the backbone of Huerta's army in Zacatecas.

Twenty-two thousand men eventually congregated on the outskirts of the city. The Nateras and Zaragoza Brigades, the troops of Aguirre Benavides, the Villa, Urbina, and Morelos brigades, the forces under Maclovio Herrera and Manuel Chao, the artillery under Felipe Angeles. Fermín Valencia wandered around the camps, smelling the food, watching the faces, searching everywhere for signs of the imminent battle, but everything he saw looked like the preparations for a celebration.

On June 23, at ten in the morning, the Northern Division's fifty cannons opened fire on the fortified hills surrounding the city. The poet's blood, already infected by the festive atmosphere, started to boil. Holding his cavalry in reserve, changing the location of his artillery, and using strategic infantry assaults, Villa wore down the Federal forces. Loreto fell in only an hour. The bombardment grew in strength. Lead rained from the overcast sky above Zacatecas.

At five o'clock in the afternoon the order came for the Villa and Cuauhtémoc brigades to move out. The poet spurred his horse into a trot along with a thousand other Horsemen of the Revolution.

Little by little they brought their horses to a gallop, the federal artillery tearing holes into their ranks. Invisible machine guns sprayed them with lead. At the poet's side, a horse was hit and its rider tumbled to the ground. The cavalry cut its way through the gunpowder smoke and the dust, leaving the explosions behind. All of a sudden a shout ran down the line, the first trench opened up dizzily in front of them. They leaped over it howling. The poet gripped the reins between his teeth, dug in his spurs, grabbed his pistols and fired on the fleeing *federales*. Next to him, one of the horsemen was singing. The first line of *federales* broke before them, sweeping along the second in their panicked retreat.

The poet reached the first houses on the edge of Zacatecas and reigned in his horse.

"Viva Villa, *cabrones!*" he screamed. At that moment Fermín Valencia was a happy man.

40

TWO ANARCHISTS IN A CELLAR

"If you didn't smoke it wouldn't be a ploblem, San Vicente," said the Chinaman in the blackness.

"Hell, I've got plenty of cigs, man. It's just that this is my next to the last match, and I hate to waste it."

Tomás had removed the crystal from his watch and he could tell by feel they'd been ten hours in that cold damp moldy cellar into which they'd fallen through the trapdoor in the floor above. Once they'd recovered from the fall they'd used San Vicente's matches to explore their surroundings, but after half an hour they'd given up. All they found was a pair of empty coffins shoved into a corner, and a few old sacks of rotten potatoes. The floor and the walls were dirt and the only way out was through the trapdoor three and a half yards above their heads, which had automatically swung shut behind them. The only way to get up or down was for someone to lower a ladder from the room above.

Their vigil had been interrupted just once in the last ten hours, when they heard footsteps crossing the floor over their heads. But the hot-tempered Spanish anarchist had cut the matter short, sending a pair of bullets flying up through the floorboards. From the shouts that followed they could guess that one of San Vicente's bullets had found its target. After that there was nothing.

San Vicente had climbed up on top of the two coffins and Tomás in turn had gotten onto his friend's shoulders, from where he could just reach the trapdoor with outstretched hands, but the spring seemed to be locked or jammed somehow from above. All they could do was give up and settle down to wait.

"What if they want to starve us to death?" asked San Vicente.

"How long can you go without eating?"

"Hell, when you're in good shape and have enough to drink, three weeks maybe. Here, who knows?"

Neither one of them was much for small talk and, once they'd arrived at the conclusion that there was nothing to do but wait, they hadn't exchanged more than a couple dozen words every hour or so.

"Listen, Tomás, I've lived pretty hard, I've lived a lot, and I've always known I could die from one day to the next. I never liked it too much . . . I've dreamed my death plenty of times, you know. There's a lot of different ways to go but, hell, I never thought it could be as stupid as this."

"It's my fault, San Vicente. I make a pletty lotten Chinaman. This is what happens to me fol not knowing my own people. This is maybe only the fifth time I've been hele in Chinatown in my whole life. I don't like the food, I don't know a damn thing about tongs ol tliads. It wasn't so bad back in Tampico, I had a bettel feel fol what was going on. Shit, when it comes light down to it, I can't haldly tell a Chinaman flom a Filipino ol a Japanese."

"Yeah, but you can tell the difference between a comrade and a son of a bitch. A few months back in San Luis Potosí another Spaniard showed me a postcard of the town where I was born in Asturias. He might as well have shown me a picture of Borneo. The whole idea of countries and borders isn't worth two shits in hell. A man's from wherever he is right now. A man's country is the two square feet he stands on. A little more when they stick you in the ground."

"How do you think it wolks?"

"How's what work?"

"The tlap dool. The hinges'le on this side, on splings. And then thele's a pin that locks in place when the splings swing the dool closed. The leason we couldn't get it open befole is because they've got it locked flom above. But what if we get up on the coffins again and shoot out the hinges? What do you think?"

"We'll never know unless we try. The only problem is we've

only got two matches left. You should have thought of it
sooner."

"Didn't you win a malksmanship contest once in Tampico?"

"Sure, dammit, but I wasn't any where near so cold back
then."

41

A HELL OF A NIGHT

The reporter finally arrived at Verdugo's apartment around two in the morning after having first tried the poet's apartment, the Chinaman's house in Contreras (which he found empty with the door open and the lights on), the Red Cross, the White Cross, the morgue, and several of the downtown police stations. He finally got the lawyer's address from a young woman of Verdugo's acquaintance whom he ran into at the morgue. She was watching over the body of her father, who'd gone on a binge and died out in the cold. The lawyer's three-story building on Tabasco Street was sunk in darkness, surrounded by vacant lots and houses under construction. The streetlights were only just being installed and the lightless posts stood like grim messengers of civilization. The moon threw a soft pallor onto the street. Manterola ran up the stairs. After his long wait at the Majestic and so many hours of fruitless searching he was convinced something terrible had happened. By the time he got to the first landing, stabs of pain were shooting up his bad leg.

"Verdugo!"

"It's about time, inkslinger," came the poet's voice through the ragged hole in the door.

The door stood ajar. Manterola groped in the dark for the light switch, flicked it on, and was greeted by a shocking sight. The poet sat red eyed in an armchair in a large carpeted room, a shotgun gripped in his hands. Verdugo and a man Manterola didn't recognize lay on a bed nearby.

The rug was stained with a trail of blood that led into the interior of the apartment.

"I've got two dead men in the bathroom, inkslinger . . . You have any cigarettes? I already finished off the lawyer's cigars and a pack of cigarettes I got off of one of the corpses.''

Manterola took out a pack of Argentino Ovals and offered one to the poet, who held on to the shotgun with one hand, resting the stock on his thigh. The reporter followed the trail of blood to the bathroom where the two dead men sat bolt upright in the tub. One of them had half his head blown off, the other had two nearly symmetrical bullet holes perforating his chest.

"It's that Frenchman and the guy who shot at me that day over at Peltzer's. It's the same guy that killed the trombonist. When I saw him at Peltzer's he was in uniform and I didn't recognize him, but now that I see him with the same hat he was wearing that first day, I'm sure it's him. Besides, he's got his holster on the left side," he heard the poet saying from the other room.

"And the cops didn't come?"

"Around here they could rape your mother and broadcast it over a loudspeaker and nobody would notice.''

"What happened to Verdugo? How long've you been here? Who's this other guy?" asked the reporter coming back into the room. He closed his eyes to get rid of the image of the dead man with only half a head.

"All afternoon and all night. Maybe twelve, fifteen hours by now. Verdugo went out to buy cigarettes around three o'clock. Round about eight these two came knocking at the door, and later on I found the lawyer down on the street. He's alive, but they must have done something to him because all he does is lie there in a cold sweat, shouting all sorts of nonsense. I don't know what to do with him . . . And the other one's Van Horn, the missing Dutchman, the one who shared a room with the Englishman who didn't commit suicide. He's in a coma. Now and then he says something but none of it makes any sense. There's only one bed so I put them both there together. I mean, the Dutchman's not a buddy of mine or anything, but I just didn't feel right leaving him on the floor . . . You know something, inkslinger . . . it's the strangest feeling, I wish my father was here, if he weren't dead I mean, and that he'd take me by the hand, tuck me into bed, give me a glass of water, and tell me a bedtime story. And then I'd go to sleep and sleep and sleep . . ."

"I wish I'd been here with you, Fermín," said the reporter.

"Yeah, me too, Manterola," said the poet, finally letting his head fall back and shutting his eyes.

The reporter worked without stopping for the rest of the night. In spite of his bad leg he carried both Verdugo and the Dutchman down to the waiting Packard, helped the poet down, put the two shotguns in the car, and shoved the two dead men into the trunk. Then he went upstairs again and carefully washed all the bloodstains off the floor and rug. Once everyone was safely in the car he drove along Insurgentes as far as Las Artes, where he turned left. Following the poet's instructions he made his way through San Rafael to the widow's mansion. It was three-thirty in the morning when he took the bodies out of the trunk and left them on the sidewalk out front. No lights came on in the neighboring houses, there was no sign of move- ment in the hulking mansion, and they drove off again into the night. They went up Tacubaya to Avenida San Angel, the moon beating softly down on the cornfields on either side. The poet snored in the seat next to Manterola. They passed a streetcar and later on a grocery cart hitched to a burro. Their headlights shone on three solitary figures walking along the side of the road. The reporter fitted his pince-nez over his nose.

"Tomás! Tomás!"

The Chinaman watched as the bulletproof Packard squealed to a stop with Manterola at the wheel, the poet asleep at his side, and two more men hunched up in the back seat. He held on to Rosa, who gripped his arm more tightly than before, and held out his hand to stop San Vicente from reaching for the gun in his jacket pocket.

"And where am I going to put you all now if I've only got one bed in my house?" the reporter wondered.

42

A RUDE AWAKENING

Manterola took charge of his beleaguered troops. They drove around for nearly an hour before finding refuge in a crib house out in Tlalpan, paradoxically named The Rest-a-While Inn. The owner, a Spaniard, owed the journalist a few favors from when Manterola had defended him from the abuses of a group of army officers three years before.

The Dutchman remained unconscious, the lawyer Verdugo, although he appeared outwardly unharmed, raved deliriously, San Vicente had come down with a violent cold, the poet was in a state of profound dejection after so many hours of violence and tension, Rosa had burns all up and down her arms, and Tomás Wong had a deep cut across his forehead, oozing blood.

The best that Manterola could get was a pair of rooms with three beds and an armchair between them, a pot of old chicken soup, and an abortionist to patch up his wounded friends. Once everything was more or less under control he went out onto the balcony to smoke a cigarette and savor the dawn. Tlalpan was a small town corrupted by its nearness to the city, living off a pair of textile mills, a handful of dairies, and a multitude of small truck farms. At that time of day, far from the highway and the factories, the town was sunk in the bucolic peace of the remotest Mexican village untouched by the years of revolution: a pair of women walked toward the market with baskets full of chiles and heads of lettuce, a dairyman drove a train of mules loaded down with huge five-gallon milk cans, a uniformed streetcar driver strolled along on his way to work. The reporter exhaled smoke and watched it chasing up toward the sky. He didn't know much about warfare, but he had the feeling the next move was up to them, whatever it was: gunfire, maneuvers, traps, newspapers. That was important, to have the power of the press behind them, the voice of God, the truth spelled out in black and white. And that was something Manterola did know about. The only thing that bothered him was the memory of Margarita, intruding stubbornly into his thoughts, naked except for her leghorn hat, a stray ringlet of hair falling across her face. He waved his hand distractedly to get the image out of his mind, as if he were waving away the smoke or shooing away a persistent mosquito. Then he asked himself what was really going on. During the two hours he'd spent driving around in the Packard he'd found out about so many things that he felt truly incapable of putting them all together. The appearance of new characters in the story, Rosa's abduction and rescue, the comatose Dutchman, and the incorporation of San Vicente into their little club—the same anarchist who, if he remembered right, had been deported by Obregón in May of '21.

The reporter smiled. He could have written a hell of a story if he wasn't already up to his neck in the whole tumultuous affair. The truth was that Mexico City was paradise for a journalist who considered his profession to be the finest of the fine arts, and his personal specialty the best of them all. "It's the real poetry of the twentieth century," he told himself out loud and then went inside to look for a place to sleep.

San Vicente snored away in one of the rooms, revolver in hand, the armchair pushed up against the door. The Dutchman lay unconscious in the bed with the poet balled up at his feet, his boots still on. Manterola stepped through the door that led to the next room, where Tomás lay on one bed, smoking, with a bloody bandage wrapped around his head, a protective arm around Rosa lying at his side. Verdugo tossed and turned in the other bed.

"Evelything okay, inkslingel?" asked the Chinaman in a whisper.

"As good as can be expected. Not sleepy?"

"I've got too much on my mind."

Manterola took off his boots, folded his socks inside them,

threw his jacket on the floor and unbuttoned his vest. Then he dropped down on the bed next to the lawyer, tugging a corner of the pillow out of Verdugo's viselike grip.

"How's she doing?" he asked.

"She'll be okay. The doctol said the bulns welen't too bad. Cigalette bulns, the sons of bitches."

Manterola turned over in the bed, leaving the Chinaman alone with his anger, and found himself staring into Verdugo's vacant eyes.

"Alberto, what's the matter?" he asked, but he realized that the lawyer couldn't hear him and that his eyes, although they seemed to stare fiercely into his own, were fixed on something far beyond: his own little private piece of hell.

Verdugo pushed back in the bed and brought his hands up to the reporter's throat.

"Hey, I'm Pioquinto Manterola, your friend," said the journalist soothingly, without trying to evade the hands tightening around his neck. "Have you got so many friends that you can afford to strangle one of them?"

Verdugo's hands squeezed tighter. Manterola stared urgently into the lawyer's deranged eyes.

"Alberto, it's me, Manterola," he said, raising his voice.

Tomás jumped out of bed with a shout: "Hey, take it easy!"

"I'm . . . your . . . friend," gasped Manterola, feeling the first effects of asphyxiation. Tomás repeatedly struck the lawyer's wrists with the side of his hand, but Verdugo refused to let up.

"No, man, no, don't let him," shouted the Chinaman. "Don't let him do it." Manterola finally reacted, grasping the lawyer's hands, trying to pry them away from his throat.

"Felmín, Sebastián!" yelled the Chinaman, the reporter's eyes starting to bug out of their sockets, locked in a death grip with Verdugo's hellish gaze.

"Leave him alone. It's the lepoltel, you idiot. Leave him alone," shouted Tomás, wildly beating the lawyer across the chest. But the lawyer held on. San Vicente and the poet ran in from the other room. Rosa was up now too, pulling the lawyer by the hair. Between the four of them they finally managed to get the two men apart and the reporter collapsed on the bed, gasping for air. Verdugo crashed down onto the floor. Manterola struggled to pull breath into his burning lungs.

"What the hell is wrong with you? That's Manterola, you idiot," the poet screamed in the lawyer's face. Verdugo started to sob.

"No, he's fooling you. It's my father. He tried to fool me, but I can tell. He's my father," murmured Verdugo, the tears sliding down his face.

San Vicente helped the reporter sit up in bed, brought him a glass of water. Rosa burst into tears, sobbing in unison with the lawyer.

"Shit, man, this is a damn nightmare," said the poet. "I'm going to wake up now and everything's going to be all right."

"He tried to fool me. He said he was my friend," said Verdugo, wiping away his tears, trying to find some way to explain to his friends the latest in a series of entirely inexplicable truths.

THE WAY THINGS USED TO BE:
ALBERTO VERDUGO IN VERACRUZ

The blazing Veracruz sun beat down on the lawyer Alberto Verdugo's white-white suit as he descended the gangplank off the *Miraflores*. He quickened his steps, trying to squeeze past another pair of passengers and catch up to the woman in the diaphanous yellow dress, the daughter of a German merchant from Campeche, who he'd been flirting with all the way from Havana.

At the foot of the gangplank a one-handed wrinkled old man held out a bowl toward the departing passengers, asking for money. Verdugo automatically put his hand into his vest pocket to pull out a coin and his eyes accidentally met the beggar's. The man smiled, pulled back his bowl, and winked at the lawyer.

Taken aback, Verdugo hesitated for a moment, then pulled out his last pack of Upmanns, Cuban cigarettes made from the best dark tobacco in the world, sat down by the beggar's side, and offered him a smoke.

The lady in the yellow dress walked off into the crowd, but the white-suited lawyer didn't even notice, bending over the beggar to light their two cigarettes under the blazing Veracruz sky.

IN WHICH THE CHARACTERS PLAY
DOMINOES AND DECIDE THAT
COLUMBUS SHOULD HAVE LANDED
AT LAKE TEXCOCO

It was the poet's idea and it was also the poet who opened with the double sixes. A madhouse like this wouldn't be complete without a game of dominoes, he said, and he'd disappeared halfway through the morning, to return a quarter of an hour later with a box of dominoes, two dozen tacos wrapped up in paper, and a pitcher of hibiscus water.

"What the hell is this?" protested San Vicente, taking a long drink from the pitcher.

"What's the mattel? You don't have any obsessions?" Tomás scolded him. "Do you believe in flee will or don't you? Have something to eat, take a siesta, and shut up, ol sit back and watch the game."

Lucky for them the room had a table and three chairs, four including the armchair the anarchist had slept in the night before. Rosa was taking a bath in the other room, humming a little tune while she washed the burns on her arms. The poet provided accompaniment with the rhythmic clack of the bones.

Verdugo, excessively pale, lined up his dominoes as if he thought he could hide behind them. After his attempt to murder the journalist earlier in the morning, he had apologized profusely and then fallen into a moody silence, alternated with spells of fitful sleep from which he would wake up screaming at the top of his lungs, covered in a cold sweat. Pioquinto Manterola seemed to be suffering from a peculiar post-strangulation form of laryngitis. The poet, who'd taken upon himself the task of raising the group's spirits, sat swollen faced and his attempts at humor come off a little too sharp edged. Tomás looked like a casualty of the Boxer War.

The poet opened with the double-sixes. It would seem like the perfect signal for their long-awaited strategy session to begin, but in rapid succession the Chinaman played the six/four, Manterola responded with the four/two, and the lawyer Verdugo played another six opposite the poet's opening bone. There was no way to hold a council of war or retell the events of recent days until it became clear whether the poet's sixes were entirely the luck of the draw or if he held more in his hand. The poet passed and the stage was set for the powwow to begin.

"I say we all tell what we've found out in the last couple of days and then see if we can put the pieces together," proposed Manterola.

"And what makes you think the pieces all go together? Whoever said it was going to be like a jigsaw puzzle where everything fits into place?" countered the poet, smoothing out his mustache.

"In my dreams just now, under the effect of the drugs, I kept thinking about a line from Shakespeare I heard once in a play in Milan. 'Life's but a walking shadow, a tale told by an idiot, full of sound and fury, signifying nothing,' " said Verdugo, playing the game's first three.

"If that's the way you fellows want it, let's just play the game and we can talk about bullfighting or baseball. It's all the same to me. With traveling partners like you all, Columbus would have landed at Lake Texcoco."

"And opened up a bakely," added Tomás.

"And called it The Flower of the Americas," said the poet, trying to ignore the fact that the sixes were coming his way once again.

"The Three Calavels," said the Chinaman.

"The Rising Sun," said the lawyer, revealing his professional inclinations.

"How about if we start with the jewels?"

"Columbus didn't bring any jewels," said the poet. "Just a lot of crummy glass beads to pawn off on the locals."

"Gentlemen, you can all go to hell," said the journalist, forced to play his last four.

"All right, have it your way. What about the jewels?"

"Two years ago two old Spanish ladies were found dead in their boardinghouse on Gante Street. Before they were killed they were tortured, presumably until they told where they'd hidden the family jewels. The jewels disappeared along with their nephew, recently arrived from Spain."

"Ramón the Spic," said Verdugo.

"Could be, although he wasn't called Ramón then. The nephew was named Dionisio. Our friend Colonel Gómez was one of the police officers in the investigation. Gómez and his men chased a mysterious vehicle out toward the Toluca high-way, a vehicle that presumably contained the murderous nephew."

"And . . . ?"

"They found the car, a Cole and Cunningham, but the driver escaped. Threes."

"Doubles," said Verdugo.

"I've got some news about a Colonel Martínez Fierro," said the poet.

"Tampico again," said Tomás.

"Martínez Fierro? When I was waiting for you all at the Majestic the other night I had a very interesting interview with a captain from the Secret Service, who mentioned Martínez Fierro and urged us to continue with our *investigation,* as he called it. He said that he got his orders directly from the president, and that . . ."

"Did you ask him what investigation?" the poet interrupted.

"He didn't give me the chance. But, he did say that two different people had tried to kill us, or me, as the case may be, on two separate occasions: Martínez Fierro and Gómez."

"Maltínez Fiello was a gallison commandel in noltheln Ta-maulipas, not too fal flom Tampico. He's plobably anothel one of Pablo González's boys."

"That makes three colonels who were all in Tampico together as of two years ago: Zevada, Gómez, and Martínez Fierro."

"So what do Obregón's goons have to do with all this?" asked the poet.

"Your guess is as good as mine. I quote: 'General Obregón is personally interested in the success of your investigation.' "

"The bloody hand of death," said the poet.

"I'll second that one," said the Chinaman, whose personal relations with the government were worse than bad. Obregón and his government had been clamping down with ferocious zeal on the red unions for almost a year now.

"The poet and I've got more about this Martínez Fierro. With six hundred pesos to loosen his tongue, a man called The Gypsy told us Martínez Fierro hired the three thugs who attacked us the other night."

"Who's The Gypsy?"

"One of this gentleman's underworld connections," said the poet, pointing at the lawyer.

"I just defended his cousin once in court," objected Verdugo, going out with the double-twos, laying the domino on the table with a flourish.

"Holy smokes, that's the game."

Verdugo mopped the sweat off his forehead with a handkerchief, and the poet, who'd been keeping an eye on him, asked with concern: "Do you want me to open the window?"

"Would you? Damn, it's stuffy in here."

"I know who killed the trombonist," said Fermín Valencia as he walked over and opened the door to the balcony. "And I also have a pretty good idea why I got shot at that day at Peltzer Tire."

"Dammit, if things keep up like this, pretty soon we're going to know everything, except what the hell's going on around here."

"Do you all remember the officer and the Frenchman? Well, Peltzer told me the officer's name was Estrada. I didn't recognize him in his uniform and all. I don't see too good from a distance. But after the shootout at Verdugo's place, when I saw him in civilian clothes and with the same hat on, I realized he was the guy that got the drop on the trombonist. I didn't recognize him, see, but he must have spotted me that day at the park, so when he saw me again at Peltzer's he went crazy and started to spit lead."

"Well, that gives us the connection between Gómez and Zevada. But why?"

"Let me see if I can't reconstruct what we know so far. First off, we've got the widow who killed her husband, or at least we can assume she did. Because I talked to the manager at the Industrial Printworks and he said Roldán never spent enough time at the presses to have died from lead poisoning. He spent all his free time playing cards, roulette, what have you. Then there's the Spic, who kills his aunts and steals their jewels. We've got a French cardsharp, a pair of lieutenants, a hypnotist, and a social secretary. And Gómez, who some way or another is at the center of everything. Elena Torres told me that Gómez has some scam going, something to do with the concession for selling horse fodder to the army here in the valley."

"That's just the icing on the cake," said the poet, returning to his chair and mixing up the overturned bones.

"So what we've got is a well-armed gang led by the head of the city gendarmery, a man up to his neck in union busting, repression of demonstrations, the whole nine yards."

"Okay, so we've got this gang, and evidence that more or less links them to the murder of the Zevada brothers, and they come down on us like they wanted to wipe us off the face of the earth . . ."

"No, not them. This Martínez Fierro," said the journalist.

"So who tried to kill you at the hospital, then?" asked the poet.

"And who kidnapped me and drugged me?" asked the lawyer Verdugo.

"And why did those other two come to your apartment? The two I finished off," said the poet, warming up to the subject.

"You know what? Instead of trying to figure out what the hell's going on, we should just go find Gómez, put a couple of bullets in his head, and that's that."

"And what about Martínez Fierro?"

"Same thing."

The poet's words were followed by a lengthy silence.

"You've got to admit the whole thing is pretty damn absurd," said Verdugo. "They shoot at us, they try and kill us, they've practically got us surrounded, and then they kidnap me when I go out to buy some cigarettes, inject me with who the hell knows what, hypnotize me, and then send me back here to kill you, Manterola."

"When did they hypnotize you?" asked Tomás with renewed interest.

"That's just what I figure must have happened. All I know is that I was walking out of the building when someone hit me over the head and I passed out. Then I remember everything was kind of hazy and I'm looking into the eyes of that redhead who talks with a lisp and she's telling me not to resist . . . I've got two needle marks here on my arm, too. And then I wake up here in the hotel and try to kill Manterola thinking that . . ."

"I'm your father. Which I didn't find at all funny, Verdugo. I figure your old man's got a few years on me at least . . ."

"Dammit, if I wanted to kill my father I could have done it without needing to be hypnotized."

"Don't worry about it, Verdugo, nothing happened in the end. I'm just a little hoarse, that's all."

"But if it hadn't been for Tomás . . ."

"I'm a little hoarse, I walk with a limp from a bullet hole in my leg, they try and poison me with cyanide in the hospital, and now hod carriers aren't even hod carriers anymore. I'd be just as happy as the rest of you to knock off a couple of colonels and call the whole thing quits, but somehow I don't think it's as easy as all that. By now Gómez probably has the whole mounted-police force out looking for us."

"What was that you said about hod carriers?"

"Forget it, it's not important."

"As long as we're getting ourselves up to date, what've you been up to, Tomás, and to what do we owe the pleasure of your friend San Vicente?"

"Foltunately that's all anothel stoly that doesn't have anything to do with this one hele, a hell of a lot simplel, the kind of stoly you can shoot youl way out of and that's the end of it."

And maybe Tomás was about to tell the rest of the story, but Rosa rushed into the room and stopped him.

"He's dead," she said.

"Who?"

"The man in the bed, the foreigner."

"Van Horn . . ."

"Are you sure?" asked Manterola.

"He's not breathing. I checked."

"That's gratitude for you. And after I carried him around half of Mexico City," said the poet sadly.

45

A GATHERING OF THE BROTHERHOOD

The poet hung a polyglot sign on the door of the women's bathroom in the Hotel Ginebra: OUT OF ORDER/ DESCOMPUE-STO/ SCOMPOSTO, then stationed himself out front to keep out any curious passersby who might not think the sign applied to them. Meanwhile, Manterola was busy inside setting up chairs and ashtrays.

Librado Martínez, the famous "bloodhound" of *El Universal*, was the first to arrive, a skeletal figure suffering from an acute case of cirrhosis of the liver. The doctors gave him two to three months to live. A minute later came C. Ortega (no one knew what the "C" stood for, it was the man's best-kept secret). Among Ortega's many accomplishments was his account—in impeccable prose—of the house fire that killed his wife and two children. He'd written the story and then collapsed onto his typewriter, overcome with grief. After Ortega came the stuttering Luis Martínez de la Garza, alias The Louse, who, un-hindered by his speech impediment, had become the ace crime reporter for *El Heraldo de Mexico*. A white streak running through his hair gave him a parrotlike appearance. Then there was *Omega*'s Juan Antonio de Blas, who lived a double life as vice reporter and transvestite, dressing up in women's clothing after work and cruising the city's most sordid dives.

The four men who had answered the call of the dean of Mexican crime reporting, Pioquinto Manterola, had little in common as far as age, dress, or personal style were concerned. However, they were all incorruptible, believing their work to be the last rampart between civilized society and absolute bar-barity, and they professed strange ideologies, greatly influenced by Nietzsche, the second act of *The Barber of Seville*, the moral stance of Victor Hugo, and the exemplary lives of Edmond Dantès and Marguerite Gautier, Epicurus and Toño Rojas.

Once they were all inside, the poet carefully shut the door and took up his post, armed with a bottle of Chianti the Ginebra's head cook had given him to pass the time. After three quarters of an hour the journalists filed out, no more disheveled-looking than was their custom but perhaps with a somewhat livelier step. Manterola was the last to emerge, with a gleam in his eye, rubbing his hands.

46

DIALOGUES, NEWSPAPERS, DISGUISES

Someone was doing his best to break the door down with the butt of a rifle and the poet barely had time to pull on his pants and let Odilia down on a rope to the patio below.

Before they'd managed to entirely demolish the door, the poet opened up.

"What's all the fuss about, gentlemen?"

"Fermín Valencia?" demanded a gendarmery sergeant. Two other soldiers stood behind him in the hall.

"The one and only. What's the matter, your sister feeling lonely?" improvised the poet, and for that he got a rifle butt across the face, knocking out two of his teeth.

"Your mother," hissed the sergeant.

Fermín spat blood. Just then the lawyer Verdugo pushed his way through the crowd of onlookers amassed around the broken door. Tacubaya was the sort of neighborhood that lent itself to spectacles, fights in the street, the kind of place where everyone loved a free show.

"Excuse me, excuse me," said Verdugo, making his way to the door.

"Who are you?" asked the sergeant.

"I'm this gentleman's lawyer. What's he been accused of?"

"The murder of an officer of the Mexican army."

"Do you know where your navel is, Sergeant? Well I'm going to make you another hole just the same size, only a little bit higher up," said Verdugo, drawing his revolver from its shoulder holster in a motion he'd been practicing all morning long in the Opera bathhouse. More prudent than his friend the poet, Verdugo had passed the night wandering around the city he knew so well, the city that hid him and protected him. In the morning he'd gone to the public baths at number 15 Filomena Mata Street, taking cold showers, swimming in a small warm-water pool, and practicing his draw in one of the private rooms.

"So I suggest you let the gentleman go, unless you want to wind up in his place, that is."

He took the poet by the arm but Fermín turned back, stripped the soldiers of their Remingtons, and threw the guns out the window into the patio below, praying that Odilia wasn't still down there. Then he dug his Colt out of the lumped-up sheets and with the gun in his hand walked back over to face the sergeant.

"Sergeant, you had orders to arrest me, but knocking my teeth out was, what should we call it, above and beyond the call of duty."

"You'll never get out of here. I've got two more men waiting in the street."

"So I want you to repeat after me: I'm a stupid copper, dumber than a swine. I went and hit a poet, and now I'll get it from behind . . . Loud and clear now: I'm a stupid copper . . ."

Figuring that there's no better disguise than the ridiculous, Manterola had dressed himself up as a Hindu prince and rented a room in the Hotel Regis under the name of Maharaja Singh Lai from Kuala Lumpur (at least all those Salgari novels he'd read were good for something). Now he went down to the lobby in a turban and brocaded shirt, to buy the morning papers.

Excélsior dedicated the entire eight columns of the crime section to a retelling of the story of an almost forgotten jewel theft and two murdered aunts, identifying the fugitive Dionisio Garrochategui as "a certain Ramón currently enjoying the protection of an officer of the city gendarmery." It went on to connect the stolen jewels with those found in the pockets of a murdered trombonist, the brother of a now-deceased colonel who had once been close friends with the officer previously mentioned.

The Maharaja rubbed his hands with glee and turned to the front page of the second section of *El Heraldo,* which revealed with abundant detail (what a genius this Martínez de la Garza was, the only serious competition around!) the story of widespread corruption in the army's purchase of horse fodder in the Vallcy of Mcxico. Bccausc the paper was owned by General Alvarado, Martínez had far more leeway than anyone else to attack certain elements of the official power structure. According to the reporter's sources, a certain unnamed colonel of the city gendarmery (there being only three in all, Gómez and two of his subordinates, the man in question was obvious enough) controlled the concession for the sale of feed and hay to the cavalry throughout the Valley of Mexico and used his monopoly to sell at 60 percent above the regular market price. The reporter wondered how this shameful situation was allowed to continue, and in a superb moralistic finale asked General Cruz to take charge of the situation and clean house, for the sake of the good name of the revolutionary armed forces.

Tired of reading standing up by the newsstand, Maharaja Manterola headed for the hotel bar where he installed himself in a dark corner at the rear, for the sake of surreptitiousness, if not comfortable reading. He opened up *El Universal* and found the page where Librado had written one of his emotionally twisted stories, asking publicly how one of the most prominent leaders of the city's graphics industry had died of lead poisoning when he had never spent any time in the leaded atmosphere of the print shops he owned. The story of Roldán's death, which in its time hadn't received more than a few lines on the obituary page, was now retold with abundant detail, augmented by several photographs of the widow and even one of the mansion in San Rafael. Almost at the end of the story, the reporter asked casually if this wasn't the same widow who had been seen frequently of late at the more stylish parties, arm in arm with a certain colonel of the Mexico City gendarmery.

Next, in *Omega,* and with a more conservative tone, de Blas explored the accusations of a nonexistent spokesman for the Aguila Petroleum Company about the activities of an armed gang headquartered in San Rafael that had kidnapped their representative Van Horn.

Manterola ordered a whiskey in Hindi, which is the same as in Spanish or English, only accompanied by a series of elaborate gestures, and unfolded his own paper, which he'd been saving until the end.

He wasn't used to rereading his own work. Journalism was an ephemeral art, and it had to be understood and lived the same way. The retelling of yesterday's events served as a link to the historical past, useful in reference to the present, but not the sort of thing you wanted to spend your life paging through again and again. Manterola often said that it made him proud to see his day-old articles used as wrapping paper for a good red snapper in the marketplace.

But today he wanted to fully appreciate the details of the journalistic siege he'd laid around Colonel Gómez and company. At the top of the page there was a rather unflattering photo of the two corpses discovered on the sidewalk in front of the widow's San Rafael mansion. The bodies had been identified as those of Michel Simon, a French cardsharp, and gendarmery lieutenant Estrada. After detailing the condition in which the bodies were found, one pumped full of buckshot and the other with two .45 bullet holes through the chest, the journalist suggested that both men had only recently been in the service of Colonel Gómez, and questioned whether it wasn't possible the colonel had had a falling-out with the dead men, for motives as yet unclear. He went on to link Lieutenant Estrada with the trombonist's murder, "according to several eyewitnesses," and brought up the close relationship between the trombonist's recently deceased brother and Colonel Gómez. "Colonel Jesús Gómez owes his superiors a thorough explanation," the article concluded, "in the interests of maintaining untainted the public image of the Mexico City gendarmery."

Manterola took his Swiss pocketknife and cut out the various articles. Diligently underlining Gómez's name every time it appeared and each reference to "a certain colonel of the gendarmery," he took all the clippings and put them into an envelope, which he then addressed to General Cruz, Gómez's immediate superior. He rubbed his hands together again until they shone. The voice of the voiceless in action, the power of the printed word, he told himself.

After leaving the union meeting at the Providencia mill, Tomás and San Vicente walked together through the back streets of San Angel. The Chinaman had found a hiding place for himself, Rosa, and San Vicente in a coal yard run cooperatively by a couple of his anarchist friends blacklisted in the local mills. Songbirds filled the bright cloudless blue sky.

"I don't get it, Tomás. First you come out against a revolutionary action in the affinity group, and now you don't bat an eye when your friends say they want to rob a bank."

"The olganization is one thing and we'le anothel. That's just the way it is, what do you want me to do?"

"Hell's bells, man, you're all a bunch of friggin amateurs. 'We're going to rob a bank,' they say, like it's as easy as jumping rope. That's the worst of it."

"That's why we need you, blothel."

"Oh, right. Well, that was obvious. The only thing is, like I said, if all you guys want is to get at the Dutchman's safe-deposit box and whatever's inside it, that's fine, but then I'm going for the money."

"And nobody said you couldn't, eithel. Once you told them you didn't want the money fol youlself, but to stalt up an analchist newspapel, evelybody said yes, including me. So what's the ploblem?"

"That's the problem right there, Tomás, that you're willing to hold up a bank, but not for the cause."

"Someday you and me'll go tlavelling alound the wold lobbing banks and taking away the boulgeoisie's money, okay, but only in places whele thele's no olganization, so they can't go and lay the lap on the comlades. Is it a deal?"

"I didn't want to kill him, but something made me keep on squeezing, I just couldn't stop. I knew it wasn't him, and still somehow it was," Verdugo said in a rush, not really feeling like talking at all.

The poet was thinking about Odilia and answered the lawyer with a nod.

"Who knows all the demons we've got bottled up inside us? That woman let one of mine out of the bottle, that's for sure, set it free to run wild in the streets."

"I think maybe you ought to ask her to marry you, lawyer. Maybe she's a little cross-eyed and talks funny, but I think she's kind of cute."

"Not a bad idea, really. I always did like redheads. Just think about the shingle we could hang outside the door: Verdugo, Attorney-at-law, Madame Celeste, Hypnotist."

"Whiskey . . . another . . . please," said Manterola, wiping away the sweat pouring out from under his turban.

"Make her a ruby red," Verdugo said to one of his contacts out toward Candelaria, who for a modest twenty-five pesos had agreed to give the Packard a new coat of paint.

"Hell, robbing a bank is an art, man," explained San Vicente, "a real art."

"What part of India are you from, sir?" asked a man with an Argentine accent. "I once served in my country's embassy in Bombay."

"Red? That's going to look like shit," said the poet as he shaved off his mustache.

"You can't get to be as old as we ale without falling in love with machines," the Chinaman told San Vicente out of the blue.

"I hate to disappoint you, poet, but you're not going to get any taller by shaving off your mustache."

"From Kuala Lumpur. I have never been to India, sir."

"Let it burn," Colonel Gómez told his men, who were busy dousing Verdugo's apartment with gasoline, the bed, the walls, the rug.

THE WAY THINGS USED TO BE: FROM
FERMÍN VALENCIA'S NOTEBOOK

I could be a gardener instead of a poet, and never have to touch a gun again as long as I live. You don't make poetry with guns. Or do you?

A PHOTO IN THE ZÓCALO

Verdugo spent the last of his lottery money on gas for the Packard and a Kodak camera and film he bought at the American Foto Shop. He listened patiently to the salesman's instructions, despite the poet's insistence that he already knew how to work the camera. Then he asked his friends to pose for him in front of the National Palace, on the Zócalo.

San Vicente ended up taking the picture, adamantly refusing to have his own picture taken.

"I had no idea you were such a romantic," the journalist told the lawyer as San Vicente clicked the shutter.

The picture, which is probably still out there somewhere after all these years, stuck in some ancient photo album or lost in an old desk drawer, shows the four friends together: Verdugo, frowning, his pearl gray Stetson jammed down almost to his eyebrows, his impeccable double-breasted gray suit, his left hand toying with the ring on the middle finger of his right hand. Next to him, the poet, sitting on a low wall, his boots dangling gaily, his arms wrapped around Verdugo's and Manterola's shoulders, looking a little baby faced with his shaved-off mustache, smiling, happy, like in Zacatecas. Manterola, his eternal English cloth cap covering his balding head, has a paternal look on his face, like an old man playing at a child's game, a half smile on his lips, chewing on a filterless cigarette. Tomás Wong, standing next to the reporter, wearing the mustache the poet lacks, looks like an abandoned child, his hands shoved into his pockets, staring with a defiant eye at the National Palace, his muscles exploding out from under his white T-shirt. The recent scar shines on his forehead. In the background, the Mexican flag flutters atop a flagpole.

After taking the picture, they went off to rob the bank.

"Good morning, this is a holdup," said a short man in a mask. He headed straight for the safe-deposit boxes without paying much attention to whether the four customers, the tellers, or the guards raised their hands above their heads, and after searching carefully for a certain number started to force the box open with a crowbar.

"I believe the gentleman said this was a holdup," said another masked figure dressed in an elegant gray suit, a dapper pearl gray Stetson on his head and a shotgun in his hands. "Well it is. So get your hands up over your heads, all of you."

"This is a holdup, dammit. Put all the money in big envelopes, no coins, no gold or silver," said another masked man in shirtsleeves.

"Shit . . . all I want is to bust open this piñata, boys," said the short man, struggling with the crowbar. After his second attempt, he walked over to the manager's desk.

"Look, mister, this is the certificate for this here safe-deposit box. That gives me the right to open it, see? It's just that I seem to have lost my ID. Now I figure you could save me the trouble of having to open it with this crowbar and get your keys. What do you say?" he said, with his Colt .45 against the banker's throat.

"This all? And you call yourselves a bank? What've you got, a bunch of beggars keeping their money here or what? Let's see some of those real bourgeois bills," said the robber in shirtsleeves. Demonstrating an agility no one would have guessed he had, he jumped over the counter and started to fill the envelopes himself.

"Ready," said the short man.

"What is it?" asked the man with the Stetson.

"Some kind of document, five pages, and then some kind of contract or something."

"That's better. That's the way I like it," said the man

with the Spanish accent, carrying off five envelopes full of cash.

"Hey, I could have said 'this is a holdup' just the same as the lest of you. Thele's no *al*'s thele," complained Tomás as the getaway car sped up Puente de Alvarado toward Tacuba.

"Yeah, and then what? You going to paint your skin white?"

"My skin's not that ycllow. I could have passed as a malalia patient with the mask on."

"A malaria patient with a mask. Hell, that's a good one."

"So read it, dammit, what's it say?" urged Manterola at the wheel of the Packard.

"Have you got a license to drive this thing, inkslinger?" asked Verdugo.

"It's a military document, a plan to revolt against the government. It's dated April 1920. That'd be one month before the Agua Prieta Revolt against Carranza. Whoever made this plan got beat to the punch . . ."

"Who signed it? No, let me guess . . . Gómez," said the reporter.

"Zevada," said Verdugo.

"And Martínez Fierro," said the poet.

"Things ale getting clealel."

"Not too bad, easier than squeezing blood out of a turnip. Sixty-three thousand pesos, one on top of the other."

49

THE WAY THINGS USED TO BE: ZEVADA, MARTÍNEZ FIERRO, AND GÓMEZ AT MATA REDONDA

The three colonels arrived separately. Zevada and Martínez Fierro drove up in their cars out of the storm, each with a small armed escort. Gómez was the last to arrive, on horseback, accompanied only by a trusted lieutenant. He stripped off his rubber poncho and joined his two associates in the salon, where they stood drinking wine from cut-crystal glasses. The five North Americans waited at the other end of the room. Two of them relaxed in voluminous green velvet armchairs, puffing away on fat cigars; a third man with white hair and a glassy stare stood at the window looking out into the driving rain; two more sat around a table talking.

"We're all here, then," announced Zevada, a tall ugly man with a scar that ran from his lower lip down to the point of his chin.

"Colonel Gómez, welcome," said one of the North Americans in Spanish, Wiliam C. Greene, general manager of the Huasteca Petroleum Company. "I want you to meet Senator Fall, and Mr. Doheny, Mr. Sinclair, and Mr. Teagle."

Gómez held his hand out to the senator, then saluted the oil barons. He clicked his heels once for Standard Oil of New Jersey, representing a third of all Mexican oil operations, then again for the owner and namesake of Sinclair Oil, and once more for the men from Huasteca Petroleum. With these three brief gestures he offered up his reverence to what amounted to 30 percent of the entire income of the Mexican treasury, acquired through export taxes and drilling rights on 194 million

barrels of crude oil a year. After that, he nodded to his two
fellow officers. The three of them together effectively controlled
military power in the whole oil country, from the U.S. border
down to the Tampico refineries and the Huasteca oil fields in
the state of Veracruz.

"All right, gentlemen, let's get down to business. The devil
himself is out there tonight and I have to be back in my barracks
at Panuco by dawn."

Greene, acting as host, led the group to an adjoining room
where they took their seats around a large mahogany table.
The manager of the Huasteca Petroleum Co. poured out wine
and offered around a tray of tiny meat-filled pastries. Aside
from the eight men assembled around the table, the huge house
was empty.

"Whenever you're ready, gentlemen," prompted Greene.

The three Mexican officers sat on one side of the table, facing
the oilmen and Senator Fall.

The colonels glanced at one another. Martínez Fierro had
risen to colonel before the others, but it was Gómez who controlled the key forces in the oil region and he was the first to
speak.

"We are ready to take arms against the government, as we
previously agreed. Colonel Martínez will secure the border,
Zevada will take care of Tampico, and I will be in command
in the Huasteca. We've considered the possible flaws in our
plan, and they are minor. Once the insurrection begins it will
be necessary to eliminate General Arnulfo Gómez, as well as
Colonel Lázaro Cárdenas in Papantla. You've got General Peláez by the nape of the neck and he will take our side. We have
men in our confidence in the garrisons at Reynosa, Laredo,
Tampico, Pánuco, Tantoyuca, Chicontepec, and Tuxpan.
Counting the troops under Peláez, we will have five thousand
men with us after the first few hours of the revolt."

Greene translated the colonel's words to Senator Fall, and
Doheny did the same for Teagle and Sinclair.

"So far so good," continued Gómez. "We can assume that
President Carranza will order Pancho Murguía against us from

the center of the country, that Aguilar will send Guadalupe Sánchez and his men up from Veracruz, and that General Marcelo Caraveo will come at us from the west. However, the conflicts that already exist among them due to the upcoming elections will immobilize them within a few days. The government can hardly rely on Obregón and his troops, and even General Pablo González is not a sure thing for them at this point. The situation works in our favor, but even so, it's unlikely that we can resist for more than a week. The rest is up to you. If after five days you're unable to resolve the political question, then you might as well go ahead and deposit the sum we agreed upon in a bank in Los Angeles, and our next meeting will take place in your country, gentlemen."

"Senator Fall has asked me to inform you of the following," said Greene. "Once you've taken up arms and your intentions are made public, the State Department will declare that the U.S. government is taking the entire Mexican petroleum region under its protection, in the name of safeguarding our national interests. On the second day of the uprising you will ask publicly for this protection, claiming that you cannot guarantee the safety of the oil wells in the face of government threats to dynamite oil operations throughout the region. I believe that we can have a squadron of marines in Tampico by the third day. You will then declare your autonomy from the central government and name an administrative apparatus to coordinate with our expeditionary forces. These gentlemen"—he motioned to the oil barons—"will apply pressure on the State Department for immediate intervention."

"Can you guarantee us a marine landing on the third day?" asked Zevada. "I can open the border at Reynosa if necessary."

Greene and Fall talked in English in low voices.

"On the third day, you'll have the Marines. In addition, Senator Fall will sound out the possibility of sending a cavalry regiment across the border at Reynosa."

"And now, with respect to the economic arrangements we discussed previously?" asked Martínez Fierro.

"In the event that the uprising fails we will deposit, in each of your names, one million dollars in a bank in Los Angeles."

"And how do we slice up the pie if we win?" asked Zevada.

"Each of you will get three percent of tax revenues due on exports and drilling rights."

"One other thing, gentlemen. We plan to form a triumvirate to govern the autonomous region, and once things calm down a bit we'll count on you to get rid of Peláez."

"Consider it done," said Doheny, pounding his fist on the table for emphasis.

Greene opened a yellow folder and took out five copies of the same document.

"This, then, is the Plan of Mata Redonda, gentlemen. Read it over. There's one copy for each of you, one for the oil companies, and one for Senator Fall, who will make use of it at the appropriate time."

"Before we sign, we want a copy in writing of your intentions, including the economic arrangements between us."

The oil bosses spoke together in English and then Doheny directed himself to the colonels.

"Agreed, with the provision that, should the operation fail, the information not be made public. What guarantees can you give us?"

"There will be one copy only, and we'll make sure that it doesn't go beyond us. Tomorrow morning I'll send my assistant to pick it up, and it will then be deposited in a safe-deposit box in the Bank of Hamburg in Tampico, as if it were a copy of a will or some other family document."

The copies of the Plan of Mata Redonda made their way around the table. Gómez, Zevada, and Martínez Fierro signed without so much as flipping through the pages.

"Have you gentlemen come up with a name for the new protectorate, should our plan succeed?" asked Greene.

"I thought we might call it the Republic of Black Gold," said Gómez. His words were translated, and the men at the table laughed.

50

MANTEROLA AND VITO ALESSIO

Manterola walked into Vito Alessio Robles's office without knocking. And without saying a word he slid the Plan of Mata Redonda across the desk of the owner and managing editor of *El Demócrata*.

Vito Alessio, the brother of Miguel Alessio Robles, Obregón's personal secretary, was an independent-minded man in the ranks of Obregón's supporters. He'd built the best daily newspaper in the country in only two years' time. With an independent outlook, an excellent labor-affairs section, detailed national news, and a brilliant crime page, well designed and provocatively headlined, the paper easily surpassed its three competitors in circulation. Alessio had made a policy of paying well for his reporters' genius, enduring their eccentricities, their manias, their unrepentant bohemianism, in exchange for an admirable level of journalistic discipline and an unsurpassed passion for the profession. So he wasn't in the least surprised to see his star crime reporter walk into his office dressed as an Indian Maharaja, and he settled back to read the document.

"All right, Manterola. What do you want to do with this?" he asked, lifting his eyes from the pages in front of him.

"I assume you've been following my campaign against Gómez. Well, this is the final blow."

"I'd like to be able to cover my ass before taking this to press. I'd like to talk it over with my brother first. You realize, of course, it doesn't merely implicate the three colonels . . . This Zevada is the one they tossed out of the window in the building across the street, isn't he?"

"One and the same. He must have been blackmailing the other two."

"We have to think about the overall impact of something like this, now that the government's about to enter into negotiations with the oil companies. What we'd be doing is accusing the four American oil companies of trying to organize a revolution to take over the oil fields. It's not these two-bit colonels I'm worried about here. It's the government's position."

"It'd be front-page news for a week, sir."

"I don't doubt that, Manterola, but I'd like to check up on it first—if you're willing, of course. If you insist, we'll go to press today. It's your story, and come hell or high water we're here to get out the news. But, with your permission, I'd like to talk to a few people first."

"That's fine with me, sir. How many days do you need?"

"Two at the most," said the editor, looking fixedly at the reporter.

"There's one small problem, sir. This document here is like my life insurance. If it doesn't get published, and they drum the two colonels out anyway, I've got one foot in the grave, if you know what I mean."

"You're safe as long as you're here at the newspaper."

"Safe from Colonel Gómez?"

"From Gómez and the entire Mexico City gendarmery, if it comes to that. You have my guarantee," said Vito Alessio. He picked up the telephone. "Get me Ericsson seven-nine-one, direct with my brother. Tell his secretary it's a matter of life and death."

"I'd like to keep the original, sir."

"Let me make a few notes, then."

"Be my guest."

"In the meantime, why don't you go down to the cashier. You've earned a bonus, Manterola."

"I appreciate that, sir. You have no idea how expensive it can be to go around dressed like a Hindu prince in a rented limousine."

Vito Alessio laughed as the reporter headed toward the door.

But not nearly as much as Gonzaga when he saw Pioquinto Manterola walk into the newsroom wearing a turban.

"Stand there a minute, will you?" he said. "This is something I've got to draw."

"Go to hell."

"Cheggidout. That reminds me, there's a message for you here. You've got a date with an army colonel who says he'll wait for you every night this week in the . . . Let's see, I've got it here somewhere . . . In the Black Circus Bar. Cheggidout. I get it now, they want to give you a job as a doorman."

51

SHOTS AT THE BLACK CIRCUS

Inside the Packard, and much to the lawyer's surprise, the poet pulled down his pants and cut out the bottom of his right front pocket with a knife. Then he loaded his shotgun and started to strap it to his right leg with a roll of sticking plaster. First he wrapped the plaster around the barrel at his ankle, then at the knee just beyond the double hammer, and again around his thigh and the gun's wooden stock. He hitched his baggy pants back up and, sticking his hand into his pocket, felt for the trigger.

"Perfect," he said. "Now all I have to do is remember not to dance, because if this thing goes off on me, you're going to see one elevated poet."

"I don't know . . . If we have to make a fast getaway, you're going to have some problems."

"If we have to make a fast getaway, I'll just take off my pants and run for it. Don't underestimate my strategy."

Verdugo checked the bullets in his revolver and replaced the gun in its shoulder holster. Then he filled the pockets of his forty-peso white linen Palm Beach suit with extra bullets.

The reporter was waiting for them at the corner of Héroes Street.

"What about your glasses?" Verdugo asked, pulling up to the curb.

"Don't worry about it. If it comes down to gunplay, everything's going to be at close range anyway," said the poet, tying a red silk handkerchief around his neck. Verdugo glanced at the poet's dull eyes and smiling face reflected in the rearview mirror. They got out of the car and walked with the reporter toward the Black Circus Bar, guided by the sound of the music.

The Black Circus was the jumpingest tropical-music joint in Mexico City, and in those days there weren't very many. Located at the corner of Héroes and Camelia in the tough Guerrero district, it was patronized mostly by working-class dance freaks, who had made it what it was: the undisputed cathedral of rumba. Tonight a twelve-piece Cuban-Veracruz *conjunto* called Extasis was officiating from the pulpit. A wave of sound, sweat, and smoke hit them in the face as the three friends walked through the swinging doors.

It was a big box of a room, with twin bars on either side, a low stage for the band at the far end, and a large circular dance floor. Around the dance floor were some two dozen tables filled with office workers, artisans, poor students, prostitutes, and musicians who'd come to learn from the new tropical sound. Extasis was just finishing off its second set of the night while a mulatto man danced barefoot in the center of the floor. Verdugo returned the stare of an officer and two civilians at a nearby table. At the next table over, behind the officer and his companions, the Chinaman and San Vicente sat drinking, pretending to be caught up in the music. While the reporter and the poet headed straight over to the officer's table, Verdugo surveyed the scene. He discounted almost everyone in the crowded bar except for a pair of men sitting with a woman three tables away from what appeared to be the center of the action. His eyes teared from all the smoke.

"Good evening, Colonel. I'm Pioquinto Manterola," said the reporter, and the man motioned him to take a seat.

The poet limped up behind his friend, pulled up a chair a little way from the table, and rested his stiff leg on another chair, his boot pointing at the belly of Colonel Martínez Fierro. Verdugo sat down on the reporter's left, an arm's length from one of the colonel's companions, a blond man with an absentminded air which made him all the more dangerous in the lawyer's eyes—Verdugo being a man who believed in anything but appearances.

"These are a couple of friends of mine, Mr. Manterola," said the officer, motioning toward his companions.

"The lawyer Alberto Verdugo and the poet Fermín Valencia, two close friends of mine," said the reporter.

"Will you join us in a drink?" asked the colonel. He was a fortyish man with dark skin and deep-set eyes that shone brightly despite the darkness of the bar. He held out a bottle of something that was either mezcal or tequila, and poured out three glasses. Manterola shook his head, and the poet politely declined. Verdugo took a glass. Whatever Martínez Fierro had in mind, it wasn't poison. The lawyer downed the mezcal with a single gulp. The band finished their set with a fanfare of trumpets. Verdugo clapped eagerly, looking around carefully for anyone who didn't, adding to the list of possible targets a man who sat at the bar several feet behind him with his head between his hands.

"Gentlemen, I'm not going to waste your time. You have a certain document in your possession, or if you don't actually have a copy of it, you're familiar with its contents. I tried to keep the representatives of the Aguila Petroleum Company who stole it from me from letting it get out but, one way or another, I was unsuccessful. It didn't belong to them, it was mine, and I should have destroyed it long ago. Now I just want to let bygones be bygones. We can all forget it ever existed. You gentlemen go about your business and leave me alone to go about mine. I'm talking peace."

"And what exactly is your business, Colonel?"

"That's just the attitude that's gotten you in trouble before. My business is my business, asshole. Understand?"

This isn't going to last very long, the poet told himself and, feigning discomfort, adjusted his stiff leg so that it pointed at the colonel's head. Then he slid his hand into his right pocket and stroked the shotgun's double trigger.

"What's in it for us?" asked the reporter, his hands starting to sweat. He knew his fear could paralyze him, and he didn't want to waste any time.

"Listen, I'm not Gómez, I don't have a whole wad of bills

to give out to whatever stupid son of a bitch comes along asking for a handout. I killed the Brit, and because you were stupid enough to try and get involved, I hired those three idiots to take care of you, too, but it turned out they couldn't shoot too good. It's not always going to be that way. Hired guns in this town are cheap and plenty. I'm offering you your own skin, gentlemen, that's all. You decide what it's worth. What do you want money for? To leave it for future generations to enjoy?"

"In other words, you're saying that if we keep quiet, we live. Now that's a hell of a good deal, isn't it, Verdugo? A Mexican Army colonel bought off by the gringos and ready to sell them a piece of his own country says he'll let us live. A hell of a deal."

"Can I say something, Manterola?" asked the poet.

"Go ahead, Mr. Valencia."

"This idiot colonel's got us figured all wrong. I wouldn't let scum like him lick my boots, let alone my dick."

"Very pretty, poet," murmured Verdugo, shoving away the blond man who was pulling his gun out underneath the table. But the lawyer wasn't quite fast enough to entirely avoid the man's first shot, which sent his pearl gray Stetson flying and traced a thin line of blood along the top of his head. The lawyer reached for his gun, but before he could get it out of the holster, Fermín Valencia opened fire with the shotgun on Colonel Martínez and his other companion, tearing apart their faces and sewing the cabaret with buckshot.

With the explosion of the shotgun blast, echoing through the room like fireworks on Independence Day, the journalist fell backward in his chair onto the floor. Verdugo whirled around searching for the man at the bar, who he found pointing a large Colt revolver in the reporter's direction. The lawyer fired three quick shots, and as the man doubled over his gun went off, throwing up splinters from the overturned table. Tomás Wong, knife in hand, stared down the men at the other nearby table, who smiled timidly at him and the steely black hole of San Vicente's .38 revolver.

On the floor, the blond gunman got off another pair of shots, but the reporter stopped him with a lucky shot to the shoulder. Verdugo looked desperately around the room for any other suspicious movements. A strange silence fell gradually over the bar. Tomás stepped over and kicked the pistol out of the blond gunman's hand. The poet hopped around trying to extinguish his smoking pants leg.

"Shit, I nearly blew my damn toes off," he announced to anyone who cared to listen.

Verdugo went and took a look at the dead colonel and his bodyguard. The colonel's face was a disfigured mass of blood and splintered bone. He couldn't help it: he started to vomit on top of the corpses. Manterola stood up, fitting his wire-rimmed glasses over his nose with trembling hands. The reporter and his four friends were the only ones standing in the entire room. Somebody sobbed from behind a table. That was the only sound there was, that and Verdugo's retching. Manterola missed the rumba.

52

IN WHICH THE CHARACTERS PLAY
DOMINOES ON TOP OF A PIANO

In the garage somewhere in Candelaria where they were spending the night alongside the ruby-red bulletproof Packard, there was an old broken-down piano where, to the poet's surprise and delight, Verdugo sat playing Chopin's Polonaises, one after the other. The poet, installed in the Packard's backseat with the door open, silently wrote some notes for an ad campaign he hoped to sell to the Stuart Company, given the sorry state of their current material (*Stuart's Hemro Ointment cures hemorrhoids, a progressive disease*).

"Good evening, friends," said Manterola, walking in through the metal door with Tomás Wong.

"We're all here. Did you bring the dominoes?"

"You bet I did. But keep on playing, Verdugo. There's no hurry."

"That's good, because there's no table, either," said the poet. "Where's your buddy, Tomás?"

"He's out meditating, Felmín. He wanted to think things ovel and figule out if evelything we got him into this week jives with his plinciples."

"And does it?"

"I think so. You could say that in a solt of indilect and sui-genelis way, we've been giving it to the state left and light."

"The army, the cops, the banks. Not too shabby," said the poet, dragging three dilapidated chairs over to the piano.

"On top of the piano?"

"As soon as Verdugo finishes with Chopin."

"Not even I can finish off Chopin," said the lawyer, pulling the lid down over the keys.

"Any word from the newspaper?" asked the poet.

"Not yet. I called a little while ago, but Alessio wasn't there. Dammit, I get the feeling they're not going to want to go ahead with it . . . The boys at the paper said there was a bunch of gendarmes hanging out on Humboldt Street. Gómez called a press conference, to make his counterattack, I suppose, but none of the reporters showed up."

"Now that's what I call solidarity, inkslinger," said Verdugo with a smile. Without the Chopin, their voices echoed hollowly in the garage.

"All the gendalmes that alen't staked out in flont of youl newspapel ale down in San Angel. They've got the whole town sealed off."

"The strike about to start?"

"If they don't set Málquez flee by tomollow," said Tomás, losing himself in this thoughts.

"And if they don't print it, what are we going to do? Are we all going to go after Gómez together?" asked the poet.

"If they don't print it it's because the government wants to hold onto Gómez—it means they're protecting him. So then it doesn't matter what we do . . . there's not going to be enough city for us to hide in. They'll hunt us down like rats."

"What would they want to protect Gómez for? What good's he to them?"

"The cops ale a piece of shit."

"I agree with you on that score, illustrious child of the rising sun. You don't need to be an anarchist to think that. But I still don't understand. The cops are a piece of shit, but they've got their rules all the same. I don't understand any of it."

"You know what, inkslinger? I've still got more questions than answers. Now we know who sent the three gunmen to kill us, but who tried to poison you in the hospital?"

"Gómez, I suppose."

"And why did he have the Zevada brothers killed?"

"I think I can answer that one," said Verdugo. "Zevada was

the idiot kid in this whole story. After the Agua Prieta Revolt the conspirators lost their chance to pull off a rebellion in the oil country. Things had changed too much. With Carranza dead, there were no longer tensions between him and Obregón's forces. Obregón had loyal generals stationed in San Luis Potosí and Monterrey, and later on Gómez, Zevada, and Martínez Fierro all got transferred out of the oil country. Their plan fell apart. Gómez, on the one hand, took up with the victors and started in fixing things up for himself in Mexico City. Martínez Fierro retained command over his troops. But Zevada was too slow on the uptake and he found himself out of the action. What I figure is that he tried to blackmail Gómez, who paid him off at first with jewels, and later on with a one-way trip out a third-story window."

"Do you really want to know what happened, poet? For now, let's just cross our fingers and hope they print the story," said Manterola, stifling a yawn.

The days had been all too long, the nights too short, and fear had been everywhere in the air.

"I give up. Get out the dominoes and let's choose partners."

"Six/one," said Manterola.

"Six/four," said Verdugo.

"Double-zelos," said Tomás.

"One/three," said Fermín Valencia.

53

A COLONEL'S HONOR AND THE DEATH
OF A WIDOW

"*El Demócrata,* section two, Manterola here," said the ink-slinger into the telephone mouthpiece.

"Manterola, this is Colonel Gómez," said a cavernous voice over the telephone. "I'm going to give you a chance, even though you don't deserve it. You have sullied my honor, sir. So I challenge you to a duel. Just the two of us, alone. Let's see if you can stand up in front of me like a man, come out of the shadows . . ."

"What honor?" asked the journalist after a brief pause. "Colonel, you can take your honor and stick it up your ass." He hung up and sat staring at the telephone. It dawned on him that he ought to remember that voice forever, those few brief words. It was the only more-or-less concrete thing he had, the only real contact with his enemy, with the man who'd turned his life into "a tale told by an idiot," as Verdugo had said.

"Cheggidout, cheggidout," said Gonzaga, walking by in his eternal mental haze. "That's some friend you've got there."

Manterola ignored the illustrator and turned back to his typewriter like a man possessed by a sacred fury. His fingers smashed the keys—time was running out. He was a professional and, although he was only waiting for his editor's decision, he couldn't keep from writing his daily piece. It was a rambling story about the rumors circulating in Durango that Pancho Villa had set out from his Hacienda Canutillo in search of buried treasure. Gonzaga read over the reporter's shoulder for a while, then went off to draw a picture of Villa in a cave, kneeling in front of a chest full of coins shining in the torchlight.

The newsroom was hot with activity just before deadline. Ruvalcaba read hurriedly through the editorials that came to him from the director's office. A pair of reporters sweated over the lead stories, one about Finance Minister Adolfo de la Huerta's comments following his return from negotiations with the American banks in New York, and the other about the general strike called by the San Angel textile workers in response to the gendarmery's kidnapping of their leader Márquez.

Suddenly the subtle odor of violets wafted across the keys of his typewriter and the journalist looked up, adjusting his wire-rimmed spectacles, to see Margarita Herrera, the Widow Roldán, standing in front of him.

"May I speak with you?" asked the widow, under Gonzaga's watchful stare.

"I'll be with you in a minute, ma'am," said Manterola, continuing to type furiously, trying to escape from the woman's piercing eyes. He yanked the last page out of the typewriter and was about to mark his corrections when a strange movement at the door to the newsroom forced him to look up again.

"Whore! Worse than a whore!" shouted Ramón the Spic, charging toward the widow with a knife in his hand.

Manterola tried to intervene but his desk stood in the way. The woman stood up, or started to, but her legs gave out under her and as she fell back onto her chair the Spic drove his knife twice into her breast. Manterola finally managed to reach the collapsed woman, taking hold of her arm and ignoring the Spic who just missed the reporter's ribs with a thrust of his bloody dagger. Gonzaga took a few steps back, the better to observe the action so that he could draw it later on. Life can be so ephemeral, so fleeting, if one isn't careful to take in all the details.

Fortunately for the reporter, Rufino the messenger boy arrived in time to bean the Spic on the side of the head with a bronze paperweight thrown from across the room. He fell unconscious at the widow's feet.

"I'm dying, sir. I'm only sorry we met so late," murmured the widow, sagging in the reporter's arms and staining his shirt with the blood that oozed slowly from her breast, masking her wounds, soaking into her white blouse.

"Some loves are idiot loves, like our own," said the journalist. That was all he could think to say as the woman lay back gulping in air that never made it to her lungs.

The entire newsroom had assembled to watch the tragedy. Like a last sorrowful honor guard, Manterola's office mates, sweating, shirtless, their extinguished cigarettes clamped between their teeth, stood in silence around a woman who had poisoned her husband, taken up with a corrupt colonel, been murdered by a Spanish jewel thief, and now lay dying in a crime reporter's arms, the same man who had once wished he could have fallen in love with her.

"The murderer's dead, too, Manterola . . . You did him right, Rufino. Holy hell, man, what an arm," pronounced Valverde, the rookie sports writer who had studied a couple of years of medicine before joining the paper.

Gonzaga sat again at his desk, manipulating the pencils and charcoal sticks like an illusionist, trying to finish the drawing before the afternoon shadows darkened forever over the dead woman's bloodstained face.

54

THE SAN ANGEL MASSACRE

It had all started two nights before, when three police agents accompanied by plant manager Julio Imbert entered the Santa Teresa mill and kidnapped Julio Márquez, Interior Secretary of the Textile Workers Federation. All the next day, Márquez's whereabouts were still unknown. At 6:05 the following morning a flood of workers entered Imbert's office, demanding Márquez's release, insulting the manager, and threatening retaliation if anything happened to their leader. Imbert took a gun out of his desk drawer, but the workers disarmed him before he could do any harm. Work in the factory was brought to a standstill, the immense looms shut down. A group of workers went out into the street and started to beat on the metal lampposts with steel bars.

The metallic, rhythmic signal paralyzed the mills all over Contreras. Workers at the Magdalena, the Alpina, the Hormiga, all quit working and went out to repeat the rhythmic signal.

Five hundred marchers left the doors of the Santa Teresa and by the time they'd reached Tizapán there were over five thousand.

The distant clanging woke up Tomás in the coal yard.

"What the hell?" asked San Vicente, jumping out of bed.

"Genelal stlike. Don't you heal the lampposts?"

"I didn't know that was the signal. Hells bells, man, are we ever organized or what?"

Rosa took the Chinaman's hand and squeezed it softly.

"Be careful. The streets are going to be full of police."

"Thele's going to be mole of us than them. Just listen to it."

Tomás went out wrapped in a heavy coat, an enormous straw hat covering his head, and San Vicente threw a scarf across his face. They joined the march as it turned onto Puente Sierra. And while they looked around for someone they knew to tell them what had happened, the workers at the front of the column ran across Imbert sitting in a car with four policemen. The marchers showered the car with stones and captured the mill manager, bleeding from a superficial cut on his face. They demanded that he publicly declare who had kidnapped Julio Márquez.

Tomás and San Vicente found their friends Paulino Martínez and Hector, and together they tried to push their way to the front of the crowd, through the enraged Santa Teresa workers.

At 8:05, on the Ansaldo Bridge, five gendarmes led by a sergeant and accompanied by several nonunion workers from the Santa Teresa mill tried to rescue Imbert. The marchers responded with stones. The gendarmes fired into the air.

San Vicente brought his hand up to his coat pocket. Tomás stopped him.

"If we file back, that gives them the excuse to shoot into the clowd. Take it easy."

The Spaniard nodded as the workers at the front of the demonstration chased the gendarmes with another volley of stones.

At 8:30 nearly seven thousand marchers entered the main plaza at the center of San Angel. Two squadrons of mounted police were waiting for them. Imbert tried to break free, but was hit in the shoulder with a stone. The gendarmes cocked their rifles. Tomás tried again to get to the front, but he was trapped in a side street while the first lines of workers entered the square. Climbing onto a windowsill and holding on to the outer grate, he strained to see what was happening in the plaza. A double row of mounted gendarmes guarded the entrance to city hall. Two officers sat on their horses behind the second line. Tomás recognized one of them, Colonel Gómez, his face and body tense, sitting upright in the saddle, shouting an order. The gendarmes retreated toward Plaza San Jacinto before the surging crowd of workers. The marchers were trying to get to city hall, where they planned to force Imbert to declare openly what had happened to Márquez.

The thousands of workers coming up from behind pushed the front of the march toward San Jacinto, but barely five hundred marchers had reached the plaza when the police opened up with their first volley. Six or seven workers dropped to the ground, and the crowd paused and fell backward. Tomás and San Vicente tried again to move ahead, but it was impossible.

"It's Gómez, did you see him? Gómez is giving the oldels."

"Let's get him."

The police opened fire again, and now the plaza was covered with fallen bodies. Some of the marchers tried to fight back, but their stones were no match for the police Mausers. Tomás was dragged along by the crowd, but San Vicente, protecting himself behind a tree, managed to get off a shot at the mounted Colonel. The bullet shattered a window at the colonel's back and he turned to try to see where the shot had come from. The gendarmes fired again, but the plaza was almost empty. The colonel made his horse caper in place for a moment, and then spurred the animal into a trot and left the plaza by the far side. San Vicente saw a ten-year-old boy with a bullet wound in his leg, took him up in his arms, and with his gun still in his hand retreated from the plaza, carefully watching the line of mounted police. Tomás waved him into the shelter of a nearby doorway. Slowly, several workers approached their fallen comrades, underneath the open mouths of the smoking rifles. Two dozen wounded lay on the ground. Two of them, the aged Emilio López, veteran textile worker, and Florentino Ramos, with two bullets in his stomach, would die within a few hours.

The bells of the Red and White Cross ambulances broke the fragile air. Tomás took San Vicente's scarf and tied a tourniquet around the boy's leg. The boy had fainted.

Another squadron of mounted police entered the plaza and headed down the streets where the marchers had fled five minutes before.

"Let's get out of here, Tomás, they're going to start arresting people."

"This is why they'le plotecting Gómez. They need him fol this kind of bullshit."

"Dammit all to hell and the Virgin Mary, man, I had him in my sights and his horse moved on me."

"Let's get him, Sebastián. He must have gone off to the gendarmely ballacks at Peledo."

"There's no way we can get through."

"Let's get him, Sebastián. This doesn't have anything to do with the othel stuff. This is something between us and Gómez, us and Gómez and all of them," said the Chinaman, pointing to the bodies lying across the plaza.

55

THE WAY THINGS USED TO BE:
TOMÁS WONG

I would have liked to have sailed away in all the ships I ever loaded, all the ships whose passengers I helped down the gangplank, carrying their bags covered with brightly colored labels from hotels, customs inspections, railroads. I would have liked to have gotten aboard those big shiny white boats in the sunshine and gone away.

I'm not from here. From this land where I was born. That's something life teaches you, if you're willing to learn, that nobody's from where they were born, where they grew up. That nobody's really from anywhere. There's some people that try to keep up the illusion, working themselves all up over memories, and knickknacks and flags and anthems. What they don't know is that we all belong to the places we've never even been before. If there's any kind of legitimate nostalgia, it's for everything we've never seen, the women we've never slept with, never dreamed of, the friends we haven't made, the books we haven't read, all that food steaming in the pots we've never eaten out of. That's the only real kind of nostalgia there is.

Another thing you learn along the way is that at some point or other the road took a wrong turn and things didn't necessarily have to turn out the way they did. Nobody should have had to eat bug-infested rice or half-rotten corn in the oil fields, paying three times the regular price at the company store. Nobody ought to have had to go out in the middle of the rains to close the valves on well number seven; muck around in the middle of the jungle laying pipe, drilling wells in the swamps, blasting dynamite, sleeping on the wet ground, taking in starvation wages while the foreman eats ham and butter out of the cans we carried in on our backs. And the bossman, far away in some big house in the city, sleeps in a bed without ever knowing who we are, without ever acknowledging the real source of his pleasure and his power, without ever having to think about us, while we carry him on our shoulders and our backs, pushing and grunting like so many ants, pushing his stocks up higher and higher every day in New York.

That's why I don't want to go on those shiny white ships. Because I'd have to pay for my dreams working eleven-hour days as a waiter, a busboy, shining the polished brass handrails, sweating in the heat of the kitchen. That's why the big boats stay far away, as I watch them come and go from every port, from all my dreams, from inside my nostalgia.

56

"SOMEDAY SOMEONE WILL TELL
ALL THIS"

Word of the San Angel shooting arrived at the newspaper by midmorning. Manterola, who'd spent the night in an armchair in the waiting room outside the director's office, prowled anxiously around the newsroom without quite daring to get involved, but leaping eagerly on every scrap of information: reports from the Red Cross and the White Cross, a statement by Gasca, the Federal District Regent, a call from the CGT central council for a general strike to begin the following day, the description of two of his colleagues who'd been out to interview the wounded and other demonstrators. A statement from the San Angel city authorities maintaining that the demonstration had been a peaceful one and blaming the gendarmery for the aggression.

"Manterola, the boss wants to see you."

He dragged himself reluctantly down the hall. As he passed the window where he'd witnessed Colonel Zevada's fatal fall he saw one of the gendarmery's paddy wagons parked in front of the building. During the night, Ruiz, who covered the city desk, had told him in a whisper that the word was out the gendarmes had gotten the order to kill him on the slightest pretext, that Gómez had put a price on his head and that a certain Captain Palomera had bet that he'd be the man to win it. That same morning, two secret service agents guarding the newspaper's entrance (Alessio Robles had kept his promise to protect Manterola) stopped an alleged salesman, who said he wanted to place an ad in the newspaper, from entering the building. The man was armed, carried no identification, and one of the agents had tentatively identified him as a wanted criminal.

"You wanted to see me, sir?"

"Major Martínez here would like to have a few words with you. It's fine with me if it's all right with you, Manterola," said Vito Alessio.

Martínez, the ex–hod carrier, sat in a leather armchair in the director's office. Next to him stood a capable-looking man in civilian clothes, wearing an earring, and with a noticeable bulge under his black jacket.

"Now remember, Manterola, the decision is up to you. If you want to go ahead with this I intend to keep my word, come what may. I didn't become director of Mexico's finest news-paper just to sell out my reporters."

"I appreciate that, sir."

Vito Alessio smiled at Manterola and left the office, closing the door softly behind him.

"I believe you haven't met my friend The Gypsy, have you, Manterola?"

"No, Major, although I've heard about him."

The Gypsy greeted Manterola with a nod. Manterola walked over to his boss's desk and sat down in his chair. The desk was covered with papers and there was a photo of the three Alessio brothers, the director of *El Demócrata,* the president's secre-tary, and an officer who had died mysteriously in a car riddled with bullets.

"Okay, Major, let's have the bad news."

"I want the document and your pledge of silence, Manterola."

"On whose authority, Major?"

"In the name of the Government of the Republic." Coming from the major, the words "Government" and "Republic" evoked days of blood and glory.

"Is the government familiar with the contents of the docu-ment and the considerable sum agreed to by Colonel Gómez and his cronies?"

"Certainly, sir. A copy of the document was given to the

governor of Tamaulipas in Tampico by the Aguila Petroleum Company yesterday."

"In other words, the government doesn't want it made public that the North American oil companies planned to finance a revolution to split off the oil producing regions from the rest of the country?"

"No, sir, it does not. At least not for the time being. I assume you understand why that is."

"Well, then the government's screwed, isn't it? If the director of this newspaper keeps his word, then the Plan of Mata Redonda will be out in tomorrow's edition."

"I don't think so, Manterola."

"What are you going to do, kill me?"

"Of course not. I want you to know I have a great deal of respect for you."

"Well then, Major?"

"I'm going to trade you the plan for something that's more valuable to you. Two hours ago, several agents of the secret police under my command arrested a Chinaman and a Spaniard who attempted to murder Colonel Gómez at the Peredo barracks."

"Did they kill him?" asked the journalist, rising up from his seat.

"No, I'm sorry to say. It would have been most convenient for everyone involved, however Gómez managed to escape with only a broken arm and a few bruises. They shot him as he was going down the stairs, and he took a rather bad tumble. Also, it seems as though he'll lose the sight in his left eye. It was all an unfortunate accident, according to the last official report I heard.

"And Tomás and Sebastián?"

"A little the worse for wear, but still in one piece. My men saved them from Gómez's men when they were about to have them shot . . . Now I've got them, and I'm willing to trade them to you for the document, Manterola . . . I don't think you really need any more convincing, but you may also like to know that I have my men surrounding a certain garage in Candelaria, and they're prepared to go in shooting in search of Colonel Martínez Fierro's killers.''

"All I can say is that your men had better be prepared to eat as much lead as they dish out if they try and go in there, Major.''

"I don't doubt that, reporter, but if need be, I'll have a machine gun placed in front of the door. That ought to take care of them. Do you understand, Manterola? I've got two cavalry regiments and artillery at my disposal. Enough of this fooling around. All I ask is for the plan and your silence in exchange for the freedom and safety of yourself and your friends.''

"What about Gómez?''

"I assume you're referring to Colonel Jesús Gómez Reyna, the new military attaché assigned to the Mexican embassy in Spain. Due to set out this very evening on a steamer from Veracruz. The sea air ought to help him recover from his unfortunate accident, wouldn't you say?''

"Well damn it all to hell and your mother, too," said the reporter. "On top of the third desk to the left of the doorway there's a manila envelope with the letterhead of a local theater company. Inside you'll find what you're looking for, Major.''

"Thank you, Manterola . . . I assume I have your pledge of silence.''

"Someday someone will tell all this.''

"Well, I only hope that neither you nor I are alive to see the day, Manterola.''

Manterola didn't see them leave the office. His eyes were fixed on the papers covering the director's desk. He felt old and tired. He would have liked to have been able to make this decision together with his three friends, together around a game of dominoes. He would have liked to have seen the headlines in big black letters and the story of Zevada, Martínez Fierro, and Gómez in eight columns in the second section . . . or better yet on the front page. And Gómez? All he had was a vague memory and a voice over the telephone talking about honor. It wasn't enough to hate, it made his hatred too rational. How many others were there like Gómez who had traded their homeland for a stack of bills? How many others like Gómez had made their fortune off the Revolution, wallowing in a pool of blood and money? But now Gómez belonged to him, to him, and to the poet, Verdugo, and the Chinaman, there was even a piece of the colonel that belonged to San Vicente. *Now we really are the shadow of the shadow,* he told himself, staring at the closed door.

IN WHICH THE CHARACTERS PLAY
DOMINOES

In the bar of the Majestic Hotel a cuckoo clock sang out one in the morning. Eustaquio the bartender looked contentedly at the domino game, the four men seated around the marble table. Everything is as it should be, he thought, as he went around turning out the rest of the lights, leaving that one solitary table illuminated in the center of the room, wrapped in the ring of light escaping from under the black shade, unreal, phantasmagoric in the otherwise deserted bar. The sound of ivory on marble rose up from the circle of light. Out in the street the hum of a car engine mixed with the neighing of a horse and the echo of hoofs on pavement.

"Too bad your buddy San Vicente doesn't like dominoes. Otherwise, he strikes me just fine," said the lawyer Verdugo. The dominoes lined up in front of him remained sunk in the shadow from the brim of his pearl gray Stetson.

"He's out thele somewhele in the darkness tlying to get his newspapel stalted. He told me to give you all a big hug fol him," said Tomás Wong, placing the three/two on top of the table. "He doesn't understand the affinity between analchism and dominoes. Not like I do."

"What about you, poet? Did you get a good look at the letter of thanks we got from the president? It's in my jacket pocket, on the coatrack there."

"Manterola, it's not my style to be so prosaic but, if the Honorable President of the Republic still had all his appendages, he could whack me off with two hands at once, the one-armed bastard. For all I care."

"It's a helluva country, gentlemen," said Manterola, scratching the scar behind his ear, and cautiously playing the double-threes.

AFTER THE NOVEL

In the course of the story, the fictional characters have mingled with historical personalities and events. For the sake of the reader's curiosity:

The four central characters belong entirely to the world of fiction.

Sebastián San Vicente was deported a second time in 1923, following his participation in the heroic streetcar strike. I compiled his brief Mexican biography in Memoria Roja, *and again, in novelized form, in* De Paso *(Passing Through). It appears that he died years later fighting in the anarchist ranks against the fascists in Spain.*

In 1926 El Demócrata *died a pauper's death, run under by debts after being sold by its original owners. General Alvarado's newspaper,* El Heraldo de Mexico, *had disappeared two years before. With the demise of the two best newspapers Mexico has ever known the once-fine art of crime reporting began its tragic decline, only to be restored somewhat in 1930 by* La Prensa, *although without the grace, elegance, and shine of earlier days. The journalist who inspired the character of Pioquinto Manterola died of tuberculosis a year before his newspaper.*

Dolores Street changed with time, and the triads were eventually forced to abandon it (or at least that's what one would suppose) following an intense campaign spearheaded by the magazine Sucesos *in the 1930s.*

The anarcho-syndicalists based in the south of Mexico City won the strike described in this book, and many more, until 1926, when they started to feel the effects of the repression unleashed by the government of President Calles.

The rebellion of a Mexican officer under orders from the foreign oil barons is a historical fact. The actual revolt was headed up by General Martínez Herrera one year after the fictional rebellion described in the novel. The oil barons never let up in their pressures on the Mexican government, although in 1923 the first agreements were reached on the payment of drilling and export rights. The end of this turbulent relationship is well known, and came about when President Lázaro Cárdenas nationalized the country's oil industry in 1938.

The wave of advertisements for patent medicines, so in vogue in the years following the Revolution, eventually died out as the number of doctors increased. By 1930, the number of ads in a single edition of the newspaper had dropped from a high of 110 to fewer than 5.

The Araña Cantina, the Cafe Paris, the Black Circus, and other cafes and dives described here disappeared only to be replaced by others of equal or greater notoriety.

In spite of the students' aggression, Fermín Revueltas's mural was finished on schedule and it can still be seen today on the walls of the San Ildefonso building in the center of Mexico City.

The criminal underworld abandoned its marginality and exoticism, learned to coexist with the law, and finally became institutionalized as an integral part of the Mexican police force.

Military bands stopped giving free concerts in the parks, the rent strike was defeated, the gendarmery disappeared and was replaced by the granaderos, or riot police; they no longer make bulletproof Packards, elegant steamers no longer dock at the ports of Veracruz and Tampico, the Krone Circus hasn't returned to Mexico since 1928, and the villages of Tlalpan and San Angel were long ago swallowed up by the city.

Times pass and things change. The authoritarianism of the Obregón regime at the start of Mexico's stolen revolution gradually turned itself into the shamelessness and corrupt arrogance of the PRI, the political party that controls the country to this day (1990).

There are no longer races run at the Condesa track, there's not even a Condesa track anymore. Sanborns, the American

Foto Shop, the Bank of London and Mexico, can still be found in the same place, but Vito Alessio Robles, de la Huerta, and Obregón are now no more than street names.

Nobody hypnotizes anyone in detective novels anymore.

Fortunately, dominoes continues to be the great national pastime, and somehow, miraculously, it has yet to fall into the claws of the mass media.

Paco Ignacio Taibo II